SPEAK EASY TO ME

TABITHA KRUEGER

©2024 by Tabitha Krueger. All rights reserved. No part of this publication may be reproduced in any form, by any means, without the permission of the author. All characters appearing in this work are fictitious and any similarities to real persons, living or dead, is purely coincidental.

Edited by Partners in Crime Book Services

Cover design by Tabitha Krueger created with Csnva Pro

❀ Created with Vellum

CHAPTER 1

LOTTIE

The sweat started pooling on my forehead. It was mid-January in Northern Wisconsin; I should not be sweating. Though my blood was running as cold as the snow blowing wind, I was burning up. I had never been this nervous in my whole life. I was leaving everything and everyone I knew to marry a man I had never met.

It had only been a week since my father sat me down at the large family dining room table and told me my life was about to change. I was to be married to a well-connected man in Chicago. I was going to go to my rich, estranged Uncle Lon's house in the city in the meantime.

My mother had not spoken to her brother, my Uncle Lon, in almost 30 years. She had been disowned for marrying my father, a lowly farmer, when her father had a well-bred man lined up for her. I was very apprehensive about going to stay with him. I had only heard through secondhand stories and whispers illustrating how awful he was. I couldn't believe my parents were going to give their blessing on this.

I had never been to a big city before, barely left my hometown of Kwahomat, spending most of my time on the family farm. I also had no clothes, nor manners, for the high society circles my uncle was a part of.

It started when my father left to run an errand for 3 days. What was actually happening was a secret meeting with Uncle Lon where he laid out an offer knowing my family couldn't pass up.

The crash of 1929 had hit my family, along with millions of other famers, hard. We were barely scraping by, having to let most of the farm hands go due to not having money to pay them. A few stayed, even though all we could provide was food and a place to sleep. Most of the men were unmarried so they didn't need much more than that.

The offer my uncle presented to my father, as if he had a choice, was simple; I would marry his business partner's son and he would pay off all my family's debts. I was the oldest of 5 girls and unmarried, so naturally my father knew I would be the most logical choice. He also knew I would be the one of least resistance. Although I am a tough farm girl, I love my family more than anything and would do anything to help ease their burden any way I could.

I hadn't spoken to my father or mother for 2 days after they sat me down at the kitchen table and told me what had transpired on my father's "trip". At first, I was so shocked I couldn't speak. Then I was so mad, I refused to talk to anyone; just stewing in my anger for 2 days. I finally broke down when I heard my mother crying in her room one night, realizing that this was hurting them as much as me.

I decided, reluctantly, that I would go and do what had to be done. Thinking about my life on the farm, working from morning to well into the night, falling asleep due to exhaustion. I had no idea what to expect except for what I had seen in the movies. My favorite being *Ladies of Leisure* with Barbara Stanwyck. Like Barbara's character in the movie, I didn't have very many options.

SPEAK EASY TO ME

Was this deal better than nothing? I had no prospects. No serious ones anyway. I was fooling around with a man on the farm, Nick, who was a few years older than me, in his 30s.

Long days on the farm and a chance encounter one night led to a physical relationship. We would spend most nights under the stars together. He was handsome enough with his sandy blonde hair and dull brown eyes.

News travels fast around the farm. He approached me on the morning of the 3rd day after my father told me. The sun was just breaking over the bare trees.

"Is it true?" he said to me as he peered at me from under the brim of his hat. I'd been trying to avoid him because I didn't know how to approach the subject. It had been easy enough the first few days since I was in such a mood. I couldn't avoid him now.

"Yes. I'm leaving for Chicago in a few days." I couldn't look him in the eye. I wasn't sure what we had, but I knew it wasn't going anywhere. He knew it wasn't going anywhere, so I wasn't sure why he seemed to be a little hurt with my confirmation.

"And you're getting married?" He seemed to be getting increasingly upset. I could only nod 'yes' in response. "To a guy you don't even know?" He threw his hands up in frustration, raising his voice a little bit.

I moved in a little closer to him and grabbed his hands in mine. "I'm sorry. I should have been the one to tell you." He yanked his hands out of mine. Looking at me with such sorrow and anger in his eyes he proceeded, "Is it because he has money? I can find another line of work if that's the case. Is that what I have to do?"

I think he could read the shock on my face as his eyes scanned my expression. I had never even considered what we were doing as anything more than just sex. I mean, we'd talked and laughed, but nothing more than that. He never

3

asked me on a date. Never even showed any interest in me other than when we were under the cover of darkness.

I had always just assumed that he wasn't interested in a more serious arrangement. I knew that no one else had ever been interested in me. I wasn't what you would consider beautiful by any stretch of the word. I wasn't a little, petite, perfect house-wife type. I was about 5'7", I towered over all my sisters. I also was fuller and rounder than any other women I knew. I did physical work at the farm, so I also had strong arms and legs that other women my age generally didn't.

I was a farm girl through and through. I had made peace with the fact that I would never marry or have a family of my own. I was fine with that. The farm; the work, the animals, my parents, that was all I really needed.

All I could manage to say was "What?" I couldn't process what he was saying. Was he confessing that he wanted to marry me?

"Tell me what I have to do." Nick grabbed onto my shoulders as he moved so close to me that our noses were almost touching. He looked me in my eyes, pleading. "I love you, Lottie." It felt like all the air was sucked out of my lungs. I suddenly couldn't breathe, the cold winter air just floating out of reach of my lungs.

I felt bad for hurting him like this when I honestly had no idea he'd felt this way. Then it hit me. He didn't really love me; he just didn't want to lose me. Now I was starting to get angry. "Why now? You've had 10 months to tell me this. 10 months to tell me you wanted me as more than just someone who kept you occupied." He just stayed silent without taking his eyes off mine. Eyes I had once found such comfort in now just looked desperate. "You're ashamed of me. You're embarrassed to let anyone know we'd be in a relationship. You don't love me." I pushed his hands off my shoulders and he let them rest at his side, still staring at me.

"Why hadn't you ever asked me on a date? Taken me into town to watch a movie or walk through the park?" His silence was answer enough. Nick looked away, down at the ground. He knew I was right. He just didn't want to admit it.

He took a deep breath and released it, the winter chill showing in a puff of foggy air on his exhale. He took my face in his hands, bent down and placed a feather light kiss on my lips. He pulled away, now with sadness in his eyes. "I just wanted to kiss you one last time. I do love you, no matter what you think." He then pulled me in to an embrace so tight that if we were any closer we would have melded into one.

"Don't let them change you, Lottie. You're perfect just the way you are. I was just a fool to not notice it sooner." I could hear the devastation in his voice. The realization that he might have real feelings for me. I hugged him a little tighter in return letting him know that I felt the same way. Wondering what could have transpired if I stayed. It was impossible to do now, no matter how much I might want to.

"I won't." I replied back, a little breathy, barely audible. I could feel the tears on the brim of my eyes.

There was a cough from behind Nick. We broke apart and I could see the tears running silently down his face. His brown eyes shone with wetness.

"What's going on here?" my father's gruff voice demanded. Nick angled his body between my father and me, ready for whatever was about to happen next. I slid my arm around Nick's stomach and pushed him behind me to stop whatever chest puffing these two were going to do.

I looked at my father and replied, "Nothing. Just two friends saying their goodbyes a little early." I could feel Nick seething behind me. Resenting my father for sending me away, forever. My father didn't look convinced.

"I've got work to do." Nick turned and walked away without looking back, leaving me alone with my suspicious father. He could always read me like a book. He just shook his head as he stepped closer. "Be careful. You're promised to another man." I shook my head in understanding. He just patted me on the shoulder twice before turning and walking back to the barn.

The rest of the week went by in a blur. One day blending into another. I wanted the week to be over with, with the tension so high in the house. Now I'm standing on the porch watching the lights of a car as they get closer. Like the lights were beckoning me into a bright, new future, full of hope and promise. All I felt though was dread and despair.

My mother released a sob that brought me back to the present. Her face was red and puffy from crying. I went to embrace her, her warm breath hitting the cold nipping at my cheek.

"Mama, I'm getting married, I'm not dead." She pulled back from my embrace. I wiped the tears from her face.

"I know. It's just not going to be the same around here without you." She grabbed me in an even tighter embrace, I swear I heard a rib crack. "I promise to write to you all the time. And I'll send pictures of the wedding." That was exactly the wrong thing to say because Mama just started crying harder and ran into the house.

My father was now standing next to me as the car finally pulled up to the porch. He hugged me as he said "Oh, Charlotte."

I hugged him back, answering "It's okay Dad. *I'll* be okay." I tried to say the last part with confidence, trying to convince him and myself of its truth, but we both knew I might not be.

We broke the hug when we heard car doors open and close. Three men in suits stepped out and approached the porch, their steps crunching in the snow. One of the men strode up the porch steps and took hold of my luggage. I didn't have much to pack. It was eye opening seeing my whole life fit into one suitcase and one carryall. I was told that I would be provided with a whole new wardrobe once I was in Chicago. I had sent my measurements with my father one day when he went into town, and he relayed those to my uncle. I was wholly embarrassed.

"We better get going Miss. Bradley." The man who had picked up my luggage said as he quickly descended the steps, walking towards the car. I turned to my father, "I guess that's my cue. I'll write as soon as I get there. Tell Mama and the girls I love them." With that, I took a deep breath and made my way to the awaiting car. One of the men in a suite opened my car door and shut it as soon as I was sitting in my seat. He walked around the back of the car, opened the driver's side back door and sat next to me, shutting the door with a loud thud. This was it. There was no turning back. No stopping what was already put in motion. I watched as the lights of the farmhouse faded into the dark night.

This was just the start of the long 6-hour drive to Chicago. I had never spent more than an hour in a car before, let alone 6. The car was cramped as the 4 of us rode in silence. My heart was pounding so hard I couldn't believe its thumping wasn't filling the car. Judging by the way everyone was avoiding looking at me, it was a pretty safe bet that I was the only one who could hear it. The *whoosh whoosh* in my ears was deafening.

I started thinking of all the things I had heard in secretive whispers throughout the years about Uncle Lon. He was my Mama's older brother by 5 years. She said that he was difficult as long as she could remember. It was always his way or no way. He was always right, even when he was completely wrong. One time he almost burned the house down when he was making soup on the stove and somehow turned it into my mama's fault, and she had gotten punished.

Mama was also a dreamer in a family full of businessmen which didn't bode well for her. She was the youngest with 3 older brothers who excelled in all things academic while her strengths were in the arts. Her father was a mean man, just for spite. He forbade her from pursuing anything even remotely artsy; painting, piano, singing. She was to marry a man of his choosing and be a perfect little housewife without complaint. When she met my father, it was love at first sight. It was a chance encounter and within a month of meeting they had secretly married. When her father found out he turned his back on her, cutting her off completely and said he would do the same to anyone else who tried to contact her.

Whenever Uncle Lon was brought up, she'd always mention how he was the spitting image of her father in looks and personality. I was essentially going to be walking into the lion's den when I arrived in Chicago. Suddenly the 6-hour drive wasn't sounding like it would be long enough. The knot in my stomach started getting tighter. My chest started to feel tighter. What the hell was I doing? Why would a high society man want to marry a farm girl who put her elbows on the table? I had plenty of time to dwell on that little fact. Was there something wrong with this guy that no other woman wanted to marry him? I guess he could be thinking the same thing about me.

I was ripped out of my thoughts by a booming voice to my left, "Your uncle wants to meet with you over breakfast to go over everything that will be happening the next few days. I suggest you try to get some sleep while we're driving." It didn't sound like a suggestion. I closed my eyes and tried to fall asleep, but it seemed to elude me for the longest time. It

SPEAK EASY TO ME

felt like I had finally fallen asleep, and the car stopped in front of a tall, cast-iron gate.

The gate opened and the car proceeded to drive up a short driveway. The house in which the man next to me had referred was definitely a mansion. The sheer enormity of it was something I had never set eyes upon before. It was dark, but the house was illuminated with strategically placed lights that somehow made it even more foreboding, intimidating. The dark brick with creeping vines going in all directions encompassing the house.

My car door was opened by another man in a suite who looked like he was part of the group of guys who had driven me here. The three men in the car seemed to open their doors in sync with each other. Before I knew it, I was flanked on all sides by this quad of suit clad men as if I would take off running at any minute. As they were ushering me up the sidewalk the oversized mahogany front door opened. In the doorway stood a woman in her mid-50's wearing a dark dress with a white apron. Once we had all entered the house, she closed the door and fell in step behind our group.

We walked through a grand open entrance room. There was a staircase on either side of the room leading upstairs. No time to stop and stare at the magnificence of this room as the men just plowed right through the house, knowing exactly where they were going. I was just hoping I could keep up because if I fell behind, I was sure I wouldn't be able to find my way back with all the twists and turns we had taken. We finally ended up at the end of a long hallway after going down three different hallways and a flight of stairs. As we approached the only opened door the men stopped, turned around and were gone before I could even take a breath. It was just me and who I assumed was a maid from her attire.

"Miss Bradley, this is your room," the woman said as she motioned for me to follow her. The room was white with light pink accents, very inviting, a contradiction to the outside of the house. The bed was at least 3 times larger than my bed on the farm. It was also covered in more pillows than I could ever want for a lifetime. The bedding was pink with white and yellow flowers adorning it.

"I hope this room is to your liking." She seemed to be hesitant, waiting for my reaction. I just smiled at her, "It is absolutely perfect. Not what I was expecting at all." It seemed she was able to relax with my answer.

"Oh?" was her response laced with confusion and maybe a little bit of surprise. "The outside and from what I've seen of the inside of the house just seems so cold and uninviting. This room is feminine and cozy."

She now had a big smile on her aged face. "Mr. Fairbanks told me to decorate however I saw fit. I'm glad you like it."

"It's absolutely lovely."

"Thank you, Miss Bradley."

"It's Lottie, please. And your name?"

"Claire." After a short little tour showing me my bathroom suite and walk in closet, Claire showed herself out, promising to come wake me for breakfast which was in just 3 hours. I needed all the sleep I could get in order to prepare to go into the viper's den.

10

CHAPTER 2

LOTTIE

After I used the washroom and changed into my nightgown I crawled into the sprawling bed, certain I would be swallowed up by the pillow mountain that lay at the head of the bed. The sheets were so luxurious that I made a silent vow to never leave that bed. I very quickly broke that vow when Claire came floating into my room right at 6am with two younger maids in tow. Between the three of them they had me bathed, primped and ready for breakfast within the hour.

I had on a simple day dress that I wore around the farm usually on Sundays. The double doors were opened to the dining room. I wasn't sure what to expect, but what I didn't expect was to see the large man at the head of the table who looked so familiar while at the same time being a stranger. He had my mother's eyes, my eyes, except his eyes were cold where mine and my mother's were friendly and bright. He stood as I entered the room, the door closing as he gestured to the seat next to his left.

I couldn't tell if it was how intimidating he seemed or how nervous I was that made my hands start shaking so bad

TABITHA KRUEGER

that I had to clasp them together and place them on my lap. He then started placing food on his fork as he addressed me. "Charlotte, I know this is all probably such a shock to you and happening so fast. It's probably very overwhelming." So much for introductions.

He shoved a forkful of eggs into his mouth. In between bites he explained how things were going to work. "My potential business partner wants his son to settle down, marry and have an heir within the year. That's why this is all happening so fast." He shoved another bite of food into his mouth, barely even closing his mouth as he chewed. I hadn't even placed any food on my plate yet which seemed to go unnoticed by my uncle or maybe he just didn't care. With the shock of everything, I hadn't even considered the timeline of events.

He took a drink of the liquid in his glass, "Today you will be going for fittings for new clothes. I have already gotten a few casual pieces for you based on the measurements your father gave me." I nodded in agreement because I was afraid that if I opened my mouth, I might scream from being purely overwhelmed. I was to be married and popping out babies as soon as the ink dried on the marriage certificate.

"You'll be meeting Cameron tonight at dinner. Not only will his mother and father be joining us, but my sons, Thomas, and Nathaniel, will also be in attendance." Oh lovely, two more just like him I imagine. This dinner won't be disastrous at all.

Uncle Lon took one more bite of food then wiped his mouth with his napkin. He pushed his seat out and started walking to the doors. He stopped just short of opening the doors, turned around and said "Do not embarrass me tonight. I know you grew up on a farm, but please act like you weren't raised in a barn."

Ah, there it was, the disgust Mama had talked vaguely

SPEAK EASY TO ME

about. Her words came flooding back to me from the day before I left "He's going to say things just to get a rise out of you, don't give him the satisfaction. You hold your head high and proud. You're a Bradley. You are strong and capable of anything." I had a feeling I would be repeating her encouraging words many times in the near future.

I had barely taken my third bite of food when the double doors burst open. Susan, one of the younger maids from this morning, came flittering into the room, a beautiful black crushed velvet coat with a white fur lined collar and cuffs held in her hands.

"Time to get going to your fittings," she said as she stood next to me, readying the coat for me to don. I pushed my chair back as I stood up and placed my arms in the softest material I had ever felt. The coat hit just below my knees and had a belt tied at the waist, hiding my overly casual outfit that had been chosen for me by the maids this morning.

"Russel will accompany you while you go out today. Marco will drive you. Russel has the instructions on what you are to purchase." All her words were matter of fact.

Without saying another word, I was escorted from the dining room though the entryway to an awaiting car. One of the men from last night was standing at the back passenger door and opened the door as I approached. I stopped in front of the tall, husky man whose blonde hair was poking out from under his hat.

"Russel?" I asked before I got into the car. He just nodded his head in confirmation. "Big talker," I teased as I sat in my seat and got comfortable. The man in the driver's seat, Marco I assumed, let out a chuckle.

"Just drive, you knucklehead." Russel did not find it very funny when I asked if Marco could go shopping with me instead, which got an even bigger chuckle out of Marco. Russel just replied, "I'm not a chauffeur," which shut Marco up for the rest of the drive into the heart of the city. My goal for the day was to get Russel to say more than five words in a row to me.

I had never really gone shopping in an actual department store before. I wasn't even sure they would have anything in my size. I wouldn't know unless I tried and by golly, I was going to try my darndest to make the best out of this weird, crazy situation. We pulled up in front of a huge building that was at least a whole city block it seemed.

Russel was out of the car and opening my door for me before I even realized he'd left the car. "Have fun," Marco teased before he pulled off. I followed Russel into the magnificent building. We went up to the 3rd floor, women's clothing. There Margaret, who would be helping me find clothing, greeted me.

She brought me so many dresses and skirts to try on, I was sure I had tried on the whole store by the end of it. The good news was that I had found, what I considered a new wardrobe, but what Russel had informed me was just the basics. We went to four more department stores and boutiques. The car was full of shopping and garment bags I almost had to sit on Russel's lap.

We had one more store to stop at before we were to head back to my temporary home at Uncle Lon's house. We approached a little boutique that had hat and scarf displays. I had never owned a proper hat. I had floppy hats that I wore outside on the farm to block out the sun, but none that were purely for fashion purposes.

I spied a simple black cloche hat with a thin white bow around it. It was truly the only thing the whole day that I wanted for myself besides a dress I had tried on earlier but deemed too risqué by Russel, so I wasn't able to buy it. The dress was a deep, rich green velvet that felt like heaven to touch. It was low cut and tight, accentuating my breasts and hips, so right back to the sales floor it went for someone else to purchase. Russel cleared his throat behind me, and I took that as my sign to go into the store.

Russel opened the door for me where we were immediately greeted by a salesgirl. She was neatly dressed in a pillbox hat strategically placed on her head. "How can I help you?" she asked, addressing Russel as if I wasn't even there.

"Mr. Fairbanks would like you to help his niece and Mr. Darby's fiancé, find a few pieces for everyday wear along with a few for more formal events." The salesgirl's eyes were fixated on Russel. I hadn't really noticed how attractive he was before, but all throughout the day every woman we interacted with had been googly-eyed over the serious, brooding man.

As soon as the salesgirl was out of earshot, gathering a plethora of accessories, I said to my chaperone, "You have quite the fan base. Every woman we have encountered has been positively gaga over you." His response was a gruff harrumph. It wasn't a straight up dismissal, so I decided I'd push my luck. "Do you have a girlfriend? Wife?"

He just stood there and gave me the side eye, "You're already engaged." I just rolled my eyes at him. I couldn't discern if he was serious or making a joke.

"I wasn't asking for me, you oaf!" Still the strong, silent type, he just crossed his arms in front of his body and stood staring at the shelf in front of him, pretending to look at the merchandise.

I was going to go a little bit further and see what would get his motor running. I was bored from the day of endless shopping. I also needed a distraction from my feet absolutely killing me. High heels were not my friend, no matter how cute they looked.

"Maggie is pretty cute, don't you think?" That got his

attention. He stopped looking at the shelf and fully turned towards me.

"The yappy maid that is constantly smiling?" That was a seven-word response, my goal for the day accomplished.

"You mean the pretty one with red hair?" I goaded him. I think I saw his cheeks turn red.

"I'm going to see what's taking this lady so long. Don't go out of this store." Russel was through placating me. He didn't even wait for a response before he'd disappeared into the back. A triumphant smile was now plastered across my face.

Since I was now left to my own devices, I decided to go look at the cloche I had laid my eyes on earlier. I walked over to the display that held it. I reached out my hand, about to grab the hat when my hand was met with a larger, more masculine hand.

I looked up into the dark eyes of the most handsome man I had ever had the pleasure of seeing. He was towering over me, at least 6'3" with broad shoulders that were complimented by the best tailored three-piece suit I had ever seen. He smelled of firewood and cedar.

His face was haggard like he'd seen one too many horrible things in his life. His eyes though, were soft and gentle and kind. Almost like they didn't belong to his face. When he smiled at me, I thought I was going to burst into flames from the heat. I could feel my cheeks redden at my embarrassment.

"Sorry, ma'am." His eyes didn't leave mine as he spoke. There was a dangerous sparkle that danced in his dark eyes. He radiated this unexplainable power. This man was bad news, but I couldn't take my eyes off him.

Our hands were still both touching, clutching the hat. I pulled my hand away quickly. I clumsily searched for words, but all I could come up with in response was, "Oh, no, your hand was there first." He just smiled bigger and handed the hat to me.

"This hat was made for you." There was something in his voice that wrapped around me like a warm embrace. He handed me the hat making sure our hands touched one more time.

"Thank you." I graciously took the hat. Russel and the soft female salesgirl's voices floating through the air grabbed my attention as they emerged from the backroom. Their hands were full of boxes. I had turned my head for less than five seconds and when I looked back, the mysterious stranger had vanished.

"Were you talking to someone out here?" Russel said as he surveyed the store. He was now on high alert as his eyes scanned the surrounding area.

"I was. It was nothing. A gentleman grabbed this hat at the same time I did." I held the hat up. "Then he handed me the hat, I turned my head, and he was just gone." I shrugged my shoulders letting Russel know that I honestly had no clue who was talking to me. He just made a grunting sound like normal then went about his business paying for all my new accessories along with my new cloche hat.

Marco and Russel had rearranged all the shopping bags and boxes in the car in order to accommodate the three of us. Once we were all situated and Marco could again see out of the windows, we were heading back to the house so I could get ready for what I knew would be an awkward dinner.

Maggie and Claire were there, ready to help unload the car of all the packages. I went to grab a bag when Claire said, "No, Lottie. Upstairs with you to bathe and get ready for dinner. We will be up to help you shortly." She then shooed me away.

I opened my bedroom door to find a beautiful dark blue, silk dress on my bed along with a matching silver and blue stoned necklace and earrings. The dress had a belt at the waist, just below the bosom and flared out just below the belt, giving the dress a flowy look. It would help hide some of my curves while accentuating my breasts, which I'm sure, was Uncle Lon's goal.

I took a deep exasperated breath as I made my way to the bathroom after undressing. The room was almost as big as mine and my sister's bedrooms on the farm; there were two bedrooms the five of us shared

I got a slight shiver as my bare feet padded across the cold ceramic white and blue tiles. The large claw tub was in the middle of the room to my left and the wall-to-wall vanity, illuminated by framing lights, to my right. I plugged the drain before turning on the water. I used my hand to test the temperature, making sure the water was as hot as I could handle, before going over to the vanity.

The vanity held an assortment of lovely smelling oils, soaps, perfumes, and lotions. I chose a light lavender scented soap and proceeded to get into the almost full bathtub. The water instantly make my sore feet and aching muscles feel relief after trudging around in high heels for hours. I never knew an all-day shopping excursion was so exhausting and taxing. I knew I didn't have much time to soak since I only had about an hour before dinner was starting. I quickly washed and made my way into my bedroom.

I had just started putting my undergarments on when Claire, Maggie and Rose came into my room without so much as a knock. I yelped in surprise and Claire, not bothered in the slightest, simply stated, "It's nothing we haven't seen before, Lottie." The three women started moving about the room.

Claire finished helping me get into the undergarments. Just like in the morning, one woman doted on my hair while one tended to my make-up, rouging my cheeks and giving my eyes a coal outline. There was also a little lipstick applied to my lips before slipping into the silk dress.

Taking one last look in the mirror, I couldn't believe that I was staring back at myself. With my hair and makeup done the dress seemed to complete the transformation from plunky farm girl to elegant city girl. The dress complimented my pale skin and dark hair. The makeup accentuated my features without overshadowing them. I looked the part I was supposed to play.

After the maids *oohed* and *ahhed* over my new look headed downstairs for the moment of truth. I was convinced I would slip and fall down the stairs, breaking my neck, which I decided would probably be less painful than this god-forsaken dinner.

I heard voices coming from a room I had not yet been in. It was to the right of the front door as you walked in. I had peered inside this morning on my way out and from what I saw, I assumed it was my uncle's study. The giant dark wood door was opened allowing the voices to carry throughout the open space of the front foyer.

There was a fire going in the fireplace giving the room a light glow along with a few lamps placed throughout the room. The talking stopped as I walked in. Taking in my now captive audience I was trying to figure out who was who. Standing by the fireplace were three people. I knew my uncle obviously, but there was an older woman, who was presumably Cameron's mom and another man about my uncle's age, Cameron's dad. Then there were three good looking men, all about my age, give or take a few years, standing around a desk. One man was perched on the edge of the desk while the other two flanked him.

"Ah Charlotte, so nice of you to join us." I was frozen in my spot. My uncle, not missing a beat, approached me, placing his hand around my waist to subtly push me into the

TABITHA KRUEGER

room. He guided me over to the older couple by the fireplace. "This is Hank and Kitty Darby, Cameron's parents." We exchanged pleasantries as I shook both of their hands while I politely smiled. My future in-laws did not hide their glares while sizing me up. My uncle then turned me to the three men at the desk.

"And this is Cameron." The man that had been perched on the desk stood up, allowing me to take in his big build. He must have stood at least 6' 1" with a buff frame that was outlined perfectly in his three-piece dinner suite. His blonde hair was neatly styled with every strand in place. His bright green eyes made him look like the most powerful man in the room.

He adjusted his coat before making his way towards me, extending his hand. I took his hand in mine and felt the smooth skin of a man who had never done manual labor a day in his life. He gripped my hand firmly as he shook it. He gave me a curt smile saying, "Nice to meet you, Charlotte."

I could tell he was taking me in, just as I had taken him in, making me instantly feel self-conscience. All the confidence I had gained in my bedroom had left my body. I met his gaze, "Nice to meet you, too, Cameron." I mustered up the best smile I could with my heart pounding so loud I was sure everyone in the room could hear it.

Uncle Lon broke my train of thought before it completely derailed. "And these are my sons Thomas," Thomas came forward to shake my hand. He was handsome enough, longer blonde hair that he just let fall however it wanted. He was a good head taller than me. "And Nathaniel." Nathaniel was good looking with a mischievous smile as he took my hand and shook it. His blonde hair was slightly darker than his brother's and stood just as tall.

I was hoping that once introductions were done my heart would settle down a little bit, but that was not the case. It was still rapidly beating as Uncle Lon announced we would be heading to the dining room. We filed out of the study to make our way across the foyer to the dining room, strategically placed next to the kitchen.

My cousin Nathaniel walked next to me as everyone else was in front. He nudged me with his elbow, whispering, "It's not going to be so bad. I heard we're having steak for dinner." His attempt at lightening my mood worked slightly because a smile crept across my face.

While looking forward I said, "Which means we'll have knives." This earned me a chuckle from him.

"Just let me know if you're feeling stabby so I know to leave the room. I'd be lying if I said there weren't more than one person who wanted to stab every single person in front of us." My shocked look was exactly what he was going for as a sly smile decorated his face.

Feeling a little more at ease as we entered the dining room I looked to see where there was an empty seat. The long cherry oak table was decorated with a giant bouquet of beautiful flowers, that clearly were not local, with lit candles a safe distance on either side.

Uncle Lon was at the head of the table with Thomas in the spot to his right and Mr. Darby to his left. Cameron was then next to Thomas and Mrs. Darby next to her husband. Nathaniel was waiting to see where I would sit before he took his seat.

"Choose wisely," his whisper was threaded with humor. I didn't want to sit in either seat, but knew I had to pick one. Cameron seemed like the better choice since his mother had been looking at me as if I had shown up covered in cow manure.

Dinner was wonderful. Let me rephrase that because that was a lie. The food was wonderful. Every dish more delicious than the last. The conversations had been few and far

TABITHA KRUEGER

between. When there was any talking it was stiff and formal. I don't think I had ever sat through something so torturously dull.

I was relieved when dinner finally ended only to be hit with "Come with me, Charlotte," by Cameron. He pulled my chair out for me and placed his hand on the small of my back as he walked me back to the study. From the way no one else batted an eyelash it seemed this was planned with me being the only one uniformed. Nathaniel followed, acting as a chaperone, and stood outside the open door.

There were two green sitting chairs in front of the fireplace, Cameron taking one and me taking the other. We sat there a beat in silence when Cameron spoke up, "I think we should go over what this marriage is going to be." His words were unfeeling, like he was leading a business meeting. "Our expectations and goals."

How do you even respond to that? I always grew up thinking about marrying someone I was in love with, not someone who I was going to be business partners with.

"Alright," was all I could muster to say, not sure what else to say. Cameron kept his eyes fixated on the fire as he continued to speak as he sunk deeper into the chair.

"My father has informed me that I am to settle down and have an heir on the way by the end of this year." I swallowed hard with the direction this uncomfortable conversation was heading. "I'm not going to beat around the bush. I don't want to get married and saddled with a baby. I wasn't given a choice though if I want to be my father's successor. I know you don't want this anymore than I do, but we need to make it work in its barest form."

I just nodded. At least we had one thing in common, even if it was that neither of us wanted this marriage to happen.

"So, here's the deal." Cameron sat up, placing his elbows no his knees, leaning closer in my direction. "We will get married, and you will provide me with an heir." Every word was laced with disdain. "After that, we are only man and wife on paper. I have my own life that I do not intend to give up or change in any way. Having a wife and a baby will not hinder my *proclivities*."

He meant he wouldn't stop sleeping with other women. My heart sank. I think I would have rather him done his running around in secret rather than outright knowing. He could have at least tried to pretend to like me, even just a little bit. As if his sleeping with other women confession wasn't jarring enough, he followed up with, "I expect you to stay faithful." I wasn't sure I had heard him correctly. I don't think I was very good at hiding my shock.

"I wouldn't think you staying out of other men's beds would be difficult for you." He was implying that even if I wanted to sleep with other men, no other men would want to sleep with me. I was so shocked that I let out a laugh I had never heard before. It was astonishment mixed with pure anger.

I abruptly stood up, not wanting to be in the same room with him any longer, not only because of what he'd just implied, but I wasn't sure I'd be able to hold my tongue. He was right on my heels as I reached to open the door his arm came from behind me, slamming the door shut before I had fully opened it.

Cameron grabbed my arm forcibly and whirled me around. "Let me out." I demanded. I was met with a credulous laugh from his beautiful mouth.

"No." He was trying to exert power over me as I stood there, back against the door, staring at him and him back at me, my anger still seething.

"Oh, so you get to go fadoodling all over town and I get to stay home waiting like a puppy by the door for you? Not happening. I'm not staying celibate due to you not wanting

TABITHA KRUEGER

to sleep with me." I wasn't keeping my voice down and I didn't care who could hear this conversation.

"You will do as I say without argument." Cameron's anger was palpable. He had me caged in between his two arms, one on either side of my head. I moved my face so our noses were almost touching. I refused to back down.

"Try and make me. See how far you get with that." We were so close I could smell the sweet wine he drank at dinner. I had been surprised there was wine at dinner since prohibition made all alcohol illegal, except in certain, special circumstances. It was then that I realized money could probably buy anything in this city.

This conversation clearly didn't go the way he'd planned. I am not sure what he expected the outcome to be after he admitted he'd cheat and then said I was so unwanted, no man would sleep with me.

There was a knock on the door, Nathaniel's voice barely audible through the thick wood, "Everything alright in there?"

Hearing Nathaniel's muffled voice pulled Cameron out of his angry trance as he pushed off the door, away from me. I turned and threw the door open so fast Nathaniel almost toppled over the threshold into the study.

Cameron pushed by me as he rushed to get to the front door with his anger trailing him like a shadow. Nathaniel's shouting drew Cameron's parents, along with my uncle and other cousin, into the foyer from the dining room.

Cameron didn't even look in his parents' direction as he stormed to the front door throwing "We're leaving," over his shoulder as he grabbed his coat.

I could not resist one more poke at the bear. As nicely and innocently as I could muster, I shouted, "Have a nice night, dear."

If Cameron was going to be a complete jerk to me, I'd

return the favor by being as sickeningly sweet as possible. Both of Cameron's parents were confused as they quickly followed him to their car.

As soon as the front door slammed shut Uncle Lon turned to me. "What the hell did you do, girl?" His nostrils were flaring. I knew he didn't like when people didn't do as he wanted and he especially didn't like being made to look bad, both of which I had just done.

"I didn't do anything," I said, spitting venom back. "He was a complete jerk." I pointed to the front door Cameron had passed through as he left.

"I don't know what you did, but you are going to fix it! No exceptions, do you hear me?" His eyes bored through me as he bellowed his demands at me.

I had already made enough waves tonight; I didn't want to push my luck and get sucked into the surf. Through gritted teeth and arms crossed I reluctantly replied, "Fine."

Uncle Lon turned on his heels and tromped to the study, Thomas close in tow. The door slammed shut leaving Nathaniel and me standing in the now empty foyer.

"Told you dinner wouldn't be so bad." He wiggled his eyebrows at me. I felt the anger slowly melt away. A giggle bubbling to the surface. Nathaniel, it seemed, might be my only ally in the house. Thomas had barely said three full sentences to me the whole night.

The giant grandfather clock at the front of the foyer, sitting against the wall between the bay window and the front door, struck 9 o'clock with its loud Westminster chimes. I was about to turn around and head upstairs when Nathaniel cut through the chimes, "Get your coat on. We're going out."

CHAPTER 3

LOTTIE

I wasn't sure where we were going. It didn't help that Nathaniel was being very vague and elusive when I would ask for details. He repeatedly asked if I could keep a secret, which made me more intrigued, but also terrified.

The chill of the night was seeping through my coat as we pulled into the alley of a few large buildings. Nathaniel parked the car then proceeded to get out. I hadn't yet opened my door not knowing if going somewhere this secluded with Nathaniel was a smart idea.

I was contemplating walking back to the house, even though I had no idea where I was, as my door was opened. Nathaniel placed his arm out for me to take. The ground was a little slippery since the temperature had dropped once the sun went down, turning the wet ground icy. I gripped Nathaniel's arm as I walked like a newborn fawn trying to navigate the slick ground in my high heels.

We walked a little farther down the alleyway and stopped when we had reached a door that was flush to a building with no visible handle or knob. Nathaniel rapped quickly on

SPEAK EASY TO ME

the door twice, then waited a beat, four more quick taps, followed by two slower knocks. The door opened allowing Nathaniel to step inside with me following closely behind.

The smell of stale cigarettes and beer quickly filled my nostrils. The music seemed excessively loud from the band on stage as blaring horns and whaling drums assaulted my ears. There was so much chatter and laughter I could barely hear Nathaniel telling me to take off my coat. I slid the sleeves off my arms and handed the coat to him, still scanning the room. A moment later his hand gripped mine as he guided me through the crowd as we headed over to the bar.

We were working our way to the other side of the room, moving closer to the bar. I watched as men and women danced to the music the band played. Legs and arms flew everywhere as people moved in rhythm to the music.

"Wild, huh?" Nathaniel yelled into my ear when he noticed me staring at the pairs of men and women dancing closely on the dance floor. I doubted there was room for a piece of paper to fit between them.

We eventually made it to the bar which took up a whole wall. Bottles of booze and various juices lined the wall. There was a giant mirror hanging on the wall making the bar appear to have twice as much alcohol as it did.

The bartender had his back to us as I took a seat at the only open stool while Nathaniel stood behind me. I recognized him before he even turned around. There was no mistaking him. The man standing behind the bar was the mystery man from earlier in the day at the hat shop. His broad shoulders and jet-black hair gave him away.

He was now donning a white button up shirt and black slacks that curved to the roundness on the cheeks of his butt. My eyes were fixated on its perfect roundness when he turned to face me. I didn't react fast enough, my eyes still

TABITHA KRUEGER

lingering in the general vicinity of his ass cheeks, only now it was his front. My face was burning from the embarrassment.

He was wearing a devilish smile when I finally found the courage to let my eyes make their way up to find his face. "Like what you see?" he asked as he rested his arms on the bar top, leaning in towards me, still wearing that cocky grin. My mouth had gone dry, and all words escaped me. I was hoping for the earth to open up and swallow me whole. Luckily Nathaniel saved me.

"Back off Emmett, this is my cousin, Lottie. She's a farm girl from Wisconsin." Emmett's smile instantly got bigger and more sinister. "She's engaged, so back off. I'm serious, she's off limits to everyone, especially you." Nathaniel emphasized "you" by pointing his index finger at Emmett. Emmett backed up, removing his arms from the bar, and putting them up in surrender.

"What can I get for you and Carrots over there?" Emmett said with a playful grin as he pointed a finger at me, indicating that the Carrots he had referred to, was me. I had had the worst day of my life and I just wanted to forget everyone and everything for a little while. Some strong giggly water was in order and quick.

"Two fingers of scotch, neat." I blurted out before I even thought about it. Emmett looked at me with amusement in his eyes. I could feel Nathaniel shaking with laughter behind me.

"This should be a fun night," he whisper-yelled in my ear over the roar of music and people. "I shouldn't be surprised though, my father has that effect on people." There was a playful amusement in his voice. He continued with his order to Emmett.

"I'll just take a beer. I'll be driving her home, and she needs the hard stuff more than I do tonight." Emmett just nodded his head in understanding before he turned to get our drinks. I was mesmerized with how smooth Emmett's movements were. Like he didn't have to think at all about what he was doing behind the bar.

He returned with Nathaniel's frothy beer first, placing the glass on the bar top in front of me. Nathaniel grabbed the glass off the bar, took a sip, held it up in signal to Emmett that it was good, then he disappeared into the crowd without a word. I was so shocked I was speechless. He brought me here just to ditch me. Nice.

When I turned back around after watching my cousin vanish, Emmett had placed a short glass filled with whiskey in front of me. He was leaning back against the counter behind the bar, arms crossed over his chest and one leg crossed over the other. His eyes danced with a challenge I was ready to take. I was beyond tired of men at this point. I just looked back at him, defiance on my face, as I brought the glass up to my mouth and downed the amber liquid in one, long drink. It burned all the way down causing me to cough a little bit.

Emmett's eyes were filled with mischief as he took my glass, "More?" He picked the glass up off the bar. I knew it was a bad idea but throwing caution to the wind felt like a good idea in the moment.

"Yes, please," I said a little roughly, still feeling the effects of the whiskey on my throat. Emmett just smiled and went to pour me more. I took the time he was away to cough a few more times trying to remedy the burning was causing.

Returning with my glass and an additional one filled, he sat mine down in front of me, then inclined the glass still in his hand to me. I guess we were going to drink together. I picked up my glass, once again bringing the glass to my lips, closing my eyes, and scrunching my nose in anticipation of the burn.

Emmett let out a chuckle. I brought the glass down

enough to say, "Just because I make a face doesn't mean I can't take it." The words were out before I could even register how they could be taken.

His eyes darkened when he said, "Really?" Before I could say anything else stupid, I downed my drink making Emmett scramble to follow suit. While I drank mine as fast as I could, Emmett was taking his time, not taking his eyes off me until the liquid in his glass was gone.

He opened his mouth as if he was about to say something when someone knocked on the bar a few stools down. Pointing at me Emmett demanded, "Don't go anywhere. I'll be right back." He went to help the man holding his glass in the air.

I watched as Emmett started running around behind the bar filling people's drinks with beer and hard liquor. He had a cool calm about him in the midst of all the chaos, giving his full attention to whomever he was helping.

His effortless smile was hard to ignore as was the way his pants were accentuating his perfectly curved butt. I was stealing glimpses as he would bend or lean over, filling drinks and handing them back to each patron. I was just mindlessly staring when I noticed that Emmett had caught me looking at his behind again. He just smiled and winked at me before wiggling his butt at me. I could feel my face turning as red as a tomato.

The room started to suddenly get hot, the effects of the whiskey kicking in, definitely not from the look Emmett had been giving me. I hadn't even noticed Emmett had returned until he was pushing a glass of water in front of me.

"Drink this, Carrots. Then you can drink the bar dry." Even though he said it softly there was a commandment in his voice. I reluctantly looked at the glass filled with water, beads of condensation already gathering on its sides.

"Why are you calling me Carrots?" I took a long sip,

letting the cool water slowly go down my throat. The cold water only cooled me down slightly. I took another sip.

Emmet saddled up to the bar, leaning in towards me. "You're a farm girl, right? Lived there all your life?" he asked those questions as if that would have been some indication as to what the newly acquired nickname he'd given me meant.

"Yes. Your point?" There was a small puddle forming under my glass making it easy for me to slide it around aimlessly as I tried to follow this man's train of thought.

"Farm girl. Carrots." Emmett spoke as if saying those words together would unlock some secret code I was supposed to know. My questioning face had him continue, "Carrots come from farms."

"We don't grow carrots." I scrunched up my face in confusion. It was my only defense to why this nickname for me should be stopped immediately.

"No, but you could," he said as if this was some sort of counter argument. It was not. I was still mindlessly passing the glass between my hands, the water puddle making the glass slide with ease across the bar top. Emmett placed his hand on top of the glass mid-slide averting my attention back to him. His eyes slid to the nearly full glass of water.

"Drink." It wasn't a question or suggestion; it was a command. He placed his hand over mine as he guided the glass to my lips.

I downed the rest of my water in a few gulps while Emmett monitored me. "There. Happy now?" I tried giving him a glare, but I think it came off as more of a squint.

He practically gloated as he said, "Extremely." He held my gaze a little too long than what was considered proper. I blinked rapidly to break the spell he was casting on me.

"I believe I was told I could now drink the bar dry." I pushed my now empty glass away from me as if the water had been the worst thing I had ever consumed.

TABITHA KRUEGER

"As you wish, fiancée." He didn't take my glass, but he turned around and walked away before I could scold him again for calling me "fiancée". I was confused until he came back with a bottle of whiskey and another glass. He filled mine up before doing the same to his. He raised his glass to me, "Bottoms up, fiancée."

I snatched my glass up and downed it before he was halfway done. We sat silently drinking, Emmett matching me drink for drink. The bottle was half gone when the urge to pee suddenly hit me. I was about to stand up when I noticed the room started spinning. Emmett noticed my unsteadiness and was out from behind the bar and at my side before I could stand up.

He placed his hand around my waist, and I put my arm around his shoulder. He was helping me stand up when my legs gave out for a second, making me lean into him as he caught me. "Whoa there, fiancée."

I looked up at him, slightly slurring my words, "Why are you calling me fiancée?" I was curious as to what his motives were.

"You said you didn't like Carrots, figured I'd give fiancée a try, since you are one and all."

"Don't call me fiancée. I am not anyone's fiancée. I'm just someone's convenience." If I couldn't tell any better, I would say I saw pity on his face. His stare was so intense I needed to divert it.

"It doesn't matter. I was going to die by myself, anyway, might as well make someone else miserable on my way out." I smiled half-heartedly as we started shuffling towards the bathrooms. "I hate Carrots less." He smiled back, shaking his head. We stumbled to the bathroom, well, I stumbled while Emmett kept me somewhat upright.

I opened the door about to step inside. "Will you be here when I come out?" I hesitantly asked.

SPEAK EASY TO ME

He smiled sweetly at me as he replied, "Absolutely. Now, don't fall in. I don't want to have to save you." I rolled my eyes at him.

"You are too funny for words. And I'm more than capable of saving myself, thank you very much." I think my words would have had more of a zing if I could have fully articulated that sentence. My tongue had stopped fully working making my words come out a jumbled mess.

I entered the small ladies' room. There were two sinks to my right and three stalls to my left. I entered the nearest stall and closed the door. I had forgotten that I had undergarments that needed another person to put on in a timely manner. I was almost inclined to jokingly ask Emmett to help, but he might say 'yes' and I don't think I would have the willpower to say 'no'. I had no other option other than to undo all the clasps and straps myself.

After what felt like forever, I was finally able to sit and relieve myself. The sound of the door opening was followed by more than one woman's footsteps on the tiled floor. Judging by their shoes, the three women who had entered were fashionable.

I could see they were standing in front of the mirror by the way their feet were positioned. One woman started talking as soon as the door closed behind them. "I can't believe he hasn't said anything to you all night." The rummaging through bags and compacts opening signaled the women were freshening up.

"I'm not worried. We have a date set for tomorrow night." More rummaging around, lipstick caps popping off.

"You might not have a date tomorrow night by the looks of it!" They all laughed. My ears perked up because I love a good bit of gossip. I heard lips smacking and lipstick tube tops popping back on.

"Emmett would never touch a cow like that. He's

TABITHA KRUEGER

worshiped my body four times now." Her voice was low and sultry. "*Ooohs*," from the other two women echoed throughout bathroom. Emmett's possible girlfriend continued, "Did you see what she was wearing? Did she think she looked good leaving the house?" They all laughed once again, at my expense.

"I bet they don't make mirrors wide enough." More raucous laughter as if it was the funniest thing any of them had heard in their lives. They finished up what they were doing and all three left, still roaring with laughter as I heard the door open and close.

I sat on the toilet, feeling utterly and completely done. I tried holding the tears back, but it was useless. By the time I was washing my hands, they were flowing freely and there was nothing I could do to stop them. I didn't care anymore. I finished washing my hands not even bothering to try to hide the fact I had been crying when I opened the door. I half expected Emmett not to be anywhere in sight, going with his girlfriend after she left the bathroom, but there he was, leaning against the wall, waiting for me.

"You were taking so long I almost sent in a search party," he said with a grin until he moved closer and saw my face, the tears still running down. His face turned serious, placing a hand on my upper arm as he took in my face. "What's wrong? Are you alright?" His eyes were searching for an answer in mine.

"I just want to go home." My voice was barely audible. I was afraid that if I talked any louder my voice would crack, sending me into hysterics. I closed my eyes as I took a deep breath to steady myself and recenter. "I need to find Nathaniel." Emmett's dark eyes scanned my face again as he nodded.

"Okay. You stay here. I will go find Nathaniel for you." I was going to do what he said, but the crowd, noise, smells, it had all been too much right then. I needed fresh air and to cool down. Between the booze, embarrassment, and the workout I had trying to get my undergarments back on, I needed to feel the cool air on my skin.

"I need to head outside. Tell him to meet me by his car." I started walking away before Emmett could respond. I felt a tug on my arm and then Emmett was standing in front of me.

"You cannot go outside by yourself at this time of night; it's dangerous, especially outside of this place," he was referring to the speakeasy. I wiggled out of his grip.

"Then I guess you better find Nathaniel quickly." My teeth gritted as I responded. I started to move around the perimeter of the room, avoiding going through the crowded dance floor. I made it to the door before realizing I didn't have my coat. I was about to turn to go back inside when I saw the wall to my left was lined with coats. I found mine and made my way outside, into the prickly night air.

I was tying the belt around the waist of my coat as I made my way to Nathaniel's car. I heard footsteps behind me thinking they were Nathaniel's. My footsteps ceased once I reached the car the ones behind me picked up in pace.

I smelled him before I saw him. I turned around to be greeted by a man in a dark coat, hat pulled down low, smelling of cigars and so much beer it was as if he'd been dipped in it. He moved closer to me, pinning me up against the driver's side of the car. His breath was hot and acidic making me gag.

"What's a pretty thing like you doing walking around by herself at night?" He took another step closer to me, the crunching of rocks on the icy concrete made me snap out of my frozen state and allowed me to react.

As he placed his hands on my shoulders I lifted my knee,

making contact between his legs. The impact forced a loud yell out of him. My victory was short lived.

It would have been a good defensive move if I had remembered that it was icy out. My foot on the ground slipped, causing me to fall, hitting my head on the side of the car on the way down while simultaneously taking this man down with me after my flailing legs hit his. He landed on top of me with a hard thud knocking the wind out of me.

"You bitch!" he screamed in my face. "You are going to be..." His sentence was cut off at the same time I felt his weight leave my body. I could finally take a sharp, deep breath. It took me a minute to realize what had happened.

Emmett had the man on his back, repeatedly punching him in the face. The sound of Emmett's fist hitting the man's face bounced off the brick buildings. He was hurling curses, insults, and threats amid each punch. I got to my feet as quickly as I could. Emmett pulled his arm back to land another blow. I grabbed onto him, stopping him. I looked down at the man's blood covered face. Emmett was breathing heavily from the combined adrenaline and exertion.

He immediately stood up, cupping my face in his hands. "Lottie, did he hurt you?" He looked me up and down, examining my clothes, making sure every garment was in the correct place.

"No, he didn't. I hurt myself actually. I slipped when I kneed him in his balls, hitting my head on the car. Then he fell on top of me, knocking the wind out of me. All my fault, really." I tried lightening the mood, but there was no humor on Emmett's face.

"When I saw him on top of you, Lottie." There was true panic still in his eyes. I put my hand on his face, forcing his eyes to look into mine.

"I'm fine. Really. Nothing happened. You came in time"

We were still looking at each other in silence, "I would also add that my virtue is still intact, but I lost that a long time ago." Emmett let out a relieved laugh.

There was a groan of pain coming from the bloody heap of a man on the ground next to us. "What about him?" I asked as I inclined my head to my attacker.

"Don't worry about him. Let's get you home, Carrots." He put his arm around my shoulders, leading me away from Nathaniel's car.

"One, I told you not to call me that anymore." Emmett just smiled as we continued to walk.

"You told me you prefer Carrots over fiancée." He wasn't going to back off the nickname. "And two?" He said with a humor laced laugh. I stopped walking and turned to him.

"Where are we going? Why isn't Nathaniel out here?" I put my hands on my hips waiting for his reply. He mirrored my gestures.

"Nathaniel is indisposed at the moment." I made a face of disgust. Judging by the look of delight on Emmett's face, he knew what my reaction to that detail would be and he enjoyed it.

"I didn't need to know that." His smile just got bigger as put his arm back over my shoulders and started leading me to wherever he had been taking me before.

"Carrots isn't growing on you?" he joked.

"Yes, like a mold that just keeps coming back," I said as monotone as I could muster as my heart was still racing.

"That's the spirit!" he said with a little too much glee. Maybe if I didn't make a big deal out of it, he'd get bored and drop it, but knowing him the little I did, he didn't seem like the type that would give up so easily.

We walked in comfortable silence for a block before we came to his car. He opened my door for me. I was settling in

TABITHA KRUEGER

my seat as he opened his door and got in. He placed his hands on the steering wheel, catching my attention.

Before I could stop myself, I exclaimed, "Your hand!" as I reached out and took his hand in both of mine. His hand was all bloody; whether any of it was his I was unsure. I was trying to examine it, but the darkness of the night made that almost impossible to do. He winced slightly as I moved it from side to side.

"I'm fine. I don't think it's broken or anything." The blood was starting to dry so I couldn't tell if he had any cuts to his hand or not. "Blood washes off," he said as casually as someone telling you about the weather.

"Well, cuts don't wash off and if you have a cut, it can get infected. Human mouths are full of bacteria."

Emmett just studied me for a minute as if what I just said was totally out of our world. "And how do you know this, Carrots?" I rolled my eyes at him. I rolled my eyes around him a lot.

"I was the designated nurse on the farm. We were too far away from town to have anyone go to the hospital for nonlife threatening injuries. With men on a farm, there were always nonlife threatening injuries." He seemed enthralled with my story, so I continued. "Gashes, burns, severed fingers. I've seen it all."

"Wait." His face was full of confusion and horror, "There was more than one severed finger?" He shivered.

"Sometimes more than one a day." I informed him wiggling my eyebrows at his obvious disgust. The look of bewilderment on his face made me burst out laughing.

I could tell he was about to ask me a question, so I beat him to it. "You can't tell a farmer anything. They also don't learn from past mistakes because they think they can do it better than the last time." He just shook his head as he started the car.

38

SPEAK EASY TO ME

"You really should let me look at your hand though. It would make me feel better." He kept his face forward, fixed at the road, but I could see his eyes glancing over my way.

I felt a slight bit of victory when he relented, "Fine. We will go to my place so you can examine my hand, Carrots."

We pulled into the driveway of a plain looking white house with a green door. After Emmett unlocked the door, we made our way into the house. The inside matched the outside. Plain white walls with no decorations adorning them. There was minimal furniture. Emmett took my coat and hung it up in the coat closet next to the front door.

"Nice place," I said, not sure what to say since I had never been to a man's house I didn't know before.

"I know it's not much to look at. I'm hardly here, so decorating doesn't seem worth it." He started walking down the hall. He opened the room to his bedroom and walked in. I stood there, hesitant. "In order to get to my bathroom, you have to go through my bedroom." He held his hands up in surrender. "I did not design this house."

I gave him a look of disbelief. "How convenient," I joked. The words spoken by the three women from earlier came rushing back to me putting me in a sour mood again. I tried to push their words back out of my head as I made my way to the bathroom. "First, I'm going to have you wash your hands with soap and water, then I'll assess the damage."

Grabbing the soap and turning on the water Emmett said, "Whatever you say, Doc." I watched as Emmett washed the other man's blood off his hands, red mixing with the clear water, turning it pink as it was going down the drain. Once his hands were thoroughly washed Emmett turned off the water and dried his hands. I carefully took his hand in mine to look it over. There was bruising already on his knuckles and a few small cuts in his skin, but nothing alarming that needed attention.

39

TABITHA KRUEGER

"What's your diagnosis, Doc?" The words came out with a playful tinge to them. I could tell he was smiling without even looking at his face.

"We won't have to amputate, if that's what you're asking." I matched his tone. I looked up at him and he was staring at me intensely. "What?" I asked as I took in his face. He had gone from playful to serious in a matter of seconds.

"It's getting late. I think I should take you home." He abruptly stood up before he left the bathroom. I heard the front door open and then slam shut. I wasn't even sure he had enough time to grab his coat from the closet. I straightened up the bathroom the best I could, wiping the little remaining blood that hadn't washed down the sink with the hand towel Emmett had used to dry his hands with.

I opened the coat closet to get my coat and noticed Emmett's was still hanging in on its hanger. After putting on my coat I grabbed his and headed outside. Once I was in the car, I handed him his coat. He snatched it out of my hands and mumbled a halfhearted, "Thank you," before putting the car in reverse leaving the driveway.

Apparently, Emmett knew where my uncle lived because he did not ask me for an address, which was fine since I didn't know it anyway. We rode in complete silence the whole way to my temporary house. I honestly had no idea what had transpired in that bathroom to make Emmett's mood change so drastically the way it did.

Emmett pulled the car right up to the iron gates. Something else I hadn't taken into consideration was how I was going to sneak back into the house now that I was here. Either Emmett could read my mind, or it was written all over my face, his voice filling the silent car, "There's a weak link in the fence over to the right. Just push it in and you can slip underneath." Gone was the cheerful tone he'd had earlier, replaced by a tone of annoyance.

SPEAK EASY TO ME

I opened the car door and got out, but before I shut the door I said, "I'm sorry for whatever happened to change your mood." He just kept looking straight ahead, no expression on his face. "Thank you for the ride home." Still no reply so I slammed the door shut. I made my way around the fence to the part he'd told me to go to. I hadn't taken four steps away from his car before he was backing up and leaving faster than I'd ever seen a car go. What a completely shitty day!

I just wanted to go inside and wash away the remnants of the whole day. The grandfather clock greeted me as soon as I entered the house, letting me know it was now 2 o'clock in the morning. I trotted up the stairs looking forward to soaking in my tub, maybe even sleeping in there.

After my bath where I soaked in water saturated with lavender oil and brushed my teeth, I piled myself into my bed and promptly fell asleep. Tomorrow, well, technically today, was a new day, things could only go up from here, right?

41

CHAPTER 4

LOTTIE

No one came to wake me up, so I slept in until 10 o'clock in the morning. The heat from the sun made the pile of blankets and pillows I had burrowed under uncomfortably warm. After taking another soak in the bathtub, this time using honeysuckle bath oil, I felt refreshed and ready to face the day. Leaving my hair down in its natural state, I put on a casual dress and my most comfortable pair of shoes.

It was unusually warm for the end of January in Chicago, so I decided to take advantage. Claire told me about a park that was within walking distance of the house. She had insisted I wait until either Marco or Russel could accompany me, but I left as soon as she made her way to find one of them. I wanted to enjoy the radiant day in solitude.

I made it to the park as the sun hit its peak, giving everything a look of happiness that made me smile. The grass was still brown, and no leaves hung from trees or blooms on flowers, but I didn't mind. The fresh air felt amazing as it filled my lungs, helping melt away the last few days.

SPEAK EASY TO ME

I merrily walked along when I heard a cough behind me. For some odd reason it sounded familiar. Slowly turning my body towards the noise, I was shocked to find Emmett standing there, in the middle of the same park I had been enjoying.

"Oh, it's you," I said with indifference as I turned back around to walk away. I could hear Emmett's hurried footsteps trying to catch up to me. I kept walking without offering him a glance back.

"I deserve that. I was an asshole to you last night and I'm sorry." He was now at my side, keeping my pace, a little out of breath. I contemplated running to get away from him. I didn't want to see or talk to him after the way he treated me the last hour we spent together the previous night.

"Don't worry yourself about it, I know I'm not." I hoped my words didn't betray the feelings that still hurt. He grabbed my wrist to stop me from walking away. His face filled with regret as I faced him.

"I am worrying myself. I want to explain my actions if you'll let me." I crossed my arms in front of me, wishing I was stronger in my resolve, but there was something in his eyes that made me want to hear what he had to say.

"Fine. If it will make you feel better. Explain." I stood there in annoyance as if this was a huge inconvenience to me. Don't get me wrong, it was, but at the same time I so desperately wanted to know his thoughts. My biggest flaw was wanting to know what made people act the way that they did. Always wanting to know what made someone tick.

"I like you," he said, his face getting a little red. Embarrassed, he was embarrassed that he liked me.

"So, you're an asshole to everyone you like?" What kind of answer was that? I was now angrier than I had been. "Thank you for clearing that up. Now I'll be able to sleep better

TABITHA KRUEGER

tonight." I threw every bit of anger into my sarcastic remarks. He was going to say something, opening his mouth then closing it, the wheels turning in his head.

"You didn't sleep well last night because of me?" There was a little sadness in his eyes, but his words suggested he liked the thought of me losing sleep over him. I refused to give him the satisfaction that he had any effect on my feelings.

"I slept wonderfully. In fact, I was sleeping before my head even hit my pillow." I started walking away, my heels clicking on the sidewalk. I was thankful to be wearing my worn in shoes for my walk today; I didn't think my sore feet could handle another full day in constricting high heels.

Emmett caught back up to me. "When I said I liked you, I didn't mean I liked you, so I treated you badly. I treated you badly because I like you."

"Well, that clears things up." I shook my head and kept walking. Emmett stepped in front of me so quickly I almost ran into him.

I stopped walking as he explained, "I tend to push people that I like away. It's a bad habit. I want to try to break that habit with you." I could see the truth in his chestnut eyes pleading with mine to believe him. He extended his hand in a handshake. "Friends?" There was an edge to his voice, but I couldn't place why.

I took his hand in mine, still a little leery as I said, "Friends." We shook hands, both forgetting that he had injured his hand, making him let out a little, "Ouch," as he recoiled from my grasp, wincing in pain.

"Oh my goodness. I'm so sorry. Are you alright?" I felt horrible about hurting his hand. It had been quite bruised last night so I'm sure it had turned into a darker purple by this afternoon when it finally settled in. He shook his hand out in hopes that it would help alleviate some of the pain.

"Don't be sorry. I'm no worse for the wear." He wore a small, reassuring smile.

We walked side by side in amiable silence for so long the warmth of the sun started dissipating into a cool breeze. My loose hair started lightly whipping around my face, forcing me to try wrangling it in. I should have put it up before I left the house. Emmett saw me struggling with the loose tresses.

"I'm glad you left your hair down. It smells good." He leaned in closer to get a better smell.

The gesture made me grin. "I used lavender oil in my bath when I got home and honeysuckle in my morning bath." As I said the word 'bath' Emmett's eyes raked across my body, up and down. There was a want in his dark eyes that he tried to cover up, but I caught that millisecond he let it lapse.

"I really should be getting home." I realized how late it was and it would be dark soon. It occurred to me that I tried to ignore Emmett so much, I had forgotten where we had turned on the path in the park. "It seems I can't remember the way we came, though." My head swiveled about, analyzing the trails from where we were standing. I was hoping he knew the way and I wouldn't have to ask him, having him conclude I was lost.

"It would be my pleasure to walk you home." He held out his arm, waiting for me to take it. The heat radiated off Emmett's arm as I took it, making me move in a little closer for the warmth. He was just escorting me home from the park; I couldn't read too much into this. He was being nice.

We were once again walking in silence when I looked over to see Emmett's face was askew. As I tried to read his expression, he shakily said, "We're friends now, correct?" He was looking straight ahead, not even glancing at me as he spoke.

"I think we've established that." I wondered where this line of questioning was going. If I didn't know any better, I

TABITHA KRUEGER

would have thought maybe his face had been one of embarrassment.

My suspicion was confirmed as he continued, "May I ask you about something you said last night?" His cheeks took on a slight pink hue. I don't think the change to his cheek coloring had anything to do with the cooler winter air approaching.

"Yes?" I said warily, more of a question than a definitive 'Yes'. Scared of what the question would be, but more curious as to what could make this man, who seems to be cool under pressure, blush.

Emmett cleared his throat, buying him some time to get the courage to ask his burning question. His cheeks were turning a deeper shade of pink verging on red. One more cough was what stood between him and his question. "When you said you no longer had your virtue..." he trailed off.

I relished this moment. I knew where this was going, and you best believe I wasn't going to just give away the answer he so desperately wanted to know. Him risking the foreign territory of embarrassment to get it somehow made this exchange that much sweeter.

"You're going to make me ask?" He caught on quick. The little bit of desperation, pleading in his voice, for me to put him out of his misery, made him endearing. The man that I saw behind the bar last night, effortlessly taking command of the room, was now stumbling over his words. It was cute, which was never a word I would have used to describe Emmett. He was a million other things: strong, confident, handsome beyond measure, charismatic, but cute? It was at that moment I figured out that he never let people see that side of him. He still was going to have to work for my answer.

"Absolutely!" I smiled as the word left my lips, feeling the

46

SPEAK EASY TO ME

victory over this battle. He swallowed, his throat visibly bobbing.

Emmett's eyes scanned the area around us, taking inventory of how close other people were to our vicinity. There was only one other couple walking their dog down the opposite path we were on. His assessment resulted in him leaning in and whispering so quietly I almost couldn't hear the question. "You're not a virgin?" Even with his words barely above a whisper his cheeks reddened even more, making me giggle. A man who works in a speakeasy, afraid to ask a woman about the state of her womanhood, was not something I had expected today.

"No," I was having too much fun with his uneasiness, that was all I was going to give him. I looked away, a smile on my face, as he turned to me, catching my glee. He let out a breath of exaggerated frustration. His playful smile turned serious as he contemplated how to ask his next question. I could feel the hesitation radiating from him. "You can ask your question, whatever it is. I won't be offended."

My invitation seemed to settle something inside him. His eyes turned soft to match his words. "Does your fiancée know you're not a virgin?" It hadn't even occurred to me to wonder if that mattered to Cameron or not. Every indication had been him not caring about me except when it came specifically to him and what I could give him, essentially.

I wasn't sure how much I should share. Emmett was a stranger for all intents and purposes, no matter how easily I was able to talk to him. I decided to err on the side of caution, not revealing too much. "We both need to marry each other for various reasons. He doesn't need to know I'm no longer 'pure', and it's not something I'm going to divulge to him." All truthful without divulging the fine print details.

"Understandable." Emmett was processing what I had

47

TABITHA KRUEGER

told him but didn't pry anymore about Cameron or why we had to get married. I wanted to chase away the dark cloud that now seemed to hang over us.

"Besides, I do have to keep up this innocent act I have going on. Don't go giving me away now." I softly jabbed my elbow into his side. He threw his head back in laughter.

"Did you forget I was there last night? I don't think you are all that innocent." His laughter ceased long enough for me to defend myself, which I couldn't.

I shrugged as I said, "I have a tattoo." Why I shared this secret so willingly, I wasn't sure. I think it was the first time I felt like someone wouldn't judge me for something I did for myself. I could bare my purest self to Emmett, and he wouldn't think any less of me.

It took me a few seconds to reconcile that Emmett's steady footsteps had stopped and I was walking alone. I turned, confusion etched on my face, just in time to witness Emmett grab his chest dramatically, mouth gaping open.

"Very funny." I put my hands on my hips in exasperation. Emmett didn't move an inch as his heady dark eyes raked over my body. He was trying to figure out where my tattoo was hidden. I casually informed him, "You can't see it unless I take everything off," before turning and continuing to walk, presumably to Uncle Lon's house.

Emmett was by my side in no time. He was out of breath from running to catch up to me. Through light gasps he asked, "Everything?" I gave him a sly grin in response. He got the message and let out a deep groan as he almost fell to his knees. I knew he had some follow up questions, but I answered enough.

He opened his mouth to speak when I cut him off, "Enough about me. I think I have earned some secrets of yours." Disappointment flooded his eyes as he nodded his head, as if contemplating. "It's only fair," I pointed out.

48

SPEAK EASY TO ME

He let out a huge breath while rolling his eyes at me, teasing. "Ask your questions." His words, although they dripped in a teasing tone, they also held an air of excitement, leading me to believe he wanted me to ask him questions.

I took a moment to let him wonder what I was going to ask him. He kept his expression steady, anticipation bubbling right under the surface. As much as he tried to contain his joy, his mouth betrayed him by slightly turning up at the corners. I was just staring at his mouth, taking in the way his bottom lip was slightly fuller than his top lip. All thoughts eluded me as I stared at this beautiful man walking beside me.

His grin grew bigger, cockier. "Are you going to stare at me the rest of the way to your house or are you going to ask me some questions?" My neck almost broke from the speed at which my head whipped forward. There was no coming back from this. I had been caught red handed ogling my friend. I could feel the heat rushing to my cheeks, no doubt making me as red as a tomato.

"You're cute when you're blushing." I shoved him slightly as we kept walking.

"So are you." The words came out before I could even stop them. My natural instinct had been to throw my hand over my mouth in surprise. The action made both of us start laughing.

Emmett placed his hand on the small of my back before he leaned in closely, whispering "Ask me your questions, Carrots." His voice was low and husky making my body tingle in places I didn't know were possible. I cleared my throat in order to chase the feeling away.

"Alright then." I scrambled to think of a question to ask to quell the sudden growing tension. "I didn't see any pictures of your family at your house. Do you not see them?" There, that should have broken the thick air of whatever was brew-

49

TABITHA KRUEGER

ing. I could tell the question hit Emmett as intended, knocking him off kilter.

It took him a minute to find the words. "My mother and father died when I was a teenager." My heart broke for him. I couldn't imagine losing both of my parents now, let alone at such a young age. I was about to give my condolences, but he wasn't done. "And I lost my younger brother, Jason, when he was five. I was seven." My heart shattered for him. As much as my sisters could drive me to the edge of insanity, I couldn't even begin to contemplate losing one of them.

His earlier confession of pushing the people he liked away came into focus. He didn't push people away because he was afraid they would leave, he was afraid they would die. It was absolutely devastating coming to that conclusion. "Oh, Emmett. I am so sorry." I was trying to read what he was thinking, but he steeled his face, surely a defense mechanism he'd perfected over the years.

"I can't handle that kind of loss again." The hurt, even all those years later, was still heavy on his heart with his revelation. Maybe this was what he had been wanting to get off his chest. Something this heavy would weigh anyone down, nearly suffocating them.

"It must be lonely. I understand your reasoning though." I wasn't sure how much he was willing to share. He had already shared more than I would have expected of anyone.

He just shrugged, "I like my privacy." A laugh escaped me at his liking privacy, garnering me a side eye.

"I am the oldest of five sisters. We had two bedrooms and one bathroom between us. There was no such thing as privacy at my house." I could see the entrance of the park coming into view, the sun starting to set, making the entrance glow in a light orange haze.

"That sounds like complete chaos." Emmett had an

SPEAK EASY TO ME

amused glint in his eye. It was better than the sadness he had just been wearing.

"It definitely was chaotic most of the time..." I couldn't think of the last time I had thought about my sisters since I had gotten to Chicago. What kind of horrible person doesn't even have a thought about her sisters back home? What was even more surprising was that I had thought about the night sky at the farm more than I thought about my sisters.

Emmett picked up on my mood change. "What is it?" Concern hiding just beyond his words. We passed the group of bare trees that seemed to have lost all their wonder from this afternoon, they looked a little more menacing as the sun dipped below the skyline.

"I thought I was going to miss my sisters more. I do miss them, don't get me wrong, but I miss being able to see the stars at night the most. Like, amid all the chaos and work on the farm, I had the stars at night just for me, for a while at least." Emmett raised his eyebrows in a questioning gesture. "That was until Nick found me laying on the roof one night, star gazing. The sky had been particularly crip that night. He joined me every night after that." It made me miss Nick, thinking about our time spent together under the open night sky. I let a small smile trace my lips. "He taught me about stars and the constellations."

"There seems to be more to the story there." Emmett seemed to be asking a question without really asking the question. I'd already shared so much with him there really didn't seem to be any harm in sharing more.

"Nick was the one who took my virginity. After spending numerous nights together, one thing led to another." Emmett's eyebrows rose in surprise. "He is also the one who gave me my tattoo." This little tidbit of information really seemed to pique Emmett's interest.

"This guy sounds like a bad influence." He cocked an

TABITHA KRUEGER

eyebrow at me. "Next, you're going to tell me he was the one who taught you how to drink." I winced at his accuracy. Emmett took my wince as confirmation. "Damn. It sounds like I have some catching up to do in your corruption."

I smiled sweetly, my words as innocent as could be. "You can't corrupt the corrupted, sir." Emmett's eyes flared after the word sir had left my lips. We turned the corner onto my uncle's block and Emmett immediately pulled me back around the corner we'd just come from. I think he could read the confusion on my face.

"I don't think I should walk you up to your door. You know, you being an engaged woman and all." His words stung a little, but they were the truth. "Do you have any plans for tomorrow?" Emmett's words were heavy.

I hadn't been informed of anything I was to do or anywhere I had to be. "Not that I know of."

"I want to take you some-place tomorrow afternoon." His eyes were filled with childlike excitement. Like when you have a gift for someone and you are too excited to wait until their birthday or Christmas for them to open it, so you give it to them the day you get it. His excitement was contagious.

"Okay," I said with a smile on my face. Anything that made him that happy, I wanted to see, to be a part of.

"I'll send a car for you at 1." I nodded. "I'll meet you under the stars, Carrots." Emmett gave a gentle wave as we parted ways.

That was an odd way to depart. The thought quickly left my mind on the short walk home from the corner. My mind was racing with what Emmett could possibly have planned for tomorrow.

I noticed Russel waiting by the driveway gate before he noticed me. I could tell from the way he was standing that he was angry. I braced myself for the fall out. Thinking I could

SPEAK EASY TO ME

sneak by him was pointless since I barely made it to the gate when he turned around, face red from frustration.

He was hot on my heels as I made my way toward the house, "Where the hell were you?" He didn't have the patience to hear my answer because in his next breath he berated me, "You cannot leave the house unattended." I kept walking. He stepped in front of me, not allowing me to pass him. "I'm serious, Charlotte. There are people out there that want to hurt you to get to your uncle or Cameron. It's not safe for you to be out in the city alone, no matter what you think." Russel was basically a glorified babysitter that took his job seriously, no matter how degrading it seemed.

"I'm sorry. I didn't think about that." I hadn't thought about it at all. What would the consequences be now that I was to become Mrs. Darby? Both my uncle and his father were rich, influential men who held a lot of sway in Chicago. Being connected to both families did put a target on my back for the men that ran the seedy underbelly of the city. It seemed that even if my fiancée didn't want me, his enemies could.

With Russel now being on guard he could put a damper on my plans with Emmett. I wanted to start planning my exit strategy now. "I will be out tomorrow. A car is going to be picking me up, so no need to worry about my being alone in the city." My words came out as assuredly as I could muster.

I was always unsure of myself in my life. As an older sister, my younger sisters came to me for advice all the time. I could give them sound advice without wavering a bit. The moment I needed advice, all my logic went out the window. Somewhere along the way I stopped taking my own advice by questioning its validity. It made me strong in regards to others while I became a self-doubting person.

I had made it to the front door, the threshold looking like some kind of beacon of safety if I could pass through it. I was

TABITHA KRUEGER

almost to my salvation when Russel came in like a raincloud on a sunny day.

"That won't work Miss. Bradley. Either Marco or I have to be with you at all times outside of this house." He had controlled anger in his tone. It made me think he had gotten in trouble for my leaving, and he was not to let it happen again. It seemed this was going to turn into an escape rather than an outing.

CHAPTER 5

LOTTIE

I woke up in the morning giddier than I had ever been. I didn't know what it was about Emmett that gave me butterflies, but every time I was around him the fluttering in my stomach would come.

I had not gotten dressed, just thrown a robe on and made my way down to the dining room for breakfast. I wasn't sure how breakfast worked around here, but the smell of food had coaxed me from the solitude of my bedroom.

My Uncle Lon was nowhere to be found, which I can't lie, was a relief to me. I followed my nose to the immaculately set wooden table. It had been transformed from the other night, not as daunting or intimidating when Uncle Lon wasn't sitting there.

I made myself comfortable as I dug into the food sitting in the middle of the table. Eggs, bacon, and fresh fruit were piled high on my plate before I started making use of my fork. I was about halfway through my plate of food when Maggie came into the room holding a box in her hand, along with a letter.

"This came for you this morning, Charlotte." The bubbly

TABITHA KRUEGER

red head handed me a white box that had been carefully wrapped with a beautiful silk red bow, card secured neatly under the bow. Maggie hesitated before she turned to leave, just as curious as I was as to what was in this box. Possibly more important, who sent it.

"You can stay," I informed Maggie before she'd started towards the door. "I may need someone incase this box is filled with snakes." I made a mockingly shocked face at her, and she gently giggled.

"If it's snakes, you are more than welcome to open it on your own." She was hovering over me by the time she'd finished the sentence, even more anxious than myself.

I debated on whether or not to open the card first, while Maggie was standing there, or wait until she was distracted by the gift in the box. I decided to take my chances opening the card first. The calligraphy was simple and ornate with the envelope simply printed with *'Lottie'*

I tore the envelope open, unable to restrain myself. I made quick work unfolding the neat creases of the paper.

'I know you will look out of this world wearing this. See you soon, Carrots.'

There was no signature. Emmett knew I'd know it was from him, but also ensured that if anyone got ahold of the letter, there wouldn't be any way to trace it back to him. Unlike the envelope the letter had been handwritten by a man as the penmanship was barely legible.

"Carrots? Who's Carrots?" I jumped at the sound of Maggie's voice. I had forgotten Maggie was standing behind me, reading every word. I clutched the letter close to my heart.

"It's not very polite to read over someone's shoulder," I said teasingly. Maggie started to mumble an apology when I had an idea. "Would you help me with something?" Maggie's eyes brightened.

56

SPEAK EASY TO ME

"Only if you open that box right now," was her only condition. We both laughed. I imagined there wasn't a lot of excitement around this house and Maggie wanted to be a part of whatever scheme this was going to be.

I gently tugged on the bow slowly watching as it turned back into a single piece of ribbon. Gingerly removing the top, I peered inside. Tissue paper obstructed the view of what lay beneath. As I took out the tissue paper my breath caught. I couldn't say anything as I slowly ran my hand over the velvety soft green fabric of the dress. I didn't need to see the whole dress to know this had been the one piece of clothing I had wanted while I was out shopping with Russel, but never ended up getting.

It was low cut with the fabric cupping the breasts in pleats. The midsection was smooth contrasting the pleated bust and gathered fabric at the hip. The skirt was a semi-wrap-around gathered just to the left of the middle. One wrong move and all your business would be showing. The cap sleeves coming down nearly to my elbow had been the most modest part of the frock. Russel had taken one look at me when I had tried the dress on and immediately told me to take it off.

I pulled it out of the box displaying it for Maggie to see. She took the dress in, running her hands along the soft green fabric. "This is stunning." Maggie couldn't seem to find the words she wanted to say. "Charlotte, you will have whoever sent this to you wrapped around your finger when he sees you in this!"

"This is why I need your help." Maggie listened intently as I explained, mostly, what had transpired between Emmett and me. I left out a few minor details but gave her the overall picture. Maggie reminded me of one of my younger sisters and it was nice to have that feeling of connection again. I think Maggie was looking for that same connection.

TABITHA KRUEGER

We carefully got the dress and card up to my room, making sure no one saw what we were doing. With our plan all worked out we began setting it in motion. I would announce to Russel I would be in my room and that Maggie would be bringing me dinner to me.

After I got ready, Maggie would distract Russell while I went out the front and through the hole in the fence Emmett had told me about the night I sneaked back in. I'd be able to meet with Emmett while Russell would be none the wiser. He'd think I was in my room.

Our plan was executed flawlessly, and I was sitting in the back seat of the car Emmett had sent for me. You can imagine my surprise when we pulled up in front of the planetarium. I exited the car and made my way to the grand stairway in the front of the magnificent building.

I noticed Emmett standing atop the stairs before I made it there. He was taking the stairs down, two at a time, as he rushed to my side. He held his arm out for me to take. Emmett couldn't see the dress under my coat, but without missing a beat he said, "I told you you'd look good in that dress." He was quite confident that I would wear the dress he bought me.

"How do you know I'm wearing the dress you sent me?" I teased.

"Are you naked under that coat?" There was heat in his voice as he asked me his question.

"No," I replied as I took in the smoldering look in his eyes.

"Then you're wearing that dress." He was so confident it was bordering on cocky, but he knew how to toe the line between the two perfectly.

I would have made small talk on the way in, but my brain was preoccupied with the dangerously handsome man walking next to me, trying not to fall going up the stairs and trying not to squeal with excitement about going to the planetarium.

The Adler Planetarium was less than a year old, so it was still a novelty to visit. It was the one place I had wanted to visit mote than everywhere else in the city. The magnificent building sat on the bank of Lake Michigan. The outside beauty of the planetarium set the tone for the inside.

Emmett must have felt my mind racing and didn't say anything while letting me take everything in. I sneaked a glance at him, and he was just staring at me with a wide grin on his face. He relished in my excitement.

As we stepped into the building, I was instantly relaxed. I was back under the stars, and everything just felt right. As we wandered around the planetarium looking at displays, I could feel Emmett's eyes on me, questions dancing around in them.

"Tell me about the stars, smarty pants." He jabbed me gently in the side with his elbow. "What did this Nick fella teach you?" I picked up a little jealousy in his words. I never had a man jealous of another man because of me. It was kind of exciting.

I wasn't sure where to start. I started pointing out the different constellations and the backstories that followed them. We had been walking for about an hour, with me dominating most of the conversation. Emmett followed me closely, taking in every bit of information I was sharing.

There was a lull in the conversation when Emmett informed me, "I'm trying to erase everything you had with Nick and replace it with me." That little revelation took me aback.

"Really?" I teased. "You want to give me a tattoo as well?" I was feeling feisty.

"Among other things," was his wicked reply. The heat

pulsing through my body almost made me burst. The nervous excitement made me test the waters a tad more.

"I think it would be odd to have two men's names tattooed on my body." From his jealousy coded attitude earlier, I knew this would get a rise out of him. I could hardly contain the laugh that escaped as I looked at the shock and bewilderment on Emmett's face.

"You should see your face right now," I said in between laughs. "The tattoo is a tiny star that's barely the size of a pencil eraser." I turned to walk away, still laughing when Emmett came up from behind, wrapping one arm around my waist, pulling my back flush against the front of his body.

"I am a very jealous man, Carrots. You like playing with fire, Lottie?" My breath caught as his deep, low voice filled my ears. His hot breath tickled my skin. "If you're not careful, you'll get burned." I turned my head. Our lips were so close that one move from either of us and they would meet.

"Maybe I want the heat." My breathes were coming out fast and shallow. "Burn me with your fire, Emmett. Turn me to ashes." I meant every word. I had never felt this way with anyone before. With Nick, our relationship had been out of convenience and boredom more than raw sexual attraction. It was nice and everything, but nothing like this. I never wanted a man as much as I wanted the one next to me, right now.

Emmett looked around before grabbing my hand and leading me down a few hallways until we came to a door. He opened it and practically pushed me in, slamming the door behind him. His hands cupped my face as he brought his lips to mine.

I never had a kiss so gentle with so much wanting. It was so light I wouldn't have thought we kissed but I could still feel the warmth of his breath as he pulled away from me.

My eyes were still closed as I took a life centering breath

trying to quell my racing heart. When I finally had the courage to open my eyes Emmett was staring at me, waiting for my reaction.

"I'm sorry. I shouldn't have done that. I was forward and I apologize." His rapid breathing made his chest move up and down sharply.

I shook my head. "No need to apologize." He looked at me like he was about to devour me.

"Good," was all the warning I got before he leaned in again, more aggressive this time. His lips filled with want and need and consuming desire. He backed me up against the wall as he kissed me harder, our tongues mingling between our mouths. He pushed my skirt open taking advantage of the ease with which it parted with the wrap around being close to the front. He pressed himself against me, grinding his hips into me. I could feel his hard length pressing into my stomach. I let out a whimper at the thought of seeing him hard and naked.

He let out an animalistic groan as he kissed his way down my neck making his way to my collarbone where he settled. His hands made their way to my breasts. He gently pulled down the velvety fabric, revealing my bra. He pulled down the cups of my bra, letting my breasts spill out. He took a step back, his warmth an immediate loss I wanted back. My chest was rising fast with my quick breaths.

"You are perfection, Lottie. Fucking perfection." I had barely heard what he said as he grabbed my wrists, pinning them behind my back with one of his hands which thrust my bare breasts up and forward. He took advantage of them being front and center as his mouth encompassed the bud of my nipple while his free hand found my other breast and started caressing it.

A moan escaped my throat which encouraged him continue his frenzied assault, not being able to control his

TABITHA KRUEGER

want. His hand wandered lower. My legs naturally parted as his hand moved over my underwear. Emmett began rubbing until I couldn't take the pleasure between his mouth on my breasts and his hand on my underwear covered clit. I couldn't hold back anymore, and my passion exploded in a mix of a moan and a sob.

He pulled back, reluctantly, as I went for the zipper on his pants. I wanted more of him. As much as I could get. "We can't," he said as he moved my hand from his pants. "We shouldn't have done this," he said, almost to himself. Like he was scolding himself.

"I'm sorry," I suddenly felt completely naked and vulnerable. I fixed my dress feeling ashamed and stupid.

"No, Lottie, I am only saying that because you're engaged. I shouldn't have let it get this far." His eyes had pain behind them. He nuzzled his face in my neck. "I want you so bad right now. Don't think that I don't want this to continue. Trust me, I do. I've never wanted anything more in my life." Then his eyes got needy again. He looked me up and down for a moment.

"Take off your underwear." The need in his voice had me immediately obeying, even if it was a little hesitant. He unzipped his pants and pulled out his full length, guiding my hand to it.

My fingers barely met as I gripped his erection. I began stroking it up and down as he took my mouth in his. His groans drove me to increase the speed of my strokes. He kissed me deeper. His tip was wet with precum. I used the wetness to make my strokes easier. A few strokes later, he grabbed the underwear I had forgotten was in my hand and placed them between us, catching everything that came spilling out of him.

We both tried to catch our breath, coming down from the high we had both been swept up in. He rested his forehead

SPEAK EASY TO ME

on mine with our noses touching. "That was..." He was panting at this point.

"Unexpected," I finished the sentence.

"I was going to say amazing, but I guess unexpected works as well." We were both still panting trying to come down from our respective highs. He gave me chaste kiss as he straightened to his full height, rearranging my dress then tending to his own clothes. He placed my underwear, now soiled with his seme, into his pocket.

He tucked a stray strand of hair behind my ear, cupping my ear in his hand for a moment before pulling me into an embrace. It was a stark contrast from his feral display just minutes ago. The hug was sweet and gentle and comforting. I could hear him as he took a deep breath. If I didn't know any better, I thought he was sniffing my hair.

"You always smell so good." He was still trying to catch his breath.

"It's this new invention called a bathtub and soap. You should try it some time." He playfully pinched my side making me giggle. He held his hand out for me to take. I knew as soon as that door opened, we'd have to drop hands and walk around as if we were only friends. I didn't know about him, but after what just happened, it felt like we could never just be friends. There was a heat between us that was undeniable. All it needed was a single spark to ignite what was smoldering underneath the surface.

Emmett opened the door and made sure no one was around. He exited first. I followed him a moment later. We started walking like we hadn't just been mauling each other in a broom closet. I felt like everyone could easily see the pleasure radiating all over my body. Emmett walked around as if nothing happened. Every once in a while, though, he'd slip up and I would catch him staring at me, picturing my bare breasts again, I'm sure.

TABITHA KRUEGER

We made our way around the rest of the planetarium in relative silence. Occasionally we would point out various things we found interesting. We made small talk when both of us knew we wanted to say so much more than that.

The end of the displays was in sight marking the end of our time together. We both started trying to delay our departure. Even in silence we still just wanted to be around each other.

We slowly made our way outside and onto the top of the steps. I spotted the same car that had brought me here awaiting my arrival to get in. I didn't want to return to my house. I hoped Emmett would tell me to get in and he'd whisk me away to his house. That way I would never have to see my uncle or Cameron again. It was never going to happen though, and I knew that.

"This is where we part, Carrots." Emmett said with sadness and headiness in his voice as he opened the car door for me.

"Thank you for this afternoon. I enjoyed myself." My face reddened with the memories of what we had done not too long ago.

"I enjoyed you too." Emmett quipped, making my blush grow as he gave me a devilish smile, knowing exactly what he was doing.

I reluctantly got into the car without another word. My stomach sank knowing that he hadn't asked me to see him again. We had no plans to see each other in the future. This was a perfect afternoon and if this was all we got, I would have to be happy with it.

I had the driver park down the block when we approached my house so I could sneak back in without being detected. I got to the front door when I was met with my Uncle Lon. He seemed surprised to see me. Like he had forgotten I was now living in his house.

64

"I wasn't expecting to see you," he said a little flustered. Why he wouldn't expect to see me around the house I was living in was strange, but he didn't seem like he thought about me, not unless he needed to yell at me.

"And yet, here I am," I said, hoping he wouldn't notice the dress I was wearing or my smeared lipstick. He seemed oblivious to my wardrobe.

"Russel said you were in your room." He was getting a little suspicious. I had to think on my feet.

"I was, but I wanted some fresh air while I stretched my legs."

"I didn't see you leave your room. I've been in the study the whole time." Had he? Was he testing me to see if I'd lie because he knew I wasn't in my room?

"That's strange. Maybe you should have Claire fasten a bell to me, so you'd be sure to hear my every move." There, hit him with sarcasm and spite. He'd get flustered and forget why he started yelling at me and now yell at me for this. Distract and redirect.

"No matter. You are going to lunch with Cameron tomorrow. He will be here sharply at noon. And lose the attitude. I will not stand for the defiance you showed at dinner." He was about to head back into his study. "Don't make me regret giving you this opportunity. Remember why you're here, little girl." I was left speechless as Uncle Lon went into his study; the door thudding shut behind him.

He had just threatened me, and I heard him loud and clear. I needed to try to make an effort with Cameron although I don't think he'd feel the same. It seemed like Cameron was set in his ways and no one would be able to change his mind. The dread that had evaporated when I was with Emmett was now back, hovering over me as a constant reminder of the deal I made.

I told Maggie I'd needed her assistance in my room. As

soon as she shut the door, I spilled my guts out. She barely had time to join me on the bed before I started telling her every detail, minus the broom closet, about my afternoon. She was giddy right along with me.

I fell asleep to the memory of Emmett's hands on my body and his name on my lips as I tried to touch myself the way he'd touched me. It was not close to the same, but my release was his all the same.

I was up before the sun had broken over the horizon. I was going to try to put Emmett out of my mind and make the best out of this thing with Cameron. I could decide to be miserable, or I could try my best to make this relationship at least tolerable, for me at least. I don't think anything I would do could change Cameron's feelings on the whole situation we've found ourselves forced into.

I mixed the lavender and honeysuckle oils together in the bathtub before getting in to get washed up. I was about to wash Emmett's touch off me, I realized. I had a tinge of sadness ripple through my body as I submerged myself in the steaming water, rinsing Emmett's every kiss, suckle and lick off my body.

When I emerged from the bathroom Claire was waiting in my room, not so patiently. She looked like she was about to burst. I could hear the minor urgency in her voice when she said, "Mr. Darby is downstairs, Charlotte." I looked at the clock showing it was only 9 o'clock in the morning. She gave me a knowing look about his surprise appearance earlier than expected.

"Are you sure he's here to see me?" I asked, knowing that she wouldn't be here in my room, waiting for me, if he hadn't specifically asked for me.

There was a sympathetic glint in her eyes, "He asked for you, dear." I just nodded before she turned and left the room.

As I was getting ready to go downstairs, I was getting

SPEAK EASY TO ME

madder and more annoyed. I put on a simple day dress that had been purchased a few days before. I didn't even bother doing anything with my hair or makeup. Cameron was early and I would bet dollars to donuts he did that on purpose. Was it a power move? Was it just to annoy me? I had no idea, but I wasn't going to give him the satisfaction of thinking I would just jump as his every whim. I wouldn't do that now and I certainly won't be doing that once we are married.

Before I made my way downstairs, I stopped at the railing overlooking the foyer; trying to calm my nerves before I saw him. I heard his voice coming from my uncle's study, but it wasn't my uncle's booming voice joining Cameron's. It was my cousin Nathaniel's easy, happy tone I heard filling the foyer space. I made my way down the stairs, trying to be quiet so I could hear what they were talking about. What can I say, I am nosy, and I like gossip.

I couldn't' make out what they were saying and as soon as they spotted me in the doorway, all conversations ceased. Nathaniel and Cameron shared a secret look and nod, and Nathaniel left the room, shutting the door behind him, no doubt just standing beyond it in case there was a repeat of the other night.

Cameron stood straight up, taking me in. He was in a nice white button up shirt with a pull over vest over top of it. He looked casual today. He cleared his throat as he straightened from his leaned back position on the wall by the fireplace. "Good morning, Charlotte."

I was still trying to figure out what he was doing here so early when we weren't set to have lunch for at least another three hours. "Good morning, Cameron," I replied, cold and guarded.

"I know we were supposed to have lunch together today, but" I hoped he would say he was canceling lunch and I'd have the afternoon free. "I was hoping you would join me for

67

TABITHA KRUEGER

breakfast and then do me the honor of accompanying me to the picture palace to watch a movie of your choice."

He could read the hesitation on my face. "I was thinking," he started moving closer to me, "we are both stuck in this horrendous situation. I figured we could try to make the best of it until things are completed." Until he gets me knocked up, he means, which was better than animosity the whole time. Could he talk to me and not insult me?

"I was thinking the same thing. We need to make the best out of our little predicament. We could both be miserable, or we could try to salvage some sort of attempted happiness." I think this caught him a little off guard. He thought I was going to be happy to be his little wife. He didn't expect me to voice my unhappiness with the situation as well. My indifference to him cut his ego a bit. He took a minute to recover that little piece of dignity I had chipped away.

"You'll join me today, then?" he asked, on pins and needles as I made up my mind.

"Yes. I will. It will take me some time to get ready though. I wasn't expecting company until noon." I scolded him.

He shook his head "No, I understand showing up here was unexpected. Take all the time you need. I'll be waiting right here for you when you're ready."

I summoned Maggie to help me get ready for my day date with my fiancé. It was still not fully absorbed into my brain that this man was going to be my husband, reluctantly or not. I was ready and back downstairs in less than half an hour, to Cameron's surprise.

I had changed into a more suitable day dress with a little flower pattern on it. My hair had dried enough from my bath to have Maggie help style it up with pins. My shoes were less high heeled and more kitten heeled, making walking more comfortable and less awkward. I wasn't trying to impress

68

SPEAK EASY TO ME

Cameron, but I wasn't trying to repel him more by tripping and falling while out.

He opened my door for me and shut it once I was in the car. He joined me, getting into the driver's seat. We pulled out of the driveway and another car followed. I looked back out the window. Cameron saw me looking and explained, "I believe you know Russel and Marco." I thought they worked for my uncle, but I was evidently wrong.

"They work for me. It's come to my attention recently that there is a man who wants nothing more than to see to my demise." There really were people out to get Cameron. "I have them with you, since now you are a target for this guy as well." I thought Russel had just been exaggerating about my being in danger. I guess it wasn't so far-fetched that someone could be after me.

"I come from a powerful family. You come from a powerful family, whether you know them or not, you're still blood and that's all that matters to these people, Charlotte" He had is eyes on the road, but kept talking. "This man would love nothing more than to get his hands on you and bring me down." He took his eyes off the road to look at me. "There have been a rash of kidnappings recently, so I am just being overly cautious."

Everything he was saying was being stated so matter of fact, like it was ordinary everyday life. Maybe it was for him. "As much as I don't want this marriage to happen, I am responsible for you and any of our future children. I want you to know that I will keep you protected." There was something so attractive in the way he was so absolute in his words that it almost made me forget that I didn't like him.

"This guy, Holden, is my reluctant business partner. He works for Petrillo, one of the most connected men in Chicago. I am the go between with the police and Holden's boss. We don't see eye to eye on the price of things." I could read between the lines. Holden wanted to pay less, and Cameron wanted him to pay more. Why is it being poor, you are happy with what little you have and being rich you are never satisfied and always want more and more, no matter the cost?

"Your Uncle told me about your connections and that is why I feel comfortable telling you about Holden. I trust you understand nothing I've told you leaves this car." There was a hint of threat in his voice.

"I am a woman of many secrets, not just my own." Assuring him that I was able to keep a secret, even if it wasn't my own.

He turned into a street and parked the car. We got out and went inside a small café. It was quaint and decorated nicely. The tables were all round with two chairs. We sat at a table and were attended to shortly after. We started talking while waiting for our food to arrive.

I was sipping on an orange juice as was Cameron. He put his glass down and asked, "How have you been settling into things?" That was a loaded question. I took an extra-long swig of my drink as I thought of what to say.

"It's...different. It's all so new to me. I'm used to having lots of people around and bossing them around, but they were my sisters and the farmhands. I feel like I earned the right to be in charge of them. Here, with the maids and butlers and drivers, it's just so foreign to me. Having people wait on me hand and foot is not something I'm exactly comfortable with."

"You'll get used to it," he said as he waved his hand in the air dismissing my discomfort.

"I wouldn't be so sure if I were you. The moment I get used to it is the moment I am no longer me." I think my words hit a nerve because he sat up a little straighter and

SPEAK EASY TO ME

rolled his shoulders. I think I had unintentionally insulted him. I felt I needed to elaborate.

"Despite what you think of me, I like myself. I am happy with who I am. I am not trying to say there is anything wrong with you or your lifestyle" I gestured to his expensive clothing that probably cost more than my last year's wages. "I'm just saying that it's not what I had envisioned for myself, is all." He was trying to be nice to me and I didn't want to mess it up by insulting him even if it wasn't meant as such.

"Would you like to see my house?" He took a beat before he corrected himself, almost regretfully. "Your house?" Until that moment this had all seemed like a game. Like this was just something that was going to happen in the future, but the future is now. This was what my life was going to be. As Mrs. Cameron Darby I was going to be part of high society. I was also going to have a target on my back for Cameron's enemies as well as my uncles. Reality started setting in and making me feel uneasy.

"We don't have to go today. Whenever you're up to it." He was being uncharacteristically nice, from what little I know of him. I smiled and nodded politely, not wanting to think about reality.

We enjoyed our food, getting to know each other a little bit better. Both of us tried making an effort. Once we had finished eating, we were on our way to watch a movie of my choice.

As we walked up to the ticket window Cameron took my hand in his. The warmth of his hand wasn't as bad as I thought it would be. We waited in line behind two other couples. It was a little chilly out causing me to shiver. The wind was whipping around as Cameron pulled me in closer to him, putting his arm around my shoulder. I let myself lean into his body. We made our way up to the window. When the

71

ticket person asked what picture we were there to see, Cameron turned to me.

I forgot that I was supposed to choose the show. After a quick scan of the marquee, I made my decision. "Little Caeser." Cameron looked a little amused as he repeated it to the ticket person, paying and then getting our tickets.

When the doors opened, I was greeted with the smell of freshly popped popcorn. Even though I just had breakfast my mouth watered at the aroma surrounding me. I must have audibly groaned because, with a smile in his voice, Cameron said "Would you like some popcorn?" I looked at him and he tugged me with him to the concession stand. We got a popcorn and drinks. I also got Milk Duds and Cameron got Raisinets.

We found our seats and settled in. The picture started and about halfway through Cameron put his arm around me and I snuggled into his side, resting my head on his shoulder. I think I heard him inhale the scent of my hair. What is with these men and sniffing my hair?

The movie had been entertaining. I enjoyed it for what it was. We were walking out of the picture palace when Cameron asked, "What did you think of the show?"

I had to respond truthfully. "It wasn't realistic enough for me." A laugh escaped his lips.

"How would you know it wasn't realistic enough?" It was a rhetorical question. I hoped it was anyway. He said he knew of my connections, but I didn't think he fully knew what they entailed. I just innocently shrugged, but there was nothing innocent about my dealings with the mob and bootlegging. That's how I met Nick, or Little Nicky, as he was referred to by everyone else but me.

I wondered if Uncle Lon knew about my relationship with Nick or if he only knew that we allowed Nick's boss's gang to occasionally stay at the farm when they were

SPEAK EASY TO ME

running booze from Canada down to Chicago. Nick had gotten into some trouble and was a wanted man, so we took him in on the farm. Most of our farmhands had some sort of criminal past, so him being a wanted man was nothing new to me. I guess you could say I had a thing for bad boys.

As we got settled into the car my mind started wandering down the road to the past. The first time I had met Nick was interesting to say the least. The memories in my mind were as clear at the picture show we had just watched.

I went out picking raspberries in mid-July. It was hot and the sun was beating down on me. I was about two miles down the road away from our farm. It was a dirt road with bushes and woods on both sides of the road, a stark contrast to our open fields on the farm.

I was mindlessly walking and picking the ripe, juicy berries, placing the ones I wasn't eating into my basket. My mom wanted to make jam for a few of the neighbors, so I volunteered to go picking.

As I bent down to pick berries from one of the bushes, I heard a rustling in the woods. Before I could register what was happening, I was staring down the barrel of 4 guns of various makes and sizes. "Whoa!" was all I could say as I threw my hands up causing my basket to drop scattering the freshly picked raspberries into the dirt.

There were four men, guns drawn, no doubt ready to shoot me at their earliest convenience. The suits they wore exuded a casual power. I exclaimed, "I didn't see anything. Whatever your business is, I don't care."

The two guys in front looked back to the older two men behind them, waiting for the order to fire. "My farm is down the road. Whatever you need should be there." I was then struck by the fact that I didn't see a car and I knew those city boys didn't happen to walk down my road by accident.

The older guy in the back who seemed to be the leader said, "Your farm, does it got gasoline?" My father had just gotten all the cans filled in town the previous day. "Yes. We do. More than enough to get you to wherever you were headed."

All of the guys turned and looked at each other making silent agreements. Before they could say anything else we heard gravel flying in the distance. The young guy with black hair said, "Someone's coming."

"Follow me." The men stood stunned as they watched me walk further into the woods. "Move it!" I said. They all silently followed behind. "Where's your car?" I had to know so I wouldn't draw attention to it or them. One of the guys pointed behind a bush, it was hidden enough that you wouldn't see it if you didn't know it was there.

I motioned towards the mouth of a small cave just beyond where we were standing. "Go in there a few feet. You can't be seen from the road, but you will be able see everything that's going on," I said over my shoulder as I rushed back to the road.

I had made it back to my basket just in time as the car made the crest of the hill right before the bushes. It was Derek, the chief of police, who was a few years older than me and his partner, Collin. I waved as the car approached, trying to act as casual as possible.

Derek stopped the car and both men exited. The sun was so bright I had to use my hand to shield my eyes. "Hello there, Lottie," Derek said. "Everything okay?" His eyes moved to the raspberries scattered on the ground and my basket in the dirt.

I nervously laughed, trying to buy a little more time to come up with a lie. "Oh that? I'm fine. I am a little jumpy right now, though." The looks they were giving me let me know this wasn't a sufficient answer. "I thought I heard a bear. Some of the guys on the farm said they've seen her around recently."

"Is that so?" Derek's questioning tone let me know he wasn't buying my story.

"It is. She got one of Mama's pies she had cooling in the window the other day." It wasn't a complete lie. There was a pie that had been snatched up by a bear, but it was two summers previous.

SPEAK EASY TO ME

"I guess no one is immune to your mama's pies, huh?" My mother was an excellent baker. Everyone in town knew it. He was reluctantly going along with my explanation.

"That's why I'm out here today. Mama wants to make a batch of jam and needs fresh raspberries." Hoping my answer was sufficient, I turned around to pick up my basket needing to also just take a breath and relax.

I bent down to pick up my basket and when I stood back up Derek and Collin had encroached on me. I got an immediate sick feeling in my stomach. This wasn't good. I had never been alone with either man, let alone both of them together. For every step I took back, the two men advanced. I was nearly in the raspberry bush when I started to feel the panic coming on.

"You know it's not a good idea for you to be out here by yourself. It's dangerous. You should let us give you a ride home." Derek wasn't trying to hide the malicious evil in his voice.

"I'm fine by myself. I have dealt with things scarier than bears before." I tried to sound self-assured, but I know it didn't come off as such.

"You better come with us." The man put his hand on my arm. His fingers dug so deep into my arm and squeezed so tight I knew it would be bruised.

"I'm making some jam for your wife with Mama. What is your wife, like, six months pregnant now?" That seemed to get his attention. "It's a good thing I know what I'm doing. Did you know that there's a berry that looks exactly like a raspberry, only it's poisonous if ingested? How easily the wrong person could hurt someone unintentionally." My veiled threat hit its mark. He let go of my arm.

His face was red with anger as he not so sincerely said, "It was nice seeing you, but we better get going. Stay safe out here, Lottie." Derek jerked his head towards their car and both men headed in that direction.

I just stood there and watched as they got into their car and

75

TABITHA KRUEGER

drove off. My heart was racing so fast. My knees gave out as soon as the car was out of sight. Adrenaline coursing through my body was now dissipating. The four men emerged from the cave and came rushing to my side. From where they were in the cave, I knew they could hear everything that had been said.

"Are you alright?" The younger guy with black hair knelt down as he helped me up.

"I'm fine. Thank you." I offered him a gentle smile as thanks. "They are local cops. A bunch of jerks with badges if you ask me."

"We had to hold ol' Little Nicky back from rushing out here and emptying his magazine on them." Nick's face was serious as he nodded his confirmation.

"As satisfying as that would have been, I don't think that would have helped your hiding." We all laughed in a relieved manner.

One of the older men then asked, "Did you really just threaten to poison that cop's pregnant wife?" This caused all four men to stare at me.

I shrugged. "I was just informing him of the truth, however he took it is on him," I sounded innocent but wore a sinister smile on my face. I had no clue if there really was a poisonous berry that looked like a raspberry, but my bluff had worked regardless of the merit.

"You also said there's a bear out here?" Nick asked. I shook my head. "Not out here. In there." I pointed at the cave. The blood drained from all four of their faces. "That's her cave. She could be in there right now or she could be out here." I motioned to the forest of trees. They all just stood there staring at me, dumbstruck.

"Remind me to never piss you off," Nick said with an amused laugh as he picked up my basket from the ground.

All five of us walked back to the farm, picking berries, talking about what brought them to cross paths with me on the road. After that, Nick was like a permanent fixture at the farm. He was the go between for his boss in Chicago, my family's farm, and their supplier in Canada.

CHAPTER 6

LOTTIE

I had a good feeling as Cameron dropped me back at my temporary residence. Temporary because I was going to be moving in with Cameron, my fiancé, soon to be husband, after we get married. This whole arrangement had still held a certain air of fantasy more than reality until he'd mentioned me coming to his house, our house. Him saying our house somehow brought the reality of the situation front and center.

We bid each other good-bye after he'd walked me to the door, taking my hand in his and bowing down to kiss it. The day date had been surprisingly enjoyable. Cameron had been nice and agreeable and interested in what I had to say. It was nice, but I wasn't about to let my guard down and think this was going to be all rainbows and sunshine. His words from our first meeting still sat in the back of mind.

The rest of the afternoon was uneventful with little to do but sit and read a book. I was in the midst of reading when Claire found me. She informed me dinner was ready and that Nathaniel would be the only one there with me. Uncle Lon and Thomas had left town for business.

I lazily made my way down to the dining room knowing Nathaniel didn't care about my punctuality. Nathaniel was sitting at the head of the table. It made me think about our disastrous dinner the other night. Nathaniel was pushed to the side of the table while Uncle Lon had Thomas to his right and now Thomas was with him dealing with business. I wondered if Nathaniel was ever jealous of Thomas being the chosen one just by being the older of the two children.

"Well, hello there Lottie," Nathaniel said with a devious grin. I sat down to his left, my place already set.

"You seem to be in a good mood," I pointed out, hoping he would reveal the source of this vibe. His smile just grew bigger as he brought his cup to his mouth, taking a sip of whatever it was holding.

"I am." He wasn't giving me any more information than that. He wanted me to pry it out of him. I figured I would play along.

"And the reason would be?" I trailed off, not sure what else to ask him.

"I want to take you to Le Mier again." I scrunched my face, trying to figure out what the heck Le Mier was and when I had been there. He just laughed.

"Emmett's place." He took another drink, gauging my reaction to his statement. I was trying to play it cool. I hadn't expected to see Emmett again after our planetarium date. I dug my feet into the floor trying to stay grounded.

I casually shrugged. "Sure." Not making eye contact as I reached for the mashed potatoes to scoop onto my plate. I wasn't sure if I covered it well enough, but Nathaniel didn't seem to notice or care.

"Excellent," he said as he took a bite of food already on his plate. He didn't bring it up for the rest of dinner. We just talked about my afternoon with Cameron and my thoughts on what was to come. He also gave me his opinion. We had a

SPEAK EASY TO ME

nice little conversation going, feeling more comfortable with each other.

"I want to ask you something and I don't mean to offend you." There was hesitancy in my voice. Although Nathaniel and I had been friendly with each other, I wasn't sure how far that friendship went.

"Ask away, dear cousin." Nathaniel was completely unbothered by any potential questions I had.

"How did you become you and not your brother?" It wasn't exactly the question I had in mind, and it didn't come out the way I wanted. "What I mean is, your brother seems like a replica of your father, and you seem so much more relaxed, nicer," I said the words as gently as I could. Nathaniel let out a small laugh.

"It's easy to be relaxed when you're the spare," he casually said. "I kind of get to do my own thing without much thought since Thomas is the one who is going to take over for our father." That made sense. Since Thomas was the focus of their father's attention it left Nathaniel to his own devices. It also meant that he wasn't around his father as much, hence why he had a wildly different demeanor than both his father and brother. "It also helped that I was my mother's shadow until she passed away. She was the sweetest woman I have ever known." His eyes got misty.

"How in the world did she end up with your father then?" Nathaniel's sharp laugh echoed off the dining room walls. My question was genuine, though. I was truly surprised any woman would put up with Uncle Lon.

"It was an arranged marriage. Sort of like you and Cameron. Although, my mother did make my father a little more tolerable while she was alive. I was lucky to have her in my life until I was 16 years old." Nathaniel had a small smile as he remembered his mother. There was kind of an uncom-

79

TABITHA KRUEGER

fortable silence that hung in the air now. I wanted to change the subject.

"Have you ever been jealous of Thomas for getting all your father's time and attention?" I was genuinely curious.

"At first, when I was old enough to understand what my place was supposed to be, maybe. Now though, I'm grateful that it's Thomas in our father's shadow and not me." There was mostly truth to what he was saying but there was also a hidden hurt that his eyes couldn't hide.

I wondered if any of my sisters had the same feelings when it came to our parents and myself. I was the oldest therefore by default I was the one in charge whenever our parents weren't around.

"Well, let me just say, I am glad that you are not like him. It's nice having an ally in this house. It's made this whole process a bit easier to take on." He gave me a smile saying that he understood what I meant.

"Finish up. We leave in an hour," he said as he pushed his chair out. "You don't have to sneak in and out of the house this time. My father is gone, and Cameron's watch dogs Russel and Marco were given the night off since I'll be here tonight."

I felt a tinge of excitement at the thought of seeing Emmett again. I walked casually up to my room before the panic started setting in. What was I going to wear? Was Emmett expecting me tonight? So many thoughts raced through my mind as I opened the armoire attempting to find something appropriate to wear to Le Mier.

I found a light blue knee length dress that had crystals and sequins sewn throughout. The dress fit snugly against my body until it hit my hips and just below my butt where it turned flowy and flirty. I found a pair of white crystal chandelier earrings while leaving my neck bare.

I am not sure how I had gotten ready on time. I was down

in the foyer placing my coat on when Nathaniel finally emerged, smirk on his face. "Quick to get out of here, huh, Lottie?" He laughed as my face turned red and I couldn't find the words through my embarrassment to retort anything. "Come on," he said as he put his arm around my shoulder, and we walked to the car.

I could hardly contain my excitement on the car ride to the speakeasy. I started to feel a little guilty for coming here after Cameron had agreed to try to make the best out of our situation. Here I was, going to see a man that I was attracted to and fooled around with.

My heartbeat raced faster with every step I took. The only sound in the alley was the clicking of my heels on the cement. Once inside, Nathaniel and I headed to the bar. It was a man I had never seen before behind the bar; Emmett wasn't in sight. I tried not to look too eager as I scanned the crowd trying to spot the tall man with dark hair. My eyes got caught on a blonde I had seen before, the woman from the bathroom the first night I had been here. It wasn't hard to find Emmett after that, he was acting as her chair. They seemed cozy, her arm around his shoulders while his wrapped lightly around her waist, resting on her hip. They were both talking and laughing to the group around them. Every once in a while, she would whisper something to him, and he would smile and nod his head.

I must not have been as inconspicuous as I thought I was because Nathaniel leaned in and whispered, "You should try not to be so obvious," with a little entertainment in his voice.

I stumbled on my words. "I don't know what you're talking about." He just inclined his head to me, not believing my lies for a second. He pushed a drink in front of me. I had not been paying attention at all because I had not heard him order anything. Like the first time we were here, Nathaniel disappeared into the crowd, leaving me alone at the bar. I

TABITHA KRUEGER

took the drink and swallowed it in one gulp, not caring what it was.

The man next to me, who was about my age, with light brown hair and eyes to match let out a laugh. He had a nice smile as he said, "Rough day?"

I just gave him a side eye and a flat, "Something like that." He laughed a heartily, bellowing laugh that was contagious, making me laugh in return.

"Hey! Another one of what she's having. Make it 2!" he said to the bartender. The bartender brought our drinks to us before the stranger next to me talked to me again.

"Leo." He held up his drink to me.

"Lottie." I held up my drink to him. We both downed the liquid in the glass, not knowing what it was but feeling the burning the whole way down. We both cringed and laughed.

"What was that?" he asked between coughs.

"I have no idea. My cousin ordered me the first one." Both of us laughed. Now I know why they called it giggly water.

"That was your cousin?" he asked, his words turning a little friskier now that he knew Nathaniel was my cousin. Moving a little closer to me, placing a hand on my bare knee. He was leaning in to whisper something to me when a menacing voice was beside us.

"She's engaged, asshole." Before Emmett was even done talking, Leo had removed his hand and stood up putting as much distance between the two of us as possible. He mumbled an apology and immediately left the speakeasy. I could see why when I turned around on my barstool. Emmett's face was murderous.

"You really need to be careful of the company you keep," Emmett warned. As if he wasn't on the list of people I needed to be careful around. I just scoffed at him.

"I am perfectly capable of making that decision on my own. I don't need or want your help." I was so angry with him. I was even more angry with myself for letting his actions get to me. I was an engaged woman and he had made no promise of loyalty to me. We had one minor tryst a few days prior and hadn't spoken since. I had no claim on him. He also had no claim on me. "Don't you have to get back to your girlfriend?" I wanted to talk to anyone else in that moment, but him. He had an amused look on his face.

"Is that what this is? You saw me with Brooke?" He smiled. He caged me in with his arms on either side of my body, resting his hands on the bar behind me, preventing me from turning back around. I was forced to stare into his playful brown eyes. "Are you jealous, Carrots?" His grin turned cocky.

"In order to be jealous, I'd have to want what she has, which, luckily for me, I don't." I was staring daggers at him. Angry that he not only was telling me what to do, but he pointed out I was jealous. The bartender came by just then, not reading the energy running through Emmett and me.

"Another one, miss?" He looked at me as he took my glass.

Emmett and I answered at the same time. "Yes," I said as he said, "No." The bartender looked between us.

Emmett looked at him and said "John, don't serve this woman anymore. She's had more than enough to drink." The bartender caught on that this was a fight he didn't want to be in the middle of and he walked quickly away.

"How dare you! Where do you come off saying what I can or can't do?" I was so mad I could have burst. I got up and started moving towards the door. I wasn't sure what my plan was, but I knew I needed to get out of there, away from Emmett.

"Get back here," Emmett said as he rushed to catch up to me.

"You telling me what to do makes me want to do the exact opposite." I tried picking up my pace but there were too

TABITHA KRUEGER

many people around slowing me down, allowing Emmett to reach me. He grabbed my arm and dragged me away from the crowd. Emmett pushed me up against the nearest wall. With my shoulders pinned he leaned in so close I could smell the hint of whiskey on his breath.

"Oh, you have no idea what I'll tell you to do, Carrots. Trust me, you will be more than willing to follow every one of my commands." His voice was low and gravely.

"Somehow, I don't believe that. I will never give you the satisfaction of finding out." My words could have been believable if they hadn't come out all breathy and wanting.

"Oh, really?" Emmett moved his body closer to mine, pinning me to the wall with his hips.

"Yes." I meant it to sound resolute, but it wasn't. Not even a little bit.

"I enjoy a challenge." A devious smile played at the corner of his lips. "I didn't get to where I am by giving up. I'm a very patient man, Carrots. I always get what I want." As cocky as he was, I believed every word he said. I believed he always got what he wanted. I was warring within myself to not be on that list of conquests.

"Too bad you can't say that anymore." My words came out heavy. I was suddenly aware of how close and out in the open we were. It must have struck Emmett as well as he grabbed my hand and took me down a hallway. I wasn't even going to pretend to protest. I would go anywhere with him.

We went down the hall and came to room on the right. Emmett turned the doorknob as he flung the door open. He couldn't get me in the room fast enough. He closed and locked the door behind us. As soon as he clicked the lock in place his mouth was on mine. Needy and furious. He put his hands on my ass cheeks, squeezing and pulling me flush to his body.

SPEAK EASY TO ME

"I haven't been able to stop thinking about you for days," he said in between kisses. I just answered with a whimper.

"Seeing that man so close to you, then placing his hand on you made me want to kill him." He moved down to focus on my bare neck. "You're making me lose control, Carrots." Our hands were all over each other. We couldn't get enough of one another. I was able to take in the room while he was paying attention to my neck. There was a desk and some filing cabinets.

"Are we in an office?" I asked making Emmett stop his actions. He just kind of chuckled.

"Yes. It's my office. Is this, okay?" Even though he was asking if us being in his office was okay, he was also alluding to what we were doing, if going forward was okay. He was waiting for my confirmation to continue. I hesitated a millisecond before I decided I didn't care. I wanted Emmett more than I cared about what the consequences were.

"It's more than okay," I said, inviting him to continue his explorations. We started where we left off. Without warning, Emmett pulled away for me and brought me over to his desk.

He spun me around so I was facing the desk, placing my hands on it while he was standing behind me. He hiked my dress up and moved my underwear to the side. "You have to be quiet, Lottie." He whispered in my ear before he turned my head towards him, taking my mouth in his.

He started lazily making circles around my clit. I let out a whimper that was muffled into his mouth. He was going so slow I thought I would go crazy with want. Before I could melt into a puddle, he placed two fingers inside me. I let out a gasp of pleasure as his fingers started gliding in and out of my dripping wet slit.

"You are so wet, Lottie. I want you to cover my fingers in your release." He started rubbing my clit with his thumbs as his fingers moved faster in and out. I felt the buildup intensifying before I exploded all over his hands. My body fell limp against his desk. He turned me over, so I was facing him. I watched as he placed his fingers in his mouth, sucking my wetness of his fingers relishing in the taste. "You taste so fucking good, Carrots. I need more."

He hoisted me up on his desk, my bottom hanging over a little. He removed my underwear before kneeling in front of me and buried his face between my legs. My clit was still sensitive when he started moving his velvety tongue around in little circles. I was trying not to make any noise but was not successful when he sucked my clit into his mouth. The sharp contrast between his licking to the suction of the sucking made me yell out in pleasure. He reached up and put a hand over my mouth, not missing a beat, while he kept devouring my pussy.

He used his other hand to grope my breasts through my dress. I pulled my top down, wanting his hands on my pert nipples. As soon as he groped my bare breast, pinching my nipple, I exploded again, this time all over his face. He growled his satisfaction and went in more aggressively as I came. I came down from my high of ecstasy as he was still slowly licking my pussy.

Pulling his hand away from my mouth he inserted his fingers back inside me, slowly pulling them in and out. "Oh my God, Lottie. I could do this forever to you. Please never tell me to stop." I just laid there reveling in the amazing spark of pleasure still rippling through my body. I gently removed his hand from me and moved off the desk.

"If you never stop, then I won't be able to do this." I pushed him back just enough so I could kneel in front of him. Unzipping his pants, the whole while looking him directly in the eyes. He sprung forward as soon as I moved his underwear out of the way. He was hard and ready for me.

I took his length in my hands and while still looking at

SPEAK EASY TO ME

him, moved my tongue slowly around the tip of his penis making him let out a low groan. I took him in my mouth and started licking as I moved up and down his length. He threw his head back in pleasure as he grabbed my head and started guiding me up and down.

"You're such a good girl, Lottie." I increased the suction a little causing him to draw in a sharp breath. "So. Fucking. Good." He started to slowly move his hips, thrusting himself deeper into my throat. I gagged a little, he got a smirk on his face and said, "You told me you could take it even if you made a face."

He thrust deeper making me gag more. "Show me how well you can take it." His words spurring me on, I grabbed his ass and drove his dick down my throat, my lips resting on the base, moving my tongue on the bottom of his length.

"I'm going to cum, Lottie." I held him in place and kept bobbing my head up and down wanting to milk every last drop out of him. He grabbed the back of my head as he drove himself into my mouth, shuddering as his hot liquid spurted in mouth coating my throat. A low growl left his throat. I swallowed while Emmett was still inside my mouth causing him to gasp at the sensation. He slowly pulled himself out of my mouth, neither one of us breaking eye contact.

"Fuck, Carrots. Of all the times I have pictured what that would be like, I never imagined it would be like that." He was running his thumb over my lips before he pushed it gently in and I sucked it a little. He was trying to catch his breath. His eyes were hooded as he bent down and helped me off my knees. As soon as I was standing, he was taking my dress off as he whispered in my ear, "Do you know how many times I have touched myself thinking of you?"

He started kissing my neck again. "How many times I have taken out your underwear just trying to smell you one more time?" He had my dress down at my feet. "I want to be inside you so bad, Lottie. Please tell me you want me as much as I want you. I want to ruin you for every man. Whenever any man touches you, you'll only be able to think of me." He stopped his work and looked at me.

"Ruin me, Emmett." That was all he needed to hear, and he had me lying on my back on a couch I hadn't even noticed had been there. He made quick work to remove his shirt and kicked off his pants. He was laying on top of me, settling in between my legs. There was nothing between our needy bodies.

He hungrily took my mouth in his, his tongue assaulting mine. I grabbed the back of his head trying to get him closer to me. His hands found my breasts and began squeezing and kneading them. Playing with my budded nipples. He moved from my mouth, down my neck and to my nipples. Taking one in his mouth and then the other one. I could feel him getting harder with each lick and suck.

I could feel his tip close to my entrance as he rocked his hips back and forth, rubbing my clit with the head of his penis. He stopped and moved above me, back to my mouth. "Are you sure about this?" He asked, wanting to make sure once again, that this is what I wanted. Knowing he would stop if I asked him to made me that much hotter for him.

I answered by wrapping my legs around his back and pulling him close. I was still so wet that the head of his dick went right in. I let out a scream of pleasure and pain. He was bigger than I expected. He started kissing me as he gently rocked his hips back and forth, working my opening to expand to his full girth. He was about halfway in when he stopped and looked at me. "I don't know if I will be able to control myself if I go all the way in."

I once again used my legs to push him all the way inside. "Lose control with me." I said. He began to thrust his hips hard and fast. Our bodies meeting was the only sound in the

SPEAK EASY TO ME

room beside our moans of pleasure. I let out a loud moan and he placed his hand over my mouth. "Your pleasure is only for me to hear." He said, each word accentuated with a hard thrust. "I want to hear you say it."

I could barely form the words. "My pleasure is only yours." He put his hand between us as he was thrusting, rubbing my clit at the same time.

His name was on my lips as he sent me over the edge. He joined me shortly after, pulling out just in time to cover my stomach in his salty liquid. I ran my fingers through the hot, white streams and licked it off my fingers. He laid down on top of me and kissed me, hard. "In me trying to ruin you, I think you've ruined me." He said as he nuzzled the nook of my neck. We laid like that for a while.

I finally said, "I think we should get back out there. I'm sure Nathaniel has been looking for me." He let out an annoyed groan and slowly moved off me. Emmett's eyes roamed up and down me as I lay naked on the couch, taking in my body as he did so. I was so self-conscious I went to move my hands in front of me. Emmett grabbed my arms to stop me.

"You are beautiful, Carrots. Don't ever cover yourself up in front of me. I want to see all of you." The honesty in his words matched his eyes. I relaxed a bit as I bared myself to him. After getting his fill of me he stood up and then took my hands, helping me stand as well.

We both were now quietly putting our clothes on. It was an awkward silence that Emmett couldn't seem to take any longer. "I didn't hurt you, did I? I wasn't too rough?" He had some concern in his eye.

I gently smiled. "No. I am perfectly fine. A little sore, but not from you being rough," I said coyly.

"What are you sore from then?" He had a wicked smile

TABITHA KRUEGER

traveling across his face. He stepped into my space, his face mere inches from mine.

"You are very big, sir." He yanked me to him.

"Sir? Hmmm. I like the sound of that coming from your mouth. I like a lot of sounds that come out of your mouth." He kissed me fiercely before pulling away and looking at me. I had a goofy grin on my face. His face went from playful to serious in mere seconds. His eyes were searching my face for something, but what, I wasn't sure. He took a step back.

"I'm sorry. We shouldn't have done this." The smile dropped from my face as I took his words in. "I take full responsibility for this. It shouldn't have gotten this far. I shouldn't have taken it this far." It was more like he was scolding himself out loud. The words hurt just the same. I was so mad. I had just bared everything to him and now he regrets it.

"I wouldn't do anything that I wouldn't want to do. I'm sorry you regret our time together." I went to walk away, still looking like I had just frolicked in the hay. He grabbed my hand, stopping me in my tracks and turning me around.

"I do not regret a single moment with you, Carrots," he said gently as he tucked my hair behind my ears, cupping my cheek. "You are engaged to another man. I should have stayed away. I thought the planetarium would be enough for me, but no amount of you will ever satisfy this hunger you have created." He kissed me softly as if this was a kiss he was trying to cherish and burn into his memory.

"I can't explain this pull you have on me either. No matter how much of you I get it will never be enough." We kissed slowly and purposefully again.

He pulled away from me, "Let's get back out there." We gathered ourselves the best we could. By now everyone would be so gone with drink that they wouldn't fully notice

SPEAK EASY TO ME

my hair wasn't as it had been, and my make-up was slightly smeared.

The room was dark enough that we were able to slip back inside without anyone noticing. Or so I had thought. There was one person who had noticed. Emmett led me to a table with two chairs and I sat in one. "The activities of the last hour have made me parched. I am going to fetch a drink. Would you care for one?" he asked.

"Yes, please. I am quite thirsty as well." He winked before turning and walking towards the bar.

As soon as Emmett left my side, Brooke was making a bee line for me. She didn't wait for an invitation to sit down. "He is quite good, isn't he?" I followed her eyes to Emmett. His back was to us as he ordered our drinks.

"He knows how to use his mouth and hands, that's for sure." I wasn't stupid. I knew he'd been with other women. It didn't mean I wanted to hear about it after what we had just done. No matter how much I disliked what Brooke was saying I wasn't going to let her know that she was getting to me.

"That little thing he does with his tongue." I cut her off before she could say another word.

"Enough. I don't care what you and he did in the past. If you could please leave, I would be most grateful." I was done with her disgusting attitude towards me. I wanted to punch her right off her chair but knew that would draw too much attention and honestly, I was trying to hide in the shadows as I was already walking a thin line.

She stood up and pushed her chair in. She didn't leave without one more jab, "I don't know what you consider the past, but we were together last night." With that she walked away and joined her friends across the room. All their eyes fixated on me hoping to watch as I broke.

I felt sick to my stomach. I was sick not only over what

TABITHA KRUEGER

Brooke said, but the fact that I was an engaged woman and Emmett is not, and will never be, my fiancé. I was a horrible person.

No matter how much I didn't want to be in this situation, I was the one who had agreed to marry Cameron. I was the one who had decided to try to make it work with Cameron. Yet here I am, risking everything, for what? A few quick sex sessions. We could never be more than that.

Emmett returned to our table with drinks in hand. I took mine and drank it before he'd even sat down. His butt just made contact with the chair when I declared, "I want to go home." There was no emotion in my monotone delivery.

He seemed put off by that and asked, "Why? Is something wrong?" Worry clouded his brown eyes.

"You were right. Things got taken too far. Now, I'd like to go home, please." I could feel the tears brimming at the edges of my eyes. Emmett could read the hurt and seriousness emanating from my eyes.

"Okay. Whatever you want," he said so gently and with so much understanding, I almost lost my composure.

He found Nathaniel for me, and we left. I didn't say anything on the ride home and Nathaniel didn't ask any questions. I went straight to my room and started a bath to soak in. I just wanted to wash the night away.

Tomorrow would be a new day. I would allow myself exactly the rest of the night to wallow in self-pity and woe is me-s. Tomorrow I would awake with a new sense of purpose and determination. I wouldn't let Emmett hold me back from trying to find a modicum of happiness with Cameron. I never thought the tears would stop coming as I drifted off to sleep.

CHAPTER 7

LOTTIE

There is just something about a good cry that is good for the soul. I woke up refreshed the next morning. It was like all the anger, sadness, and confusion had been purged from my body, tear by tear. I put my robe on before heading down to grab breakfast. I wasn't sure if I was going to eat in my room or in the dining room. I quickly made up my mind as soon as I entered the dining room and found Uncle Lon sitting at the table.

I didn't know when he would be back, but I didn't expect him to be back so soon. I took a seat next to him. I started filling my plate with food when he spoke up, "Is this how you dress for breakfast?" The tone was the most condescending he'd used this far. I wasn't going to rile him up anymore.

Without looking up I said "I wasn't expecting you back so soon. I was going to bring food up to my room." I was hoping he wouldn't say anything else, and we could just eat in awkward silence. He gave me a halfhearted grunt and continued eating without giving me a second glance.

After Uncle Lon was done eating, he got up to leave the room. He was right by the doors as he turned around and said, "You and Cameron will be going to the symphony tonight. It's business, so remember your manners, no matter how little you have." With that, he left the room. He did that a lot, waiting until the last minute to tell me anything, as he was leaving a room. I wonder if that was a power technique he had picked up. You can't argue with someone if they have left the room.

I had all three maids helping me get ready once again. I had a blush pink silk gown with lacy flutter sleeves that went down to my elbows. The bodice was cinched and pleated where it met in the middle, between my breasts. There were two triangles of silk at my hips and the rest of the skirt matched the flowing lace of the sleeves. I donned a pair of pearl earrings with a matching pearl necklace. A simple clip held my hair back on the left side while the rest remained in loose curls. Most women, especially in the city, had short hair. My long hair, which was easier to manage on the farm, made me stand out here.

Cameron arrived a few minutes early and asked to see me in the study. We greeted each other pleasantly and he asked me to sit down in one of the sitting chairs. I obliged him and did as he asked. He seemed nervous as his eyes danced about and his couldn't stop fidgeting.

His voice was a little unsure as he spoke. "I know this is not what either of us want, but here we are." He took a deep breath. "If you are to be my wife, you need a proper ring." He knelt in front of me and pulled out a dark green oval box.

"Charlotte Bradley, would you be my wife?" He opened the ring box and my breath caught in my throat. There sat the most beautiful piece of jewelry I had ever seen. The white gold band was adorned with small diamonds on either side, drawing my attention to the giant, light blue gem. I had never been so close to a diamond before, let alone one that big.

SPEAK EASY TO ME

Cameron let out a small laugh as I took the ring in. I couldn't even hide the shock and awe on my face. "Is it okay?" he hesitantly asked.

"Is it okay?" I said mockingly. "It's the loveliest thing I have ever laid my eyes on." He smiled as he slipped it on my left ring finger.

"Good." He looked at me. "It's a 3-carat emerald cut aquamarine diamond." I was just admiring it on my finger, even if it was a little big and looked ridiculous on me.

"Thank you," I said to him as I kept my eyes on my new ring.

"Is that a yes?" he asked curiously. I had forgotten he'd even asked me a question.

"Yes. It's a yes," I said as I vowed to myself to make this work with him. He had gone out and gotten me a very expensive ring that he didn't have to. He's putting effort forward and I would match it. He grabbed my hands and pulled me to my feet. Throwing his arms around me as soon as I stood up. It was a friendly hug, no zing or spark.

Maggie cleared her throat at the study entrance. "You will be late if you do not leave now." She said before she quickly walked away.

Cameron helped me with my coat. We made our way to the car with Marco driving. Cameron had his hand on my knee the whole car ride. It felt familiar but lacked the heat of Emmett. I needed to get him out of my mind.

"We are going to the symphony tonight because I heard Holden will be there. He can't ignore me in public, since he wants to privately." He tightened his grip on my knee slightly as he spoke, "He is a dangerous man, Charlotte. Please be careful when we arrive. I don't want you wandering off. If you need to go somewhere, I or Marco will escort you. Holden and his men are dangerous. They have killed before for far less than what I am trying to do." He was

95

as serious as serious could be. I nodded my head in agreement.

Being around criminals was nothing new for me. Most of the men on the farm had some sort of criminal history. My father didn't judge anyone but made it crystal clear that if anyone hurt one of us girls or Mama, it would be the last thing they do on this earth. I didn't want to undermine Cameron and tell him about my resume with criminal dealings, so I just kept quiet.

I got one more warning speech before we exited the car to enter the theater where the symphony was being conducted. "Holden is an enforcer. He will try to intimidate you, don't let him. You are my fiancé. I will protect you. You hold your head high." I again placated him with a nod before Marco got out and opened my door.

We made our way up the grand steps in front of the theater. Once we got inside it was a grand room full of lively chatter. Everyone was dressed immaculately in tuxes and dazzling gowns. We checked our coats and proceeded to head further into the building.

I was holding on to Cameron's right arm putting my left hand on full display, my ring catching the light and shining brilliantly. We made our way around the room greeting people Cameron knew, him introducing me to anyone we spoke to.

I glanced up at the ceiling not able to look away once I had seen the intricate details that adorned it. I was being guided blindly by Cameron while I couldn't take my eyes off the work of art that was the wood carved ceiling.

I heard Cameron say, "Holden." Which immediately grabbed my attention causing me to look in the direction of the man Cameron was addressing.

Time stood still. I looked forward. This man, Holden, had his back was to us, but if I didn't know any better, I would

SPEAK EASY TO ME

have said it was Emmett. The way this man in front of me filled out his tux was exquisite. He turned around, confirming my fear. I felt all the blood drain from my face. The walls were closing in and my lungs suddenly couldn't get air. My head was trying to wrap my brain about what was unfolding.

"Ah, Cameron. So nice to see you." Emmett, or Holden, whatever this man's name was, clearly was not happy to see Cameron. Brooke was draped on Emmett's arm like she had always belonged there. The only sliver of a silver lining in this situation was the look of shock on Brooke's face when she saw me with Cameron.

"You are a very hard man to get ahold of," Cameron said with disdain dripping from his words. Emmett gave him a condescending chuckle.

"I'm easy to find if I want to be found." Emmett looked at me and it all clicked. He used me. He had let me come to him each time. It had all been a game to get to Cameron. I wasn't sure what his end game was, but I knew it had something to do with ruining Cameron. Maybe he wanted me to leave Cameron so he'd lose his inheritance, or whatever nonsense he would lose, if we didn't get married.

Emmett looked at me as if he was seeing me for the first time. My heart stung so bad I almost grabbed my chest from the pain. "Your fiancée?" Emmett inclined his head in my direction.

Cameron pulled me closer to him, "Yes. This is my fiancée, Charlotte Bradley. Charlotte, this is Holden Emmett." Emmett stuck his hand out for me to shake it and I panicked. I didn't want to shake his hand. If I was around him for another minute, I was going to give us away.

As soon as he stuck his hand out, I blurted, "I need to excuse myself for a moment." I turned and walked away without so much as a look back. I had left so abruptly I

TABITHA KRUEGER

wasn't even sure I had spoken loud enough for anyone to hear me. At that moment I didn't care. If Cameron asked me later about what happened, I would play up the whole 'he is a bad man and made me nervous' act.

All the sounds of the lobby faded. The lights were so bright I could hardly see, everyone and everything were just blurs in my peripheral vision. I walked with no real purpose except to escape. I followed a hallway and opened the first door on my right. There was a stairwell, and I went down it, having no idea where it led. At this point, a stairwell straight to hell would be a welcome change of scenery.

I hadn't heard the door open or close behind me while I was making my way down the stairs. I only knew someone had followed me when I heard the shuffling of feet coming down the stairs. I thought it was Cameron and started talking before I turned around to face him. "I'm sorry, I just needed to get out of the crowd." To my surprise it was Emmett standing there with his hands in his pockets.

Now that his secret was out, I had no idea what he was capable of doing. Would he kill me so I wouldn't tell Cameron what he'd done? If you had asked me ten minutes earlier, I would have told you that Emmett would never hurt me, but this wasn't Emmett, was it? This was Holden. Emmett had just been some role he was playing to make me gain his trust.

"What are you doing?" My words came out as a mixture of terror and anger. Emmett put his hands up in a defensive move while he took a step back.

"I came down here to explain." He was talking like I would eat up whatever bullshit he was about to tell me. He didn't know me at all if that is the kind of woman he thought I was.

"There is nothing you can say to me right now that I want

SPEAK EASY TO ME

to hear. Now, please move so I may leave." I moved towards the door. He grabbed my left hand as I tried to pass him.

"He gave you a ring?" There was anger behind his words. He held my hand and moved it from side to side as he took in the ring that now sat on it.

I ripped my hand out of his hand. "He is my fiancé. Why wouldn't he give me a ring? More importantly, why would you care? I don't appreciate being made a fool and you, sir, have accomplished that by leaps and bounds."

I went to step up the first stair when he grabbed my arm to stop me. I whipped around so fast he faltered in his step, stumbling a few paces back. "You don't get to ever touch me again, *Holden*." I threw so much venom on his name, Holden, it sounded like a curse word. "If you do, I will cut your hand off and mail it to your mother's grave." He didn't follow me after that exchange. I made it to the top of the stairs and threw the door open wanting to get as much space between me and Emmett as possible.

I ran right into Cameron as I emerged. He took one look at me and knew something was amiss. Before he had a chance to say anything the door opened behind me. Emmett was now standing there. Cameron's gaze went from Emmett to me, noticing my upset demeaner. Without warning Cameron punched Emmett square in the face. Emmett flew back against the wall. He hadn't even defended himself.

In one motion Cameron had pulled me behind him as he stood over Emmett. "You ever come near my fiancé again, you will wish you were never born." Cameron turned his attention to me. He cupped my cheek with his hand as he took in my face. "Are you alright?" I sniffed as I felt the tears welling up.

"I'm fine. Really." He brushed his thumb over my cheek before he put his arm around my shoulders, and we started walking away.

TABITHA KRUEGER

Emmett couldn't let Cameron have the last word, "You'll have to let me know how I taste on your wedding night." Cameron was back by Emmett in no time. Punches flew. I knew it really didn't have anything to do with me. Their animosity towards each other had been simmering below the surface for some time. I was just the catalyst that it took to bring it fully to the surface.

I tried to break up the two of them, but in the melee, I ended up getting knocked to the ground. My dress tore as I fell backward. Emmett was the first one to notice I had fallen and ran to help me up. He bent down to help me up. I slapped his hand away; same I did when Cameron offered me his hand. I was pissed at both men. I was also mad at myself.

"You are both Neanderthals," I said as I dragged myself off the floor. "Kill each other for all I care. I am going to find my seat." Cameron followed behind me. He had to jog to catch up to me before we made our way back to the main lobby of the theater. He had a bloody lip I hadn't noticed in the hallway. I reached out my hand and touched just below his lip.

"You should go clean yourself up." I could also see him opening and closing his hand. "Is your hand alright?" He looked at his hand as if contemplating if it hurt or not.

"It's fine. I'll take you to your seat before I clean up." He waited until I was seated before he went to the bathroom to make himself a little more presentable.

How could I have misinterpreted things so badly? I prided myself at being able to read people easily. Growing up with four younger sisters I had gotten really good at reading body language and feeling people out. That is also what made me good at being the go-between with the bootleggers when I lived at the farm.

Although my father was gentle and understanding with my sisters and me, when he was in any other situation, he

SPEAK EASY TO ME

was harsh and stubborn. My father was not a businessman by any stretch of the word. We would have lost the farm long ago if it had been left up to him. My mother, as brilliant as she was, did not possess the ability to not trust someone. Put plainly, she was kind of gullible and took everything at face value.

When I had walked back from the road with the four men who would eventually become our business partners at the farm, I had made the deal to let them use our farmland as a resting and recouping site between Canada and Chicago. I had left the farm in the hands of my father knowing I had worked out a deal that didn't need to be renegotiated. It was a win for everyone with minimal monetary loss for Nick's boss. We needed just enough money to keep the farm afloat and they needed a cheap place to lay low in between runs.

Nick would stay at the farm, becoming a farmhand of sorts, to make sure everything was kept on the up and up and no one was the wiser. It also helped him lay low when he was wanted in connection to a few shootouts on the streets of Chicago.

Before I got too lost in thought, Cameron sat in the seat next to mine and wrapped his arm around my shoulder and pulled me in. He had cleaned up his lip which now only had a slight cut on it. I grabbed his right hand in both of mine and looked at it a little closer. "It's fine, Charlotte," he said with a slight reassuring smile.

From my seat I could see across the theater when Emmett and Brooke entered the room, finding their seats. I looked away as fast as I could. I had to get over Emmett and let the fact that he used me sink in. All that had happened between us had felt so real though.

The lights went out and the curtain came up indicating the symphony was about to begin. I snuggled in closer to Cameron to enjoy the sounds of the strings and winds.

CHAPTER 8

EMMETT

I fucked up. I fucked up big time. Lottie was pissed at me. I couldn't blame her. She had every right to be as mad at me as she was. I was an asshole, and I had no excuse. I wanted to tell her the truth so many times. I was just a coward. I knew if I told her the truth she would never want to see or talk to me again and being the selfish bastard I am, I couldn't risk that.

I had decided I was going to come clean with her and let the pieces fall as they may. Now, I'll never get that chance because that bastard Cameron beat me to it. I might have had a chance to explain myself if Lottie had heard it from my mouth, not pulling the rug from underneath her in a very crowded public space.

I have no idea how Cameron knew I would be here tonight. It wasn't a secret, obviously, but it wasn't public knowledge. I'd have to let Simon know so he can figure out who's blabbing. I keep my circle small and tight. I've seen what can happen if you let too many people in. People cannot be trusted, especially when it comes to money and bootlegging brings in a lot of money.

SPEAK EASY TO ME

I started making my way back to the lobby a safe distance behind Lottie and Cameron. She was so hurt. I couldn't stand the way she looked at me. It was pure and utter betrayal in her eyes. Hurt and anger were there too, but it was the betrayal that flared brightest in her eyes as she looked at me. I would give anything to take that away. I have been shot, stabbed, beaten, someone even tried to drown me one time, none of that compares to the pain I felt the moment I saw that look in Lottie's eyes.

From the look on Brooke's face as I approached her, I knew I was looking worse for the wear. I was debating on whether I should go clean up in the bathroom or walk around with defeat clearly written on my face. My mind was made for me as I saw Cameron enter the men's room. My feet started leading me before my brain could stop them. "Go find our seats." I snapped at Brooke.

It was going to take everything in me not to cold cock him the second I got close enough. He didn't notice me right away as I entered. He looked up in the mirror as he wet a towel at the sink. "Come back for more, Holden?" He said as if I hadn't just stood there as he hit me the first time. He was either too stupid or too proud to conclude that I never raised my hands up in defense. I'd allowed him to hit me square in the jaw. Something I wouldn't be doing again.

"If I was, you wouldn't be standing upright right now." I spewed with as much hate as I could muster, quelling the dragon of fury inside. He just smiled in the mirror as he started wiping his lip with the wetted towel.

"Whatever you say, lover boy." He was checking to make sure he'd wiped all the blood away. "I knew you were going to try to pull some bullshit, but going after my fiancée, tsk tsk, not a good look for you, Romeo."

He tossed the towel into the laundry basket. "Not sure what you were going to accomplish with that, but she will be

TABITHA KRUEGER

my wife and she will be pregnant with my baby soon enough." His baby. I could barely stand the thought of him putting his hands on her. Her being pregnant with his baby was unimaginable.

"I guess I should thank you for breaking her in for me. I do want to have fun on my wedding night and virgins usually aren't too fun." He was just goading me now. Wanting a reaction, I didn't give him one.

I felt I had already betrayed her enough with the quip about Cameron tasting me on their wedding night. I didn't want to further violate her, even if she wasn't present to hear what I said. "You don't deserve her." Neither one of us did. She was too good for us, as much as it pained me to admit and lump myself together with Cameron about something.

Cameron left me in the bathroom feeling defeated. I'm a fixer. I fix problems for my boss without feelings or regrets. The people I deal with are bad men. There has never been a man who hasn't deserved what I dished out. People fear me, with good reason. Yet here I was not having a clue on how to fix this situation with Lottie. I couldn't just go kill Cameron and drag Lottie away by her hair like some caveman, although the idea was starting to sound pretty good, not to mention, the most logical way to right things.

I grabbed a towel and cleaned my face off the best I could without really caring all too much how I looked. Walking around with blood on my face would help perpetuate the idea people had of me. I walked a fine line between the upper crust of the Chicago elite and the dirty underbelly of corruption and criminality that was peppering the city. The two recently started overlapping.

I tossed my towel on top of Cameron's in the laundry basket. That should give the laundry service something to talk about. Violence started to run a little too rampant on the streets of Chicago lately and we were all told to cool it for a

SPEAK EASY TO ME

while until the heat was gone. We were only to do necessary jobs and nothing more.

Brooke was still standing in the lobby when I made my way out of the bathroom. She knew not to ask any questions. That was about the only good thing about her. That and she was an occasional decent fuck. I hadn't touched her since my run-ins with Lottie and I had no plans to change that any time soon. Brooke had been a means to an end, but after having Lottie, I knew no one else could compare to the way she made me feel. I would just end up feeling disappointed with anyone else.

Brooke looked meek as she said, "I wanted to wait for you before sitting down." I just nodded and kept walking. I was over her and her desperate desire to make this thing between us into more than it was. She threw herself at me at every opportunity and it was starting to wear on my nerves.

As we took our seats, I scanned the room. Lottie was hard to miss in her light pink silk and lace dress that hugged every delicious curve of her body. Her long, curly brown hair was a contrast to most of the women's short bobs. I watched as she and Cameron got cozy in their seats. I could have sworn I saw Lottie looking at me as we sat down, but she never even glanced in my direction the rest of the night.

The conductor raised his baton starting the hour and a half long concert. I couldn't take my eyes off Lottie the whole concert. It had been that way since the moment I laid my eyes on her. My plan had been to seduce her and ruin things with her and Cameron. It was going around that Cameron would get disinherited if he didn't clean up his act and settle down. His father had given him an ultimatum; marry whomever he chooses or be cut off, nothing in between.

Nathaniel had found out that his estranged cousin was set to marry Cameron and we set our plan up. Nathaniel and I both disliked Cameron for different reasons. For Nathaniel,

TABITHA KRUEGER

Cameron was someone his father held above him, after his brother Thomas. Nathaniel wasn't second in line in his father's eyes, he was third. With Cameron out of the way Nathaniel could take over his role in Lon's business.

My issues with Cameron stemmed from something a little deeper than that. Cameron's father was my ultimate enemy, and by default, Cameron was now, too. My father was a chronic gambler. He owed some bad people a lot of money and he didn't have it. It would have gone unnoticed for the most part, but Cameron's father turned my father in, therefore, bringing attention to his debts. He was killed by loan sharks when I was 14.

Despite his flaws, my father was basically a good man; generous when he was able to be, kind, gentle. He was the only person I had left in the world. My younger brother died when he was 5 years old, and I was 8. My mother then died a few years later. I had my whole world torn apart in six years' time.

Cameron's father's legacy is his biggest source of pride. I wanted to strip him of that pride in any way I could. I had to bide my time in order to figure out the best way to strike and do the most damage. My plan had been to seduce Lottie, have Cameron catch us in the act and Cameron would end things. I can be a heartless bastard when I need to be and some woman I didn't know was the least of my concerns. Besides, she was desperate enough to marry Cameron, sight unseen, it wouldn't really matter if she didn't marry him.

I was going to do some surveillance when I learned she was in town. Nathaniel had been able to get a schedule to me of where she was going to be the day she went shopping with Russel in tow. Russel was Cameron's number one enforcer. He was one of the scariest men I had ever had the unfortunate pleasure of meeting. He never talked and would just

SPEAK EASY TO ME

hang out on the fringes of meetings and gatherings, observing everyone and everything.

I was surprised when I first saw Lottie. She was plumper than I thought she would be. I never was one to judge anyone on their body, but I knew Cameron was shallow and he wouldn't be pleased that Lottie didn't look like she stepped off the cover of Flapper magazine.

She was talking to Russel like he wasn't the most terrifying person she had ever encountered. Lottie also was making Marco laugh. I realized then that Lottie may be more than the poor country bumpkin everyone thought she was.

I was planning on just following her for an hour or two. The time flew by and before I knew it, I was four hours into this surveillance, not able to take my eyes off her. She was shopping, but not looking like she was enjoying herself, except when she would talk to Russel, which was starting to get on my nerves.

It was hour six into this shopping spree when I had finally seen her eyes light up. She was holding this beautiful dress and went to try it on. She looked absolutely stunning when she emerged. Her smile was beaming making her eyes sparkle. I was outside, observing through the giant window in the front of the store. Russel said something that made her smile drop immediately. She went back and changed into her own clothes and handed the dress to her attendant. The attendant placed the dress back where Lottie had gotten it.

Russel is one of only a few men that I am intimidated by, which I would never admit out loud. I know my own limitations and going up against Russel would not be good for my health. Although, in that moment, him taking away her happiness made me not care how much bigger or stronger Russel was, I was more than ready to take him on. I should have taken that as a hint to stop what I was doing immediately, but I didn't. I couldn't.

TABITHA KRUEGER

I stupidly decided that I needed to get close to her that day. I wanted to be in her orbit if only for a minute. I ceased the opportunity when Russel went in the back of the hat store with the saleswoman. I had no plan going in. I watched as Lottie went back to the hat she had stared at when she had entered the shop. I went to it too.

When our hands touched as we both went for the hat, my heart almost beat out of my chest. Her hands were surprisingly calloused while being soft and smooth at the same time. Her sheepish smile when she looked at me almost had me fall to my knees. She was absolutely breathtaking. The sounds of Russel and the saleswoman returning to the front of the store was enough of a distraction to allow me to exit.

I should have phoned Nathaniel and told him right then and there that the plan was off. I was out. This woman had cast such a spell on me in the short amount of time I had been around her, most of it was from a distance. Her not being with Cameron was more than just a simple plan now, I truly didn't want her with him for my own selfish reasons.

Nathaniel called later that night to inform me that he would be coming to Le Mier with Lottie. I should have taken that opportunity to tell him then that I didn't want anything to do with her. The gentlemanly thing to do was stop this before it became anything more. Too bad I'm not a gentleman.

Nathaniel cleared his throat once he reached the bar, letting me know he was there with his cousin. My back was to them as I fixed a drink, but I glanced up at the mirror sneaking in a glance at Lottie. I noticed she was starting at my ass. I smiled at the thought of her starting at other sections of my body in the same vicinity. I turned around fully knowing she wouldn't be able to look away in time.

The look of embarrassment that colored her pale cheeks

SPEAK EASY TO ME

made her that much more enduring. Her soft brown eyes eventually made their way up to mine. I had her full attention and I was more than happy to keep it. I never felt this way before.

I purposely never dated anyone. If I was with a woman, she would know my intentions before anything happened. I was not husband material. My line of work wouldn't make me a good boyfriend or husband for anyone, let alone someone I could care about. All I had to worry about was myself and I liked it that way.

There were a few women who tried to change my mind over the years. Brooke was the latest one attempting to change me because she believed she was special and different from any other woman I had in my life. That was simply not the truth. She was exactly the same type of woman I'd let in my life from time to time. There was nothing special or unique about the way Brooke would throw herself at me. There was nothing special or unique about the way she would fuck me the few times we did get together. She was a version of a woman she thought I would want.

Brooke's arm brushing mine brought me out of my thoughts. I looked across the theater and saw Lottie all cozy with Cameron and my stomach sank. I had to close my eyes and breath slowly through my nose to prevent my dinner from making an appearance. Seeing her with him, knowing he didn't care about her, hurt something down in my core. If she wasn't going to be with me, I'd rather her be with someone who cared about her, even the slightest bit. Cameron had shown his true colors of only wanting Lottie as breeding stock for his father's approval.

I would give Lottie a week to be mad at me. After that week, I would do whatever I could to make sure she knows the truth about me and Cameron. I would confess every-

TABITHA KRUEGER

thing. Whatever she wants to know, I'll divulge. I just need to figure out how to live until then because right now, feeling like this, dying would be easier to handle.

CHAPTER 9

LOTTIE

The orchestra strings and winds were intermixing melodies that I would normally enjoy. This time they brought tears to my eyes. As the notes were hit and crescendos flowed, my tears dropped silently and slowly. If you didn't know what I was going through, you'd think the music was moving me to tears.

I was so full of sadness and anger over the whole Emmett situation. Sadness that someone I had thought was my friend, someone I had trusted with secrets and my body, betrayed me so deeply and thoroughly. Anger that I let myself be a pawn in a man's game. Anger that I had been so completely blinded by a good-looking man I was considering risking not only my future, but my family's future as well.

Never again will I let someone in so wholly. I truly thought Emmett, or should I say Holden, cared about me. I could have sworn I saw pain in his eyes when I was confronting him. No matter, he would be out of my life for good now.

I could focus on what I came here to do; marry Cameron and have babies. The thought of that made me readjust in my seat, pulling away from Cameron's arm casually wrapped around my shoulder. He didn't even look at me as he now rested his hand on my leg.

I needed a plan to get over Emmett and quick. If I didn't think about him long enough, eventually my feelings for him would disappear. If I could find a distraction, something to occupy the part of my brain that held Emmett, I would be set.

The orchestra played one last song that ended too soon. The lights in the theater came on and everyone applauded. I knew once we were in the car alone, Cameron would want answers and I didn't know what I would tell him. I couldn't very well tell him the whole truth, but he also knew too much that I couldn't skirt around what Emmett and I had done. I was hoping that Cameron would be like me and want to put the whole ordeal behind him and move on.

On the way out of the theater, arm in arm with Cameron, an older couple stopped us. The man was unremarkable, dressed in a tux, as was every other man in attendance with nothing astounding setting him apart from anyone else. The woman on his arm though was stunning.

As Cameron and the man exchanged pleasantries, I took the older woman in. Her graying hair was pulled into a bun at the base of her head, showing off her strong shoulders and very defined collar bone. Her dress was black silk, fitting like a glove, looking like it was made only for her to wear. Her blue eyes shone with years of wisdom and lessons learned.

"Charlotte, this is Hugh Montgomery and his wife Elsa." Hugh stuck his hand out to me. I shook his hand and then Elsa's. "This is my fiancée, Charlotte," he said as I exchanged greetings with the couple. "We just need to discuss business real quick," Cameron said before he kissed me on the top of the head and walked away with Hugh.

Elsa causally informed me, "Men. They do this all the

SPEAK EASY TO ME

time. As if they won't spill the beans to us on the drive home." She gave me a light smile. "Are you new to the city? I don't think I have ever seen you around." Elsa had this calming energy about her.

"I moved to Chicago recently. This is the first time I've come out since I've been here." I realized it sounded like I was locked away, so I tried to correct myself. "I meant, this is the first event we have been to publicly. I don't know anyone in the city, so I have been keeping to myself for the most part." Which isn't technically true, but it's not like I can tell her I have been to Le Mier or the planetarium. I needed to deflect the attention away from me and back to her. "How long have you lived in the city?" She seemed more than happy to answer my question.

She had to think for a moment while doing the mental math. "It'll be 20 years next month." She let out a "phew" as she laughed. "I just aged myself, huh?" We both let out a giggle.

"I won't tell anyone." I said as I made a cross on my heart, "Cross my heart." That made her smile shine through. Elsa absolutely beamed when she fully smiled.

"Have you made any friends since coming to the city?" The only person I considered a friend had just betrayed me. Maggie didn't really count as a friend since we had never gotten together after she was done working. Nathaniel was also on my list of lying liars that would get an earful the next time I saw him.

"No. I have just been keeping myself entertained." Worry clouded her eyes. Being new in town was hard and it was even harder when you were out of your element and not sure how to navigate anything in your new environment. Elsa moved in closer and lowered her voice as she spoke, as if she was revealing a secret only the two of us were to know.

"I remember when I first moved here. I didn't know a

soul. I was holed up in our house for a month before Hugh made me go out and have lunch with his golf buddy's wife. She was so kind and welcoming. Because of her, I was able to flourish in Chicago society. She also encouraged me to open my own dance studio." That would explain her shoulders. She had a dancer's body. She took a step back as she fell into her regular talking voice, "Do you dance?" she asked.

"I don't know if what I do would be considered dancing. It's more of my body convulsing while music plays." I had occasionally danced at parties and such, but nothing like they do in the movies. The coordinated steps were something I never could get the hang of. "I have cleared more than one dance floor in my life, and it was not in a good way."

I was reminded of my cousin, Therese's wedding. Everyone was having a good time on the dance floor while the music played. I started dancing, ended up falling and taking out the groom. He had a concussion from his head bouncing off the floor. I had a bruised ego. I don't know which one of us was hurt worse.

"Sounds like you need some work," Elsa said between laughs. "Why don't you come to my dance studio, Elsa's Ensembles, tomorrow. We can start your dance lessons and 'Wow' everyone at your wedding." She was just too sweet. I couldn't say no to her, no matter how much my pride wanted to remain intact.

"As long as you know the risks, I will accept that offer." Her smile reappeared at my agreement. She grabbed both of my hands in hers as a little squeal escaped her throat.

The men reappeared from wherever they had gone to chat. "What's with all the excitement?" Hugh asked as he wrapped his arm around Elsa's waist, bringing her as close to him as possible.

"Charlotte here had agreed to dance lessons with me." She

SPEAK EASY TO ME

was beaming up at him and he was equally as enamored with her. Hugh turned to me to gauge my reaction.

"I am a horrible dancer, so I really hope Elsa can perform miracles." This made Hugh laugh. He had a hearty laugh that didn't seem to match his looks, which were quite lackluster. What he lacked in appearance he made up for with his infectious laughing.

"She can be quite convincing when she wants to be." Hugh said as he hugged Elsa tighter. "Maybe we should leave before she talks you into something else Cameron has to pay for." With a smile on his face, he winked at me as he turned and walked away with Elsa tucked under his arm.

"You just charm everyone, don't you?" I could hear the slight jab as Cameron said those words. His cool calm attitude made me think his even keeled demeanor was just an act until we would be alone.

I smiled at him, trying not to lose it right in the middle of the lobby where we'd have a captive audience. My hope of him dropping the subject seemed like a fantasy that would not come true. I didn't want to face the consequences of my own actions.

The walk to the car was like walking to my own wake. There was a heaviness in the air between us as we approached the car. The chilly air showed as our breaths intermingled in clouds of white. He opened my door for me and practically slammed it on me, almost, before I was fully in the car. When he got in and slammed his door, I was surprised the glass didn't break from the force.

I was shocked when the ride to my uncle's house was quiet. My heart was racing, waiting for Cameron to say something in order to somehow start the conversation I knew was inevitable. He just stared out the window the whole ride, sitting as far away from me as possible.

It wasn't good for me to stew in the madness that I was

TABITHA KRUEGER

carrying. I was mad at myself, at Cameron and Emmett. I was mad at my parents for agreeing to this idiotic plan. I was mad at my Uncle Lon for existing, really. The more I thought about the last week or so, the more this ball of anger was building. I went from being scared to have this conversation to being ready to throw down the gauntlet as soon as Cameron said something.

When we got to my house, I yanked my door open, not waiting for Cameron or Marco to open it for me. I was at the door when Cameron had caught up to me. He opened the door before I could and barged in front of me, then proceeded to try shutting the door on me.

I was furious. I channeled all that anger and frustration as I slammed the door behind me when I entered the house. Cameron had disappeared, I hadn't seen where he went once he entered the house. I had just taken my coat off when Cameron appeared in front of me. I still had my shoes on, dripping with a mixture of half melted snow and water.

Cameron grabbed the top of my arm so hard; I knew there would be a bruise there the next day. He dragged me into the study as my shoes slipped on the moister from both of our shoes making the floor wet. He prevented me from falling by grabbing my arm and yanking it even harder. My fiancé pushed me into the study so forcefully, I was lucky I had caught myself on the desk before I fell on the floor. Cameron entered the study and slammed the door so hard it made me jump.

I gripped the edge of the desk as I turned around to face a very angry Cameron stomping over to me. He grabbed my face in his hand forcing me to look at him as he spoke with deathly calm anger.

"Charlotte, you are going to tell me right now about the extent of your relationship with Holden." His grip on my face getting tighter. "Trust me when I say this, if you lie to me, I

116

SPEAK EASY TO ME

will know it and there will be steep repercussions." There was fury in his eyes as his chest was rapidly moving up and down.

I had to remember who I was. I wasn't this scared little girl who needed Cameron's approval for anything. The worst thing he could do was send me back to the farm, no worse than when I had left, minus a broken heart not caused by him. I refused to bow down to anyone.

"I will not tell you a damn thing." I quickly threw my words back at him as I ripped his hand off my face. "What are you going to do, call off the wedding? Then what of your inheritance? Don't you do everything your daddy tells you to?" I barely got the words out before the back of his hand hit my cheek. The sting of the contact made my eyes water as an audible gasp left my lips.

He just stood there, staring at me. Daring me to say anything. I instinctively raised my hand to my cheek, cupping it as I walked to the door. Before opening it, I turned to Cameron. "If you ever lay another hand on me, you won't get it back along with your other appendages." I heard glass shatter as I walked to the staircase across the foyer.

There had only been one other time that I was hit out of anger. It was the summer I had turned 19. A new man who had just been release from prison started working on the farm. Most of our farmhands had criminal pasts, so this was nothing new to us. Each farmhand was given the same speech as soon as they arrived on the farm; touch any of my father's daughters and you would be six feet under, but not before certain body parts were cut off. The men always got the message loud and clear.

Well, this man, Henry, didn't get the message. He found me alone in the barn one afternoon and ceased the opportunity to attack me. He came up behind me as I was bending down to pick up something I had dropped. He wrapped his arms around my arms and middle in a bear hug. "I have been waiting to get you alone

117

TABITHA KRUEGER

since the moment I got here," he whispered in my ear as I thrashed about.

I went to scream as he placed his hand over my mouth, preventing any sound escaping. "We wouldn't want to draw attention to us, now, would we?" he said as if I wanted this to happen. I knew what he was going to do, and I wanted to prevent it with every fiber of my being.

In a state of panic, I whipped my head back, causing a crunching sound as my head connected with Henry's nose. His arms immediately left my body as he let out a painful scream. With blood spurting out of his nose, spraying the top of my head, I ran to the barn door as fast as I could.

All the other farmhands that had been within hearing distance were running towards the barn. The look of horror was all over their faces as I emerged from the barn covered in blood. They thought I had hit my head by the amount of blood covering my hair. It wasn't until Henry, angry and as mad as a bull at a bull-fight, made his way out of the barn.

"Hold that crazy bitch while I teach her, her place," he said as if these men would do anything to harm me, let alone sit by and watch as another man did. Henry was holding a handkerchief to his nose which did little to stop the flowing blood from pouring out.

Mitchel, an older gentleman, had been working on our farm for almost 10 years. He just looked at me and said, "Go inside, Lottie. Get cleaned up." I hesitated for a second and Mitch barked "Now, Lottie!" I turned and did what he said.

I got inside our small farmhouse and found Mama in the kitchen baking as usual. There were a lot of mouths to feed on the farm and she cooked every single meal for all of us. She dropped her rolling pin as I walked through the door.

Running over to me with concern all over her face she grabbed my face to examine me. "I'm fine, Mama. I just... Henry." I couldn't form a full sentence through the sobs that burst forward. The adrenaline coursing through my body had started dissipating.

SPEAK EASY TO ME

Mama just held me in her arms and cried with me. When I didn't think I had any more tears left to cry, Mama led me upstairs to the bathroom and ran a hot bath for me. I rinsed my hair out in the sink not wanting to sit in bloody water.

Mama helped me take my blood sprayed clothes off. She would later burn them that night. My father was in town when this incident took place. No one told him what happened because by the time he'd gotten home, Henry had left the farm, never to be heard from again. I had doubts he ever left the grounds.

I passed Maggie as I went to my room. I watched as she went into the study after hearing the glass breaking. I was too over everything to tell her Cameron was in there and he wasn't in a good mood.

I went to bed as soon as I got changed into my nightgown. I didn't even bother washing my face or doing any of the other nighttime routines I had started with all the products Claire had gotten me. I don't think I ever tossed and turned so much in bed.

119

CHAPTER 10

LOTTIE

*E*ven though I had a fitful night of rest I woke up feeling refreshed and ready to take on the world. I didn't want to admit that it was because my dance lessons would start today but getting to see Elsa again was like gasping for air and finally being able to breathe. She was the only one who had shown me sincere kindness since I'd been here. I learned my lesson from Emmett, and I won't fully trust her, at least not for a while.

I had to take a few extra minutes lingering in the hot bath water. I grabbed my towel as I exited the now cooling water. Taking a glimpse in the mirror I was horrified by what I saw. My eye had a light purple ring under it highlighted by a very red cheek. I then took in the bruising on my upper arm. Every one of Cameron's fingers were imprinted on my skin, making it look like I had a handprint on my arm.

I moved closer to the mirror not wanting to believe that my fiancé left me bruised. I inspected the mark under my eye, hoping that maybe it was just a shadow, or some leftover coal I hadn't scrubbed away good enough. It was in fact, a black and blue mark. There was no denying the handprint on my arm, so I didn't even bother examining that further.

I went to my closet to find a long-sleeved dress to wear that would be suitable for dancing though I had no clue what I was looking for. I chose a plain light gray dress that was for everyday wear.

Next, I used the powder I had to try to diminish the appearance of the under-eye bruise. I looked utterly ridiculous. I wiped it off and decided I'd tell everyone I slipped on some water in the foyer and hit the side of my face on the marble table in the center of the room as I fell.

As I was walking down to the dining room for breakfast it hit me, Elsa had never told me a time to be at her studio. The whole time I ate, I debated on what to do. It was around 10 o'clock in the morning when I finished eating. I settled on finding Russel and having him take me to the studio. If I was too early, I could explore downtown.

I searched the whole house to no avail. Russel was nowhere to be found. I oddly seemed to be the only one in the house at the moment. I left a note with my whereabouts on the giant table in the foyer. Armed with a book and some money Uncle Lon had given me when I had first arrived, I put on my shoes and coat and made my way to the trolleybus.

I had to walk a few blocks in the blustery cold. It felt refreshing to feel the wind on my face, even if it was a bit chilly. I had only been driven through the neighborhood except for when I had walked to the park almost a week prior. My walk to the park felt like a lifetime ago.

I was able to take in the neighborhood in a way I was not able to while I was zooming around in a car. None of the houses were as grand as Uncle Lon's, but they all looked well cared for despite the brown grass and bare trees due to the time of year.

TABITHA KRUEGER

I could feel my nose and cheeks turning red from the nip in the air. It was a little warmer once I got on the trolleybus, but not by much. At least the bus kept the wind mostly at bay. You could still hear it as it fought against the windows for entrance, making a light hissing sound as we moved along the road.

Because it was mid-morning the bus was only half full with about 15 other passengers aboard which made finding a seat easy. I wasn't sure where I was going. I was feeling adventurous today, so I would get off when I felt I was in the middle of the city and go from there. Knowing I had a little bit of a ride in front of me, I opened my book and started reading. I had gotten about three chapters in when I looked up seeing tall buildings surrounding me. I decided this was the perfect spot to get off the trolleybus.

As I was leaving, I asked the conductor if he knew where Elsa's Ensembles was. He pointed me in the direction he thought it was and with a "Good luck" parting, he shut the door and continued on his route. I stood on the curb in awe at the sprawling city in front of me. I had always had someone escorting me around the city. Being here on my own was a little daunting.

If I sat and stared long enough it would intimate me, all the tall buildings and people bustling around me. I willed my feet to start moving in the direction the conductor had told me. Everyone seemed so sure of themselves, moving along the sidewalk mindlessly to their destinations. I, on the other hand, didn't know if I was going in the right direction, taking small, hesitant steps.

My attention wasn't fully in front of me and a man, in a hurry, wearing a suite, bumped my shoulder with his as he passed by. "Watch where you're going, dick!" I heard as someone shouted behind me. Only, it wasn't directed at me, but at the man who had bumped me. It took me a second

SPEAK EASY TO ME

to process the voice with its familiar huskiness to it. Emmett!

I made an unsuccessful attempt to pick up my pace. The people all around me seemed to have slowed down to a crawl leaving no space to weave betwixt them for me to pass. Emmett was by my side in no time. I had nowhere to go.

"Good morning, Lottie," Emmett said with a friendliness that was way too casual for my liking. I tried to keep my eyes forward, not giving him the benefit of a glance, but my eyes betrayed me.

"Morning, Holden." I gave him an exasperated side eye that would let him know I was annoyed with him. "It was good until you showed up." He placed his hands in his pockets casually.

"I am sorry to have put a damper on your morning. It wasn't my intention." The cocky playfulness his voice carried a moment ago was gone. In its place was a more melancholic tone. "You just so happen to be traveling in the same direction as I."

"At the same time?" I questioned accusatory. He just wore a soft smile on his face.

"Seems so," He retorted. His smile quickly faded as I fully turned my face to him. The crowd in front of us was slowly dispersed into the various buildings and shops we passed. At the next sight of an open door to a shop Emmett wrapped his arm around my waist and tugged me with him into the shop. I didn't even have time to protest.

He shut the door, flipped the lock, and told the young woman behind the counter to come back in five minutes after handing her a five-dollar bill. As soon as the woman was gone Emmett looked at my face again. "What the fuck is that?" He said with so much anger I jumped back a bit. I didn't answer right away because truthfully, I didn't know what he was talking about.

TABITHA KRUEGER

"What?" I asked, confused. He pointed to my eye.

"That." His gentle touch under my eye was in stark contrast to the way his words were coming out. "What. The. Fuck is that, Lottie?" He was beyond angry at this point.

Emmett had no right to know what happened in my personal life behind closed doors. "It is none of your damn business Emmett, or Holden; whoever you are today." I spit the anger right back at him. His anger was directed at Cameron, not me, while my anger was fully directed at Emmett. I went to unlock the door.

"Lottie," Emmett pleaded as he placed his hand on my upper arm, right where my new bruise sat. I yelped in pain. He let go of my arm as quickly as he had grabbed it.

"I am so sorry Lottie," Emmett said, concern filling his eyes, thinking he grabbed my arm too hard. I hadn't realized how bad and deep the bruise went until that moment. Emmett had barely even placed his hand on my arm when the pain hit. His eyes went from concern to menacing.

I was now holding my hand over my arm as if that might stop the pain. "Show me your arm," he said through gritted teeth. He was seething with anger. I was not about to take off my top in this random shop in downtown Chicago with a man who in all reality, was a stranger.

"I will do no such thing," I informed him. My words came out a little fast and high pitched.

"Look, Carrots. You can either willing show me your arm or I am going to rip that dress off you myself to look at it. The choice is yours." He folded his arms in front of his chest. The movement pulled his jacket tighter around his shoulders.

I begrudgingly started to unbutton the top of my dress after I dramatically rolled my eyes at him. He placed his hand on mine as I undid the first button halting me in my tracks. "Go behind there." He pointed to a tall display shelf. "I want

124

SPEAK EASY TO ME

to see it, not let the whole city of Chicago see it." It hadn't even dawned on me that the window to the shop was fully open and anyone walking by could see inside.

I resumed my partial disrobing as soon as we were safely shielded behind the wooden display case. I slipped my dress down far enough for the top of the bruise to show. I wasn't going to go any lower, but as soon as Emmett saw the bruise, he pulled the arm of my dress all the way down to my elbow.

He carefully inspected the deep purple marks outlined in blue. "Cameron did this?" he asked without looking up from my arm as he slowly turned it back and forth. It was more of a confirmation question than an actual inquiry.

"It doesn't matter. It's already done." I just wanted to put my arm away and get as far away from Emmett as possible. It wasn't good for me to be this close to him. His scent floated into my nose as he bent down closer to my arm. It filled me with a familiarity I didn't want to revisit.

"It does matter, Lottie." He let go of my arm, letting it fall to my side. "I'm going to kill that prick." There was so much conviction in his voice, I knew he would.

"There is no need for any of that. I took care of it." I was hoping to diffuse the situation. I started buttoning my dress back up. Emmett just chuckled as he crossed his arms.

"Really? You took care of it?" His mocking tone was condescending at best.

"I told him that if he ever touched me again like that, I would cut off his hand," I paused for a moment before finishing, "along with other appendages." A small smile danced across my lips.

Emmett let out a high-pitched whistle. "Oh boy, I bet old Cameron liked that." The joy that was radiating off him was contagious. "What did he say to that?"

"I have no idea. I left the room before he could reply, but

TABITHA KRUEGER

if the breaking glass I heard was any indication, he wasn't too pleased."

"I'm proud of you Carrots. You surprise me at every turn." The smile on his face was filled with pride. He was proud of me? I smiled back before remembering that I hate him. I am supposed to be ignoring him and moving on with my abusive fiancé which sounds absurd when I put it that way.

Blinking rapidly a few times, I came to my senses. "Now, if you'll excuse me, I have a date to be somewhere. Thank you." I could tell from the way his face shifted from triumph to serious he had thought he was forgiven.

I made my way to the front of the store. Emmett was unlocking the door and opening it up for me without a word. I was a little disappointed that he wasn't putting up a fight. Even a little push back would be welcome. What the hell was wrong with me? I liked fighting with Emmett though. Our little back and fourths were, I don't know, comforting? Exciting? As twisted as it seemed, I looked forward to my little tiffs with him.

"Not going to follow me?" I teased, letting a smile draw the corners of my lips up ever so slightly.

"As much as I know you enjoy it, it would appear I have been traveling in the wrong direction." We were now outside the shop door, standing under the eve of the awning.

"Good. Your neediness is not a turn on." Emmett's eyes burned with a fire I knew I couldn't extinguish. As he inched closer to me, I quickly said, "Good day, Holden." I used his first name to really drive home the point of me being mad at him. Then I slipped into the crowd of people passing by.

I had no idea what this hold was that Emmett had over me. It was like all sense went out the window any time he was around. If I could just avoid him for longer than *a day*, I think this silly schoolgirl crush could be quashed. Dancing would be a good distraction.

CHAPTER 11

EMMETT

I didn't last a week. Hell, I didn't even last a day. I overheard Elsa telling her husband she was going to be giving Lottie dance lessons as a wedding gift. I never miss an opportunity to take advantage of knowledge I shouldn't be privy to.

Brooke was not happy with how the evening ended; her alone in her bed without me there to warm it. I didn't even pretend to be a gentleman and walk her to her door, nor did I open her car door for her.

With Brooke in my car, I got to thinking about the first night Lottie had come to Le Mier. When I had helped her to the bathroom I witnessed a scene that didn't sit right with me and I analyzed it while I drove.

Before helping Lottie to the bathroom, I made sure Don and Louis were tending the bar. I had a perfect vantage point from the hallway where the bathrooms were. My eyes were on the bar, but my ears were trained to the women's bathroom door. I was listening for any signs of a splash so I would have an excuse to go in there and save Lottie.

I was so lost in thought that I had barely registered as Brooke

TABITHA KRUEGER

and two of her minions walked past me. Brooke's fingers glided across my chest as she walked by. She flashed me a seductive grin as she filed into the bathroom with her group.

I couldn't hear what was being said behind the bathroom door, but sounds of high pitched laughter that could only be described as cackling came rolling out in waves. I knew nothing any of those women had ever said, combined, warranted the enormous amount of laughter coming from behind that door.

Brooke could be cruel. That is why I thought we had been on the same page. Her heart was as cold as ice and anyone in her way would feel her wraith. I had made it perfectly clear to her that we would never be more than two people who fucked. I didn't mince words in order to avoid situations like this. It was not my fault she expected more than she knew I was willing to give.

The door swung open and all three cackling hens walked out, giant shit-eating grins on their faces. Brooke's was more of the cat that got the canary variety. I should have gone in there right when they made their way out, but I didn't. I left Lottie in there after whatever Brooke had said to her.

It was a long time from when Brooke left the bathroom to when Lottie finally made her way out. She had tears streaming down her face. I had never felt my heart sink to my stomach before and it was a feeling I never wanted to feel again. The hurt in Lottie's eyes made me want to end whoever put it there.

When Lottie said she wanted to go home I didn't hesitate to find Nathaniel. I would have driven her myself, but with her being an engaged woman, it wasn't appropriate at the moment. I didn't want to push anything on her in her condition. I found Nathaniel with a woman and they were practically eating each other's faces. He barely acknowledged me as I told him I was bringing Lottie home.

She hadn't listened to me and went outside. A speakeasy full of drunk men, a dark alley, and a woman did not a good combination make. I walked outside to the sight of a man on top of Lottie. I am not sure how I was able to transverse the slick concrete to make it to

Lottie without slipping. I pulled the drunkard off her, throwing him on his back to the ground and made his face my punching bag. Blow after blow didn't quench my thirst for his blood. I felt a soft grip on my wrist as I wound up to hit him again. It was Lottie. She was up. I checked her over to make sure she was physically okay.

She told me what happened. I wasn't completely sold on leaving the man who almost violated her alive, but he would be feeling his hangover and his face in the morning. As soon as Lottie spotted my hand she wanted to take care of me. I didn't know anywhere that would be appropriate for us to go except my house.

While we were in the bathroom of my house, watching Lottie tend to my hand, I had an overwhelming feeling of guilt. I couldn't do this to her. My plan wasn't only going to ruin Cameron's life, but hers as well. If she had been anyone else, I wouldn't care. I could easily destroy anyone and not feel a morsel of remorse. This woman though, my Carrots, how could I knowingly hurt her?

It would be best to cut ties now. Bail on my plans and try to figure out another way to hit Cameron where it counts. When Lottie looked up at me with those warm brown eyes, my mind was made up. I stood up abruptly and made my way out to the car. It would be easier if I was a dick. At least, that's what I told myself.

Pulling up to Brooke's house was almost mindless at this point. She sat for a minute, waiting for me to open her car door. Once she realized that wasn't going to happen, she had a few words for me before throwing the door open and then slamming it shut. I didn't even wait to see if she made it in safely. Truthfully, I didn't care. Not after remembering those tears running down Lottie's face.

I had a few things to do before I would be ready to "bump" into Lottie on her way to her dance lessons. I hadn't heard a time for the lessons so I would need to be up bright and early to make sure I wouldn't miss Lottie.

I got home and picked out a suite and matching tie. I took out the coat and shoes I would be wearing. I made sure to shower and shave, putting on cologne before dressing. My stomach was feeling a little queasy. I needed to calm my nerves somehow. I rubbed one out and felt a little bit better, but my stomach still wasn't feeling right. I was nervous. I didn't get nervous. Everything I was ever taught was to override any feelings of self-doubt since your enemies could sniff out any bit of leverage they were able to gain over you.

All these new feelings were so foreign to me. Nervousness was just the newest of the feelings Lottie was bringing to the surface. She made me feel longing and want in a way I didn't know was possible. She made me want to do anything I could to put a smile on her face.

I made sure I was at her house before the sun had even risen. It was four hours before Lottie finally made her way out of the house. She was alone. Marco and Russel were nowhere in sight. She started walking towards the trolleybus. I almost blew my cover to drive my car up to her and give her a ride.

Was Cameron so pissed about last night that he was going to pull her security duty to spite her? There were plenty of people other than myself who would take any opportunity to get at Cameron any way possible. I made a mental note to bring this up to Lottie whenever she allowed me to talk to her again.

I followed her to the bus. She got on and I got on right behind her. She was so distracted that she didn't notice me. I kept my head down and sat as far away from her as possible. She started reading a book, completely ignoring the people around her. She really wasn't aware how dangerous it could be for her. I knew where Elsa's studio was, but I wasn't sure Lottie knew evident by her getting off three stops past the dance studio.

I had gone over in my head how I was just going to follow her; no interactions would take place. That was until some

SPEAK EASY TO ME

random prick bumped into her without even apologizing. I gave myself away by yelling at the buffoon. She had to have heard me, so there was no hiding anymore.

Lottie would barely glance my way the whole while we were walking together. Her eyes kept darting around, looking for an escape. When she finally turned her face fully towards me, my stomach dropped to my feet. Her eye was bruised. Blind fury took over as I shoved her into the nearest store I we passed.

That son of a bitch Cameron did this to her. I knew I shouldn't have said my last little jab in the hallway at the orchestra because Lottie paid the price. I knew she didn't want to tell me. I wasn't going to give her that option. If she confirmed it was Cameron, that would be my go ahead to end his life. No one would disrespect Lottie like that and remain breathing. I've killed men for less.

Her eye was just the tip of the iceberg. Her arm had a deep purple handprint engulfing the top. Cameron had to have grabbed her arm extremely hard to leave a mark like that. I felt my blood boiling with white hot rage. Lottie could read my expression and tried to calm the situation.

When she told me she handled the situation I found it comical. I didn't see any marks on her hand indicating that she didn't fight back. She told me what she said to him and how she just walked away afterwards. Cameron hates not being in control. He could not stand that he couldn't control Lottie the way he does everyone else.

I had been so focused on her injuries that I completely forgot to lay everything out for Lottie. How my plan had gone from messing with Cameron to falling for her. I needed her to know the truth. I don't know what her knowing the truth would do for the situation. My delusion is thinking that she would leave Cameron and end up with me. Now would have been my perfect opportunity to take advantage

TABITHA KRUEGER

of the fact Cameron had hurt her to make my case seem more sympathetic.

Lottie had already divulged way more than she wanted to and I didn't want to press her any further. I would take the next opportunity I get her alone to put my heart out there to her. If she rejects me, then I will leave her alone. I didn't know how easily done that would be for me, but I would have to relent if she chose Cameron.

CHAPTER 12

LOTTIE

The last week had been fairly uneventful. After my run in with Emmett I hadn't seen or heard from him again. I was having an inner conflict with whether that was a good thing or a bad thing. I haven't yet decided.

I have been going to dance lessons every day. Elsa is amazing and plays off when my two left feet make an appearance. I forget all that is going on when I walk through her studio doors.

I had flowers from Cameron waiting for me when I arrived home from my first dance lesson. There was a note attached apologizing for our "misunderstanding" as he put it. He knew he messed up and he knew my threat of cutting off his body parts was valid. Cameron has been a perfect gentleman ever since. He is going out of town with Uncle Lon for business for a few days now so I'll get a little bit of a reprieve from both him and Uncle Lon.

I'm on my way to my second partner dance lesson. Elsa believes, no matter how delusional she is, that I have advanced enough to need a partner. Tripping on my own feet

TABITHA KRUEGER

isn't enough, I should change it up and trip over someone else's feet.

Charles, my dance partner, is 25, no wife or kids. He works at a local factory and has always wanted to take dance lessons, but had been too afraid to. Elsa had seen him and thought he would be a perfect dance partner for me. His tall stature and strong build would compliment me while dancing. She was right. We fit together like a glove. It didn't hurt that he had no clue what he was doing as well. We both walked off the dance floor limping more than a time or two.

I have gotten very comfortable with taking the trolleybus and navigating the city on my own. I leave early to walk the streets before they get so crowded it makes them hard to navigate. I also take time after my lessons to visit new shops I hadn't been to before. Immersing myself in city life seems to have helped take some of the stress off my shoulders.

I made it into the studio with a few minutes to spare. Elsa was already there, getting the studio set up. Yesterday we had learned the basics of the waltz. I was excited to see what we would be learning next. Just because I wasn't good at dancing, didn't mean I didn't like do it.

"Good morning, Elsa." I greeted her happily. My new routine had me feeling like a new person. Like I had some semblance of control in my life.

Elsa stopped what she was doing and turned to me, "Good morning, Lottie. How was the city this morning?" This had become our daily conversation starter. I would tell Elsa what I had seen in the city that morning and what shops I had been to the previous night. She would give me tips and tricks on where I should go next, her favorite spots and hidden gems that no one else knew about.

I described the people I had seen; some new and some I had seen every morning since starting my dance lessons. "The sunrise was extra beautiful this morning," I told her as I

SPEAK EASY TO ME

remembered how it was displaying a vibrant orange haze as the sun emerged from its slumber. The cold air making the oxygen I breathed in slightly burn as it entered my nose. There was a feeling of being alive today that I couldn't quite describe, not correctly anyway. "It's going to be a good day." I told her with a bright smile on my face.

There was a smile until the door to the studio opened. I turned, expecting to see Charles, but to my utter horror, it was Emmett. My brain felt like it was malfunctioning. I had finally lost it and gone mad. There was no way on God's green earth that the man who just walked through the door to my dance lesson was Emmett. I kept blinking as if this was a mirage I was seeing, and I just needed to clear my vision to see properly. All the blinking in the world wasn't going to change who I was staring at.

The foxlike smile on his face confirmed he knew exactly what I was thinking. He seemed to throw Elsa off as well. She turned to him and stumbled over her words. "Hello, sir. May I help you?" She was just as perplexed as I was.

He said from the doorway, "Charles couldn't make it this morning. He is incredibly sorry about that. I told him I would come in his place. I'm Emmett, by the way," He smiled at Elsa, using his charm so she wouldn't ask any questions. "If that is alright with you?" He said to her and then turned his attention to me, "And you, ma'am." His smile grew bigger. Emmett knew I wouldn't say anything. It would bring up too many questions that I did not want to answer.

I was sure there was steam coming out of my ears from how hot my anger was in that moment. The one safe space I had that was fully mine where no one else in my life would interfere. I weighed the risk of picking up the phonograph to hurl at him. I didn't have the money to buy Elsa a new one, so I stayed put.

Elsa took a minute to say, "It's fine with me as long as

TABITHA KRUEGER

Lottie is on board." Elsa's eyes were on me to see if I was comfortable with the change. Now, I had two options and neither of them were great.

My first option, accept that Emmett would now be my dance partner. I'd have to touch him and him, me. We'd be in close proximity for an extended period of time. I was just starting to get over him and the betrayal he'd made me feel. I felt like I was finally accepting my path in life and what that entailed. Him being here may start me questioning my choices again.

My second option, flat out refuse him as a dance partner. There was no logical reason I could give Elsa for my doing that without giving her some back story. There would be too many questions if I refused him and didn't explain why. Questions I didn't want anyone to ask especially since I didn't know how I would answer those questions; how I truly felt about everything.

I cleared my throat a moment before I spoke. "It's fine." I gave a tight smile to Elsa before glaring at Emmett. My glare seemed to be what he was aiming for as he smiled right back at me.

Elsa clapped her hands together. "Great. Now, places everyone." Elsa stood at the front of the studio where the mirror was placed. "Yesterday was the waltz." I was now standing in front of Elsa as Emmett was still hanging his coat. "Today we are going to be learning the Tango." I heard the coat hanger drop from Emmett's hands as it hit the hardwood floor.

"Sorry." He said as he picked it back up, quickly hanging his coat up. Making his way to my side he addressed Elsa, "Wouldn't something like the foxtrot be more appropriate?" I could see he was more than a little uncomfortable. I am not sure what he was expecting when he crashed my dance lesson, but this was not it.

136

SPEAK EASY TO ME

Elsa just smiled, not missing a beat, "Yesterday I noticed Lottie seemed a little stiff. The tango will help loosen that stiffness making her movements more fluid. The tango is a dance of passion, unrequited love, and longing. It makes you *feel.*" She emphasized the word "feel" with such conviction, clutching at her chest. I could feel Emmett's eyes on me. I just nodded. Oh, the irony.

"Whatever you say teach." Was Emmett's response because why not? He just wanted to torture me little by little. Both Emmett and Elsa were looking at me to confirm we could start the lesson.

"Let's get started then." I said with very little enthusiasm and a lot of hesitation. Elsa was so excited to get started she didn't pick up on the reservedness of my tone.

As Elsa walked to the phonograph, her back to us, Emmett closed the distance between us. "I'm sorry about this. Charles said you had done the waltz, I figured you'd be doing some other hoity toity dance. Not the fucking tango." Elsa started heading back our way and Emmett moved a few steps away from me, looking all innocent.

"Now, move closer together." We did as Elsa instructed as she placed a hand on either one of our backs and guided us to close the gap we had. We moved closer, facing each other. "Next, Emmett, you are going to be placing your right hand on Lottie's lower back, like this." She took his hand and placed it on the small of my back, bringing me in closer to him, his arm extending around to almost the other side of my back. "And Lottie, you will place your right arm on his shoulder." Elsa guided my hand to Emmett's shoulder, adjusting it slightly. "Perfect. Now, Lottie, raise your right arm and bend it at a 90-degree angle." Once again, she adjusted my arm to the correct position she wanted. "Yes. And Emmett, you will place your hand in hers, like this." She took Emmett's hand and placed

TABITHA KRUEGER

it over mine. He gently wrapped his fingers around my hand.

I was staring at our joined hands, letting my eyes wander to Emmett's face, where I met his warm eyes. He was tensing up. I watched as he slowly swallowed, his Adam's apple bobbing noticeably. I wondered if he could tell I was tense too. I was too close to him. Emmett holding me like this was not good for my resolve to hate him. I remembered the way he held me after our tryst in his office. Which then also reminded me what an asshole he had been afterwards.

I could tell the moment Emmett read the change in my face. He went from tense to confused, confirming he could not in fact read my mind like I had previously thought. Elsa began instructing our movements. I was angry and took this chance to purposely, on accident, step on Emmett's feet. After the foot stomping, Emmett got annoyed, realizing it wasn't accidental at all.

"Elsa, would it be okay if I had a small chat with Lottie, alone?" He said so nauseatingly sweetly I almost lost my breakfast right then and there.

"Of course. Dance should be about open communication between partners." She looked between us. "I'll just be right over there in my office." She now directed her attention to me, "So if you need anything, just give me a holler." She patted my shoulder as she left the room.

As soon as her door shut Emmett started in, "What the hell is your problem, Carrots?" He was pissed. I wasn't sure why since he was the one that invited himself to my dace lesson. I never asked him to be here, he could deal with the consequences of his own actions.

I just smiled sweetly and batted my eyelashes, "I'm sure I don't know what you are talking about."

"You know exactly what I'm talking about. Stop stepping

138

SPEAK EASY TO ME

on my feet." His voice was barely above a whisper as he scolded me. I looked at him like he was an idiot, and to me, in this instance, he totally was.

"I'm a bad dancer. Why do you think I need lessons?" It was a rhetorical question. I didn't want him answering. So, I answered his earlier question. I brought my voice down to a quiet yell, matching his. "And what the hell I'm doing is what you deserve. You think I will just forgive you for everything you've done to me? For all the hurt and betrayal, *you* caused?" I was trying to read his reaction, but he just stayed stoic with no expression passing his defenses. I resorted to pointing my finger at him. "Don't you dare shut down and tune me out when you can't handle the truth, pal."

Emmett snapped his eyes down to mine. Seeing the disappointment and regret in his eyes almost made me lose my resolve. "I am so truly sorry about everything, Lottie. Please let me take you to lunch to explain myself. Please?" He sounded so sincere. I would go to lunch with him, not for him to feel better, but for me to feel better.

"I will go under one condition." There was a spark of hope in his eyes. "Once lunch is finished, you leave me alone. You don't follow me anymore. You don't show up randomly where I am. I will just be a memory to you." I had to establish this hard line before being alone together so if I would fall for his line of bullshit, I would have already extradited myself from any further dealings with him. Future me might not be as clear headed as present me.

The hope left his eyes, not what he was expecting me to say. "That's fair." He said sadly.

Elsa emerged from her office, hesitantly opening the door and peeking her head out. "Everything okay out there? Mind if I join you?" We both let her know we were ready to resume our lesson.

TABITHA KRUEGER

The rest of the lesson was much less dramatic than the first half. I miraculously didn't step on Emmett's feet anymore. There were a few times Emmett held me closer than he needed to, causing our pelvises to meet more than once. I had to keep reminding myself that he was not a good person.

CHAPTER 13

EMMETT

I wouldn't have come today if I had known it would be so personal a dance. Then I am glad I had come because if Charles had danced like this with her, I would have lost my mind with jealousy. Lottie is making me think crazy things.

I caught Charles as he left the studio yesterday. I offered him fifty dollars to let me take the lesson with Lottie the following day. He couldn't accept my offer soon enough. He happily took my money, and I was never happier to give someone money.

Today, I was taking advantage of all the closeness the tango afforded me to relish in Lottie's body. This was the last time I was going to be this close to her and I was going to squeeze every drop out of it as I could. Feeling her soft body against mine, breathing in her scent, everything about her was perfection personified.

She could say she was a bad dancer all she wanted to, but the way her body moved once she had relaxed was spellbinding. Catching glimpses of her curves in the mirror as she moved was almost my undoing. I had to keep taking deep, calming breathes to soothe my inner beast wanting to burst through.

After an agonizing two hours of being so close to Lottie, the lesson was over. She moved so far away from me you would have thought I had the plague. I was afraid I had pushed it too much and she'd relinquish her acceptance to lunch. To my delight and surprise, she said, "Where are we going for lunch?" She didn't look at me as she spoke, but I would take any crumbs she was willing to give me.

"There's a little place I know on Toothpick Row. You won't be disappointed." She gathered her belongings and we walked to my car. We drove in silence the whole way. The drive wasn't far, but the silence made the usual five-minute car ride seem like hours.

I pulled in front of the little luncheon café. Lottie went to open her door, "Don't. Let me do it." She pulled her hand back and placed it on her lap. I went around to her side of the car and opened the door for her, holding my hand out to help her step onto the sidewalk.

She stood for a moment, taking in the brick and cement building in. "This is cute." She said before I placed my hand on her lower back and ushered her inside.

We found a table in the back and sat down. A waiter soon came over with water and took our order. Now that we were finally alone and not to be bothered for a while, I was going to confess everything to Lottie, no matter how uncomfortable it made me feel.

I had thought about what I was going to say to her a hundred times, but now that the moment was here my words escaped me. Every cohesive thought I had abandoned me simultaneously. Lottie was the first to speak, "If you have anything to say to me, now is your chance," She crossed her arms in front of her chest as she leaned back in the seat, giving me the floor to explain my actions.

SPEAK EASY TO ME

My mouth was suddenly drier than a desert. I took a sip of my water then cleared my throat. "Lottie, I am so sorry for what I did to you. I have been trying to come up with an excuse good enough for the hurt and pain I have caused you. The irreparable damage I have done to our relationship." She was not reveling anything as she stared blankly at me. That was almost worse than her just getting up and walking out, indifference meant she didn't care.

"I initially wanted to screw up things between you and Cameron, plain and simple. The short story is that him and I don't get along, we never have. Our fathers didn't like each other, and we have faithfully kept that legacy going." I steadied myself for what I was about to tell her next. "I lost my father when I was about 12. He had a gambling problem and owed some money to a bookie, who just so happened to be working for Harris Petrillo, of the Petrillo family. He was a very mean and hateful man, but he generally let little things slide. He said he would let the little things go in order to keep people on the hook for favors when he called them in. Well, my father was one of those men who would owe little things and in return, do small favors when asked. Nothing outlandish, basically piddly little jobs that were seen as beneath one of Petrillo's men." This was going to be the hard part of the story. Lottie must have sensed my uneasiness because she moved closer to the table, closer to me.

"My father, like usual, had owed Petrillo some money. It wasn't any more than he normally did. For whatever reason, I was never privy to the truth about this, Hank turned my father in to the police. Claimed he was a bootlegger from what I was told." I took a deep breath, not sure how I would handle saying this out loud. It had been years since I'd thought about my father's death and even longer since discussing it. "While he was in custody, my father was killed in his holding cell. Rumor has it that someone told Petrillo my father was a snitch and was going to revel all of the jobs he had done. My father was a lot of things, but a snitch wasn't one of them. He took his secrets to the grave."

The look of complete sadness and hurt for me was written all over Lottie's face. She took my hands in hers. "I am so sorry that happened. And you were only 12? I couldn't even imagine going through that now, let alone at such a young age." I gave her a sad smile.

"Thank you." I turned my hands upward to hold Lottie's hands in return, but she pulled them away so quickly you'd think my touch burned her. It threw me off, but I regained my composure and kept on going, "My vow to my father was to get back at whoever had turned him in. There is nothing more important to Hank than his legacy, having an heir. I just wanted to mess things up for Cameron so he couldn't fulfill his father's wishes. You were just going to be collateral damage that I was fine with."

She looked at me, shocked. I held my hand up to stop her from saying anything. "That was my plan, until I met you. Until I saw you shopping downtown, actually." I saw the puzzle pieces fall into place as her eyes turned to mine.

"The hat store?" She had come to the realization that it was a set up of sorts.

"Yes. I was planning on following you, gathering as much information on you as I could. What I had planned to be only a few hours turned into an all day event." Lottie sucked in a deep breath as she figured another piece of the puzzle out.

"The dress! You knew I had tried it on and didn't buy it." All I could do was nod my head yes.

"I saw the look on your face when you tried it on. You were positively beaming. It didn't hurt that you looked drop dead gorgeous in it." I smiled at her as her cheeks turned pink from embarrassment. "Then I saw your face when you didn't get it."

SPEAK EASY TO ME

Lottie cut in, "Russel had said it wasn't an appropriate dress for someone of my build." Her words were meek. Russel made her feel bad when there was no reason for her to feel anything other than beautiful. I'd have a little talk with Russel the next time I see him. I'd let my brass knuckles do all the talking. I will not be afraid to play dirty, not when it comes to Lottie. With Lottie all the rules were thrown out.

"You are so beautiful, Carrots. I have fallen so hard for you I don't know which way is up or down. You have made me feel things that I had only ever heard of. Feelings I didn't know I was capable of feeling. I wish we had met under different circumstances, but I can't change the past and I can't change the way I've made you feel. All I can do is ask for a second chance to prove to you that I was who you thought I was. I never portrayed myself to be anything other than who I truly am to you. You're probably the only person in my whole life I have been completely honest with."

I wasn't trying to hide the tears welling up in my eyes. I told her I would be honest with her, and this was me baring myself wholly to her. I wasn't going to hold back an ounce of what she made me feel. This was the first time I was living. I was looking forward to the next day. I cared about what happened to me. I never had that sense of self-preservation before. When I looked into her eyes, I saw my future. A future I never knew I wanted before Lottie. A future I don't want unless it's with Lottie.

I was looking at Lottie, waiting for a reply, any form of communication that she understands where I'm coming from. She shifted uncomfortably in her seat as the waiter approached with our plates of food. He sat them down in front of us. Neither one of us moved to eat anything. We both sat there, mostly staring at our food, not talking, or eating. I had finally taken a bite of my French fries and Lottie followed suite.

TABITHA KRUEGER

As we worked on our food, the silence was sliced with the sounds of forks scraping plates and patrons chattering about their days. The noises were a welcome distraction from our awkward silence.

Lottie wasn't halfway through with the food on her plate when she abruptly stood up. "Thank you for lunch, Emmett, but I think I should be going now." After I poured my heart out to her that was all I got. She didn't give me any indication on how or what she was feeling. "I will assume you remember our deal. I would appreciate it if you stick to it or my fiancé will not be very happy." Did she honestly threaten me with Cameron?

Out the door she walked not even giving me the benefit of a glance back. I just sat there in my chair as I watched the woman who held my heart walk out of my life for the last time. As much as I wanted to run after Lottie, I knew that I had to respect what she asked of me. If this is what she truly wanted, I would grant it to her. I would do anything for her even at the expense of myself.

I took a few minutes to compose myself and gather what little dignity I had left over before I could leave the restaurant.

146

CHAPTER 14

LOTTIE

Walking out of that restaurant was the hardest thing I ever had to do. It was even harder than leaving my family behind. Emmett had laid everything out on the table for me and I left it there. I knew if I didn't leave then, I never would. If I stayed there another second, all my resolve would have disappeared, and I would have done anything for him. I broke his heart and knowing that I was the one responsible for the look of desperation on his face will haunt me, always.

I wasn't quite sure where I was, so it took me longer than normal to get back home. Waiting there for me was Nathaniel. He was staying at the house with me while Uncle Lon and Cameron were out of town. Russel and Marco had to accompany them on their business trip. I didn't ask questions because I didn't want to have the weight of the answers.

"Hey there, Lottie. How was your daily lesson today?" Nathaniel knew my daily routine just as well as Elsa. I wasn't sure if I should divulge the Emmett situation to him yet. I had still been on edge around Nathaniel since I knew he was in on the lies Emmett had told me or didn't tell me. Lies by

TABITHA KRUEGER

omission were still lies. Nathaniel had tried to win my trust back by being at my beck and call for everything. I basically have had breakfast in bed for a week straight.

"Emmett showed up." I figured I should tell him. He would most likely hear it from Emmett anyway, or maybe he already knew and didn't tell me.

He got a devilish smile on his face, "Now there is something to spice up a boring day. Tell me everything." He got ready for me to spill all the details of the afternoon, but I wasn't going to do that. I wanted some things to remain private, only for me to know.

"There's not much to tell. We danced and then he took to me lunch trying to apologize, but I walked out halfway through the meal. I'm sure whatever was in your mind is far more interesting than what actually happened today." He looked like I took away his favorite dessert and placed vegetables in front of him.

"That was very anticlimactic. Boo to you!" He gave me a thumbs down and I slapped his hand away.

"I am so very sorry my life wasn't dramatic enough for you today." I laughed as we made our way towards the library. Our nightly routine was reading quietly together in the massive library I had just discovered on the first floor of the house. We would read for a few hours and then make our way to the dining room for dinner. This night was no different.

Charles was back dancing as my dance partner the next day and everything was as it had been. My routine was pretty routine. No surprise Emmett popping up, no deviation from day to day. That was, until three days later.

I was sound asleep when Nathaniel burst through my bedroom door. He rushed to the side of my bed in a panic. "Lottie. Lottie." He nudged me until I finally opened my eyes. "Lottie, you have to get up and come with me right away."

SPEAK EASY TO ME

There was an urgency in his voice that alerted me to the seriousness of the situation. I had no idea what this could be about, but I had a feeling it wasn't going to be good.

"We don't have time for you to get ready. I'll explain everything in the car." He tossed a robe at me and my house slippers. I followed closely behind him as we descended the stairs and ran out the front door, barley having time to grab my coat.

I got into the car just as he slammed his door shut and started the engine. The night air was freezing. "What the hell is going on?" I demanded to know what the reason was for him dragging me out of bed in the middle of the night.

"There's been a stabbing. Emmett called the house asking for you. He said you used to fix up the guys on the farm. That you'd know what to do." My mind started racing. Was Emmett the one who was stabbed? Where was he? I could feel the panic and dread creeping into my veins.

"What? He was stabbed?" I needed answers now before I started spiraling and couldn't get reeled back in.

"Him and two of his guys. He said it wasn't horrible, they'll probably just need some stitches." Here I was thinking he was bleeding out and he just needed stitches. Is he serious?

"So let me get this straight. You got me out of bed because three grown men couldn't handle a few cuts themselves? You have got to be kidding me right now!" I went from panic to seriously pissed.

Nathaniel slowly side eyed me, gauging my level of anger. "They're pretty big cuts."

"They better be or I'll finish the job those other guys started." Nathaniel was very quiet the rest of the car ride there.

We pulled up to the speakeasy. I was debating on not even getting out of the car. Nathaniel opened my door, "Come on,

149

Lottie. You're here already." He encouraged me out of the car. We quickly made our way into the building.

I took in the three men as we entered the main room. Two of the men I had never seen before. All three men were wearing white button-down shirts in various saturations of blood and tatters. Emmett's shirt had the most blood on it.

The easiest way to assess the damage was to have all three men remove their shirts so I could see their injuries. "Shirts off." I didn't have time for pleasantries. All three men started unbuttoning their shirts. I removed my coat and set it on a table. I took my engagement ring off and placed it in my coat pocket.

I went over to Emmett first. I was trying my hardest to treat him like the other two men; like I didn't know him. That was too much to hope with Emmett though.

"If you wanted to see me with my clothes off…," He had a smile on his face I wanted to wipe off.

"I can easily walk back out that door. Your choice." I was tired, pissed, and not ready to deal with Emmett in any capacity.

"Sorry." He said with caution. I proceeded to exam him. There weren't any significant marks on him. He had one superficial cut on his upper arm, nothing that would warrant the blood on his shirt. He must have read the confusion on my face.

"Most of it wasn't my blood." He informed me. There was a relieved breath that escaped my throat. As mad as I was at Emmett for how dumb he was, I was thankful he wasn't hurt all that much.

I went to the other two men and looked over their wounds as well. All three had superficial wounds, not even needing a single stitch between the three of them. The ride to the speakeasy took longer than it took me to tend to these three Neanderthals.

I was going over to put my coat back on as Emmett approached me. I shrugged my coat over my shoulders and began buttoning it slowly.

"If I would have known that getting stabbed would get you talking to me again, I would have done it sooner." He was smiling at me. I was so relieved he wasn't seriously hurt, I let it slide and returned the smile.

"I think you just like the dramatics of it." I jabbed at him. He didn't disagree.

"I'm surprised you showed up tonight, if I'm being honest." The words were interwoven with his husky voice.

"Nathaniel wasn't completely honest with me when he told me about this emergency. I use emergency very loosely in this case." I gestured between him and his two minions. "He didn't tell me you would be here until we were already in the car and driving here." I told him, not sure where this conversation was going. "I wasn't sure I was going to get out of the car when I knew you would be here."

"Thank you for not letting me die." He bumped my shoulder with his.

"Well, it would be hard to ignore you if you were dead, so I didn't really have a choice." He was smiling at me, reveling in our conversation. His eyes wandered down to my left hand.

"Where's your ring?" He asked with hope in his eyes. I pulled the ring out of my pocket and placed it back on my left ring finger.

"I didn't want to get blood on it." He took my hand to take a closer look at my ring.

"This ring isn't you." He almost was saying it to himself.

"Really? What kind of ring do you think is me?" I was offended at his remark. How dare he presume what is me and what isn't.

"A simple diamond on a silver band. Like you, simple

elegance that makes a statement. Looks good with every-thing." He was still holding my hand in his. I looked at our joined hands before looking up at him. I slowly removed my hand from his.

"Stay safe Emmett." I left him standing there as I walked away. There was so much I wanted to say but walking away spoke volumes more than any words would have. This thing, whatever it was between us, needed to be over. I walked with Nathaniel to the car.

The whole last month or so had been a big whirl wind of emotions. I reflected on events as we drove home. If I were to look at it from an outsider's perspective my falling for Emmett didn't seem so bazaar. I was ripped away from life as I knew it, put in a position to marry a man that had no interest in me and made it very clear of his intentions. It was no surprise I clung to the first person who showed me inter-est. I was looking for a way out and Emmett seemed to be my savior, my last hope of not entering a marriage I wouldn't be happy in.

I turned to Nathaniel while he was concentrating on the road. "I do not wish to see Emmett anymore, in any capacity." My words were quiet but absolute. Nathaniel continued staring ahead as he nodded his understanding.

I spent the next three weeks keeping busy. Dance lessons, wedding planning, endless dinners and parties with Cameron filled my schedule from morning to night. I felt I had finally had enough time and distance away from Emmett that I could think more rationally.

Although we were going to have a small wedding, the planning and prepping for a society event was immense. Food, decorations, cake, flowers, it all seemed never-ending, but it gave me a sense of purpose. I had an appointment I had to get to for finalizing the flowers today at four pm.

SPEAK EASY TO ME

Cameron couldn't make it but was going to meet me at Uncle Lon's house after.

Nathaniel was with me, giving his thoughts on the flowers I had narrowed the selection down to. My two choices were roses and sunflowers or white dahlias and pink peonies. Nathaniel was looking mindlessly outside as I was trying to show him the different flower arrangements. I followed his eyesight. The big window at the front of the store was framing the falling snow outside like a portrait. I snapped my fingers in front of Nathaniel's face, breaking his concentration. He turned to me, still a little hazy eyed, and smiled. "I got lost in thought for a moment. What were you saying?" He said as he shook his head slightly, trying to fully come back in focus.

"I asked what you thought about the colors of the flowers." I held up the samples of flowers in my hands. His eyes still had an air of distance in them. I let out an exasperated sigh as I turned, dropping my hands down.

"I think we should go. The snow is really starting to come down. I don't want to drive through snow tonight." I looked back out the window and sure enough, the snow was now coming down in droves. It was starting to stick to the ground, quickly accumulating.

By the time we left the flower shop, the wind was whipping the snow around so hard I had to squint to see anything. I was glad we left when we did. Driving back home was not a fun experience. The car was veering all over the road almost side swiping a few other cars that were parked on the side of the street. The slick roads while driving through a wall of white had my eyes closed until we had pulled safely up to the house. Nathaniel didn't pull in the driveway.

"I remembered I must be somewhere. I am just dropping you off." I went to protest him driving any more in these conditions, but he preemptively countered with, "I have

153

TABITHA KRUEGER

driven in much worse. I promise to drive slowly and carefully."

I knew no matter what I said he wouldn't listen, so I just said, "Alright. Be safe." He nodded his head once and was off as soon as I shut my door. I walked through the thin layer of snow on the driveway. The snow was crunching under my shoes until I got to the porch where the awning had prevented most of the snow from entering.

I was trying to decide if I wanted to make myself a cup of tea first before getting in a hot bath to rid my body of the chill that had made its way in. I shivered as the warm air circulating in the house hit me as I opened the door. I shut and locked the door, about to take my coat off, when I heard a sound coming from the study.

I moved closer and heard more noises. The sound was muffled. I moved slowly towards the door and eased it open. What I found on the other side of that door will forever haunt me. There was Cameron, bare ass hanging out, with Maggie splayed out on the desk, ramming himself into her. The sounds I had heard were their moans. I stood in stunned silence for a moment, taking in the scene before me. The two of them so wrapped up in each other they hadn't noticed the door was opened with me in the doorframe.

I was disgusted by what was happening in front of me. It would be hypocritical of me to judge him for this indiscretion when I had done various intimate activities with Emmett. My problem was the fact he was doing this in my current residence, with a woman who I thought was a friend, while I was out finalizing wedding flowers. It made me wonder how long this had been going on.

I am not sure how I was able to keep my composure as the thrusting increased and the sound of skin slapping together got louder. That's when I struck. I shouted, "This is your business you had to attend to?" Cameron stopped mid thrust and pulled out of Maggie, exposing himself, and her, to me.

Maggie jumped down off the desk pulling her dress down to cover herself up. Cameron stood there, unmoving. I took my ring off and threw it in the fire going in the fireplace. "Both of you can go to hell." I couldn't leave without getting one last lick in at them both. "No wonder she had to fake all the moaning." I let my eyes wander down to his fully exposed semi hard rod. I heard Cameron say "Shit," under his breath as he bent down to pick up his pants.

I slammed the door as I left. Russel must've heard the ruckus from whatever room he had been in because he was standing there in the foyer now. The look of shock and pity was on his face as he took in the scene. Cameron was opening the door behind me as he buttoned his pants. Maggie was disheveled in the study following after Cameron.

I walked right up to Russel, "Take me to Le Mier." His eyes were darting from me to Cameron, trying to figure out the best way to navigate the situation. I wasn't going to give him a choice. "Listen here, you can either take me there or I will walk there. Either way, I am going. I refuse to be in the same house as either of those assholes." I didn't even wait for a response.

I turned and walked outside. I was really hoping my threat to walk would make Russel come after me. The big flakes were still falling rapidly as I made my way down the driveway. I couldn't even see my previous tracks in the newly falling snow. I heard crunching footsteps behind me.

"Charlotte. Get in the car." It was Russel. He gestured his head toward the car he wanted me to get into. He made quick work of wiping off the snow that had piled up on the windshield. As soon as we were on the road, Russel was about to say something.

TABITHA KRUEGER

He opened his mouth, "I," was all I let him get out. I didn't know if he was going to apologize to me, sympathize with me or try to convince me this wasn't a big deal. I didn't want to hear any of it.

"I swear to God Russel, if you say anything to me at all, I will grab that steering wheel and crash us into the nearest structure. Do not try me." I saw his hands grip the wheel he was holding onto even tighter, his knuckles turning white. At least he was taking my threat seriously.

Familiar buildings were hardly discernable through the sheets of snow making their way down from the sky. It took nearly double the time it usually would, but we eventually made it to Le Mier. When I first told Russel to take me here, I had just wanted to go to a place I knew.

Emmett wasn't as out of my system as I had thought. The first person I wanted to go to when I was in trouble was Emmett. I had made up my mind in the car. I couldn't live a life where my heart will be broken a million little times. It would cost way too much to fix that amount of hurt and pain. There's no way I have that much strength. My soul wouldn't survive that torture. I wanted to be with Emmett, consequences be damned.

CHAPTER 15

EMMETT

There had been a finality in Lottie's words. I willed her to turn around. To come running into my arms. Instead, I had stood there as she walked away. This time was different. This time I would let her go. I needed to let her go not only for her sake but mine as well.

Nathaniel gave me a sympathetic look as he turned to follow her. I hadn't needed her to come here. It was a whim that I called Nathaniel to tell him I needed Lottie's specific set of nursing skills. None of us were hurt nearly bad enough to warrant more than a band aide.

My two associates and I had to go take care of a problem for Petrillo. There was a guy in his inner circle who was selling out his secret bootlegging routes. Four of his shipments had already gone missing and he had a big one scheduled to come in the next few days. We were to get as much information out of him as we could before giving him a Chicago burial. He was a slippery snake and had managed to escape the ties we had him in.

When Louis looked away, slippery Mike struck. He grabbed a knife from a table nearby and began wildly swinging it around. It took all three of us to wrangle him to the ground, wrestle the knife out of his hands and restrain him once again. All three of us had gotten sliced with the knife, barely breaking the skin.

We eventually broke him, in more than one way, and the details came pouring out of him faster than his blood was gushing out. The blood Lottie had seen was the result of the final slice across his neck with the knife he tried to slice us with. I figured that was only fitting.

We left Le Mier to clean up and change before reporting to Petrillo. He was more than happy with our findings. His regular enforcers were sent out to discuss the new discoveries with the perpetrators.

I crawled into bed at 8 o'clock in the morning. I was used to late nights. I wasn't used to coming home feeling absolutely defeated. I couldn't fall asleep despite the feeling of extreme exhaustion coursing through my bones. I tossed and turned until it was time for me to start getting ready for another night at Le Mier.

This was the first time I had dreaded going into my hideaway. Louis was there getting the bar ready for the patrons to enter. We were all ready by the time the first knock sounded on the entrance door. As the night dragged on, I found myself drinking more and more. Slipping into the sweet oblivion the alcohol promised. This was the start to how I spent the last three weeks.

I was preparing to start imbibing when Nathaniel showed up. He slid up to the bar with a blank face. He had no snarky remark or joking. "She's going through with the wedding. We looked at the final flowers today." He took a swig of the beer I had just placed in front of him.

"I don't know why you're telling me this." I took a shot of whiskey. After this conversation I was going to move to the

SPEAK EASY TO ME

moonshine we had gotten from Tennessee, that stuff makes you forget you're even on planet earth.

"There's still time to stop this." He was pleading with me. He was fond of Lottie and knew Cameron was completely wrong for her. He would stifle her in ways that would damage her forever.

"Lottie made up her mind. She chose him." I took another shot. "This is what she wants." I was pouring myself another shot waiting for the numbness to come. I don't know why I bothered with the small glass when it would be easier to just drink directly from the bottle that I'd empty by the time daybreak was making an appearance.

"You are going to lose her forever if you don't do something soon, you moron." Nathaniel pushed off the bar swinging off his stool. I watched as he was engulfed by the crowd. He could stay lost in the crowd for all I cared.

Time was starting to blur together. It could have been five minutes or three hours since my conversation with Nathaniel had taken place. The alcohol seemed to hit me all at once. The room started spinning. Suddenly everything was too much.

I told Louis to tend bar as I headed into my office. I had to get away from the noise of the music and the people. I entered my office taking a direct path to my couch. I laid down and placed my forearm over my eyes. I took a few cleansing breaths hoping that would help the room stop from spinning.

The office door creaked open. I heard heals on the floor clicking closer to me. "Emmett," I heard a voice say low and needy. I moved my arm from my eyes. The bright lights of the office made it hard for me to focus on the blurry figure standing at the foot of the couch.

The figure kneeled beside me. I breathed in the sweet scent of floral notes of the perfume as the figure started to come into focus. She wasn't fully in focus yet as she bent down, her lips meeting mine. I was thrown off which took me a moment to comprehend what was happening. When her hand moved down to my pants, working on the button and zipper, I snapped out of my drunken stupor.

I rolled off the couch, landing on my back with a thud. Before I was able to move, the figure, who was now fully in focus, was Brooke. She took my position on the floor as an invitation to straddle me. My pants were still unbuttoned with my zipper partially down.

"What do you think you are doing?" I put my hands on her hips to move her off. She grabbed my wrists and pushed my arms down to my sides.

"I know this is what you need." I used my body weight to spin us, putting me on top of Brooke and her with her back to the floor.

"I never want anything to do with you, ever again. Every minute I have spent with you was a mistake I wish I could take back." She wrapped her legs around my hips pulling me closer to her. I let go of her wrists to unfurl her legs from me.

The door of the office swung open at that moment drawing both mine and Brooke's attention to Lottie as she stood there. She was gawking at the position we were in. I stood up with Brooke still trying to keep her legs wrapped around me. I turned towards Lottie. I followed her eyes down to my undone pants.

"This is not what it looks like." I said quickly. I had wanted to see Lottie for so long and this was what she walked in to.

"Brooke's legs weren't wrapped around you with your pants halfway off? You are all fucking assholes. You all deserve each other. I'm so done here." Tears were running down her face as she turned and ran away.

SPEAK EASY TO ME

"Fuck!" I stormed after her buttoning up my pants as I followed behind. Brooke blocked my path.

"You are still going to go after her?" Brooke had been trying to get back into my bed as soon as she heard Lottie was done with me. Word travels fast in the speakeasy. If I was going to get under a new woman to forget Lottie it definitely wouldn't be Brooke.

"What part of this are you not understanding? I do not want anything to do with you whether or not Lottie is in my life. I want you out of my life forever. I do not care if you went outside right now and got hit by a train. I would not shed a tear. I would not mourn your loss. You were a wet hole for me to get off to a few times, nothing more." I shoved her out of my way as I pursued Lottie.

I quickly scoured the room stupidly thinking she didn't leave. As soon as I didn't see her, I headed right for the door, exiting the Le Mier. The snow was heavy as it was making its way down. I looked to my left and saw nothing. I spun my head to the right and saw footprints in the snow. I began following them. They lead to a car, but there was something off about it. The snow made it hard to see until I was right next to the automobile. The driver's side door was open with a body in the front seat, slumped over in a pool of blood.

Panic started filling my veins as I made my way around the car. There was a flurry of footprints in the snow mixed with blood. There was also blood spray on the side of the car, covering the windows in a fine mist. There was no sign of Lottie anywhere.

I went back around to the driver's side to confirm my suspicion. I moved the body, so it was sitting up. I was looking at a very recently dead Russel. I leaned him back against the seat as a car pulled into the alleyway.

The car stopped and Cameron jumped out of the driver's

side. It took him a short while to take in the scene before he had me pinned against the car with Russel's dead body in it.

"What have you done?" He accused. I pushed him off me. Both of us almost slipped in the snow as we separated.

"I have no idea. Lottie came in, saw me in a compromising position with Brooke and then she came out here. I followed her, but this is what I came across." I was talking so fast I wasn't sure if what I was saying was making any sense. It must have because Cameron punched the side of the car.

"This is all my fault. Lottie caught me and Maggie going at it on the desk in her Uncle's study. She threw her ring in the fireplace and demanded Russel bring her here." Cameron tipped his head back and let out a loud, long sigh.

She was coming to me after severing ties with Cameron. After walking in on Cameron and Maggie, she walked in on Brooke and me. It didn't matter that we hadn't done anything despite Brooke's advances, what she saw looked like we were about to have sex.

There was a cough that came from the passenger seat of the car. Turned out Russel wasn't as dead as I thought. I hadn't even thought to double check to see if he was still breathing. My mind was on Lottie and her whereabouts.

Cameron and I both rushed over to Russel. He was coughing as he was trying to take deep breaths. We grabbed him and dragged him from the car, placing him in the freshly fallen snow next to the car.

"I am so sorry, boss. They took her." He was coughing up blood now. "I didn't even see them coming." He knew he was going to die. All three of us had seen enough men die to know the gurgling cough of a dying man. "She fought back. Broke one of the bastard's noses." That's where all the blood on the other side of the car came from. They took her alive.

The white snow was now saturated with the warm blood leaving Russel's body. His dying words barely audible, "Find

SPEAK EASY TO ME

her." Russel's eyes rolled back in his head. Cameron and I just sat there hunched over in the snow.

My adrenaline started racing. I got up and sprinted down the alley to the main road. At this time of the night there wasn't much traffic downtown. The road was covered in tracks. No way to discern which tracks were newer or older. All of them getting filled in by the steadily falling snow.

Cameron pulled up next to me in his car. I hopped in the car with him. He turned right onto the main road. "There is no way to tell which way they went." I said, defeated.

Following an endless group of tracks in the snow wasn't going to help us find Lottie. Time was crucial. They had her alive, but we didn't know for how long. Or why they wanted her alive. There were a million thoughts going through my head on the possibilities.

Cameron pulled the car over indicating he also knew aimlessly following an endless number of tracks was counterproductive. "I don't know what to do." Cameron said hopelessly, resting his head against the steering wheel. We were both powerful men who got what we wanted. Finding Lottie should be easy for us. Why are we already feeling defeated before we even try?

"Go back to Le Mier." Cameron lifted his head to look at me. "We can use it as a headquarters. Neutral ground for now." Cameron wasn't someone you wanted in your speakeasy. His type was bad for business. He answered by driving back to the speakeasy.

We walked through the door together, both covered in Russel's blood. By the look on everyone's faces when we entered it wasn't going to take much to clear them out. "The bar is closed until further notice." I bellowed into the room. The lack of movement from the people who were supposed to be leaving was pissing me off. "Get out! Don't make me

TABITHA KRUEGER

say it again." The sound of shuffling feet was the only sound through the whole place.

Prior to coming inside Cameron and I had moved Russel into the car then moved it to the side more. The blanket of fresh snow helped to cover the blood that had been visible 20 minutes ago. When the last person was out the door, I immediately locked it. Briefly explaining what was going on the Louis had him on the horn putting a call out to our men to gather here.

Cameron made use of the phone once Louis was done. Now it was a waiting game for everyone else to arrive. In the meantime we would try to come up with some sort of game plan. We went over what we knew. Cameron had a lot of enemies from his line of work as the middleman between corrupt cops and bootleggers so we didn't even discuss why she was taken, it was a given.

"Whoever did this must have known she was going to be here. But how?" I was just throwing out ideas.

"They were probably following her. She had scheduled appointments today that she cut short. Maybe they wanted to take her after one of them, but she changed her plans, so they had to improvise."

"Russel said she broke one of their noses. If that is true, he'll be sporting two black eyes shortly, if not already." It was somewhat comforting knowing that she fought back. I was proud of her. I couldn't wait to tell her that as soon as I seen her. "Write down anyone you think might be involved." I placed a pencil and piece of paper in front of Cameron. He began scribbling names down.

An hour after both of our phone calls had gone out we had over 20 men sitting in the Le Mier awaiting orders. I stepped to the front of the crowd. "Along with Cameron's fiancé Charlotte being taken tonight, Russel was killed in the process." The men in this room were not easily phased over

SPEAK EASY TO ME

anything, but hearing that Russel, the indestructible man he was, had been killed so easily sent a stunned silence through the room. The feds had been listening in to phone calls so the message over the phone had been extremely vague; the men were to get here as soon as possible.

Cameron cut in, "Charlotte is my ex-fiance, but she needs to be found regardless of her relationship status to me." Cameron was rocking from leg to leg, it was a nervous movement. "There are a few things you need to know about Charlotte." Cameron dipped his head to Little Nicky sitting in the back of the group of men, I hadn't even seen he was there. I didn't even know Little Nicky had been back in the city. He had been MIA for months since the feds had been looking for him.

Little Nicky worked for Morelli. Morelli was a bootlegger who got his supply from Canada. Morelli was also the biggest supplier of alcohol in the Chicago area. He was the only man in town who had a free pass to sell to all the families in the city.

Little Nicky made his way up to the front by Cameron and me. He took a minute before addressing the men. "First, there are a few things you all should be made aware of. Charlotte, or Lottie, is someone none of you have probably heard of, which is what we wanted. You would know her as Charlie." There was now a murmur going through the group.

Little Nicky didn't have to elaborate on Charlie, we all knew who he was talking about. Charlie was the talk of the town for the last year. Morelli had found a secret route to the Canadian border where none of his men had been pinched for almost a year. The only clue to his secret route was it was headed by a man named, Charlie, who turned out to be Lottie. Only Little Nicky and three other men knew the identity of the mysterious Charlie.

My jaw was on the floor. Who the fuck was this woman?

Everything I learned about her was astounding. Just when I thought I had her figured out, another layer was peeled back.

I had this strong urge to punch Little Nicky after putting the new information together. Little Nicky was Lottie's Nick. He was the one who had sat under the starts with her every night for months. He was the one who had taken her virginity. She was permanently marked with his tattoo.

I was looking down at the ground trying to recover my composure as Little Nicky continued, "Second, we will not be meeting any ransom demands." My head snapped up in his direction. The murmuring grew louder amongst the men. Cameron also looked shocked as he stared at Little Nicky. I don't think Cameron was expecting him to say that.

"What?" I said astounded. There had been string of kidnappings around the city. Men were being taken all over the city, from every family. Once they were abducted, a ransom demand would be made and then met. There were no negotiations, no questions. It had become such a normal routine it wasn't shocking anymore. "Why wouldn't the ransom be paid?" I felt myself getting worked up.

"She is collateral damage at this point. Whatever happens to her, Morelli washes his hands. No one is to pay the ransom." I couldn't contain my anger any longer. I socked him. I swung my right fist into his face knocking him backward into Cameron, who managed to catch him.

"You son of a bitch! After everything she's done for Morelli and *you*, you have the nerve to stand up here and say she's nothing more than collateral damage?" I took a step in his direction, but Cameron stepped in the middle separating us.

"Look man, I tried to change Morelli's mind. He won't budge. He has what he wants. I don't think he likes the fact he had to have a woman's help to move his supply." As much as I wanted to take another swing at him, he was only doing

SPEAK EASY TO ME

what he was told. That is the life we take on in this business. What your boss says is law. Morelli wasn't my boss though.

I stared daggers at Little Nicky as I spewed, "You can tell your boss that I don't accept his orders. I will tear this city down brick by brick to find Lottie. If anyone gets in my way, they will wish for death before I am through with them. If Morelli tries to stop me in any way, he will find out what a waking nightmare feels like."

I could not look at Little Nicky for another second knowing he was betraying Lottie the way he was. I turned to walk to my office, not even addressing any of the other men in the room. I heard Louis dismissing the other men.

I had slammed the door to my office shut the second I entered the room. Just a few hours before I had been caught in a very compromising position with Brooke in this room. If I hadn't gotten so loaded, I would have had more control of my actions. I never would have allowed Brooke to get so close. If only I had stayed out at the bar for a few more minutes Lottie would have found me as a drunkard on a bar stool, not looking as if I were about to be balls deep in Brooke.

The what ifs and shoulda-coulda-wouldas would haunt me for the rest of my life. I am not proud to admit that I have done a lot of bad things in my life, things that would make a normal man's skin crawl, but hurting Lottie, that is the one thing that I cannot get over. The look on her face when she saw Brooke and me, that will haunt my dreams until the day I die.

I stalked over to my safe, the dial clicking as I opened it to retrieve the two guns inside. I would need to be packing more heat than usual if I am going to get Lottie back. Whoever has her, his days are numbered.

My office door flung open with Cameron, Louis, and Little Nicky entering. Good thing my guns weren't loaded or

TABITHA KRUEGER

I would have ended Little Nicky right then and there. Anyone who would betray Lottie, betrays me as well.

I was about to let my tongue lead the assault on Little Nicky, but Cameron cut me off. "He's not our enemy Emmett." My eyes were locked on Little Nicky's. His blue eyes were full of worry.

"Give us a minute." I dismissed the other two men. Neither of them argued before exiting the office, closing the door behind them, leaving Nicky and me alone in the room.

The door had barely shut when Little Nicky began speaking. "Emmett, I know how bad this is. And I know it looks like I don't want to help Lottie, but I do."

I didn't even want her name on his lips. "You do not get the privilege to call her Lottie."

He got a smirk on his face, "I called her even more intimate names. More than you have." His words hit me worse than a punch to the gut. "If you want to turn this into a pissing contest, I will win every time." We were now standing nose to nose. "You can either stop with the tough guy act, or we can have it out right now. Beat each other bloody while who knows who has Lottie. The choice is yours, Emmett."

He was right. This was getting us nowhere. My rage was pulsing so loudly through my veins it was blinding my logic. My priority should be who took Lottie, not beating up the guy who took her virginity. "You're right." I shook my head to rid it of every thought of Lottie with Little Nicky.

I nodded at Nicky, indicating he could let Louis and Cameron back in. Once all of us were gathered around my desk, Nicky laid out his plans. As mad as I was at him, the fact he was here talking to us about getting Lottie back, going against Morelli, I couldn't fault him any longer. He did love her, and I knew she loved him from the fondness in her voice when she had recalled their time together.

"I have eyes and ears all over this city. I have given the

168

word to watch out for anyone that may have a grudge against Cameron, Emmett, or Lon." He had already had this plan in play before he even arrived at Le Mier. "I let one of my guys know to look for anyone with two black eyes." Little Nicky turned his attention to me. "She broke one of the guy's noses?" There was unmistakable pride in voice.

"Based on the blood everywhere and Russel's account, very much so." I said, reciprocating his prideful tone. The smile that was painted across his face was that of satisfaction.

"Let's go find our woman." Little Nicky slapped my shoulder as he exited the office, Cameron and Louis closely behind him. I was hit with the fact that she was our woman, with the exception of Louis. Little Nicky was her past. Cameron is her present. With any luck, I will be her future.

We decided the best course of action was to split up. We'd each talk to our guys since we each could cover different ground. Cameron had his cop buddies and political partners that he put on notice. I had my guys that were spread out within the city. Little Nicky couldn't be quite as obvious as Cameron and I could, but he had his close associates spreading the word.

After 24 hours we reconvened at Le Mier. None of us had any new news to share. We were all met with dead ends. That was, until I decided I needed to get some fresh air to clear my head. Maybe with some time to think on my own, I could come up with a better plan than torturing men for information they didn't have.

I had rounded the corner to the biggest department stores in Chicago. The massive building took up multiple city blocks and was six stories high. Imagine my surprise when I spotted a man with two black eyes and a very bright red, crooked nose. That freshly broken nose was attached to a very familiar face to me; Arnold Prescott.

Prescott was one of the slipperiest weasels I had ever had

TABITHA KRUEGER

the displeasure of meeting. He was the lowest of the low. Nobody seemed to pay him any mind due to the fact he was pathetically a follower. He never posed a threat to anyone which let him get away with being a spineless weasel. He didn't spot me until it was too late.

I had him by his collar a second before he registered my presence. His feet slipping and sliding along the sidewalk as I dragged him behind me heading to his demise. Prescott's pleading words fell on deaf ears. He was babbling about not knowing what was going on, but by the time I made it to my car he was singing a different tune.

In a shaky voice he pleaded, "I'll tell you whatever you want to know." His eyes were darting back and forth in pure terror.

"I know you will." I said as I shoved him in my car. "If you attempt to escape, I will cut off your legs right here, right now, in the middle of this damn street." His silent obedience was a testament to my reputation following me. He knows I have no qualms about following through with my threat.

Prescott was shaking so bad the car vibrated the whole drive to Le Mier. I got out of the car and went around to let him out when he made a break for it. His feet fighting through the snow the only sound in the empty alley. It didn't take me long to catch up to him. I had gotten close enough to push him to the ground. I had to skid to a stop as I passed him.

The poor pathetic weasel was face down on the ground. If he thought I was playing around he was going to be sorely mistaken in a few minutes. I grabbed him by the hair and slammed his face as hard as I could into the snow-covered cement. There was a crunching sound accompanied by his cries. Bright red blood was flowing down his face. "Did you think I was fucking joking when I told you there would be consequences to your actions? Good thing

SPEAK EASY TO ME

for you we're going into Le Mier. I won't cut your legs off out here."

I had him by the collar of his shirt so tightly, it was choking him. I didn't let up. He could pass out for all I cared, I'd wake him up by ripping his finger nails out one by one. I was not a pleasant guy when I was mad and right now, I was piping hot angry.

As I pushed Prescott into the speakeasy, the three men already inside ran to see what the commotion was. Prescott's cries hadn't rescinded an ounce since I rebroke his nose.

"I found this piece of shit outside a department store. He has a freshly broken nose." All three men looked at his newly bleeding nose and then back to me. I threw my hands up, "He had a broken nose already before I had to remind him who he was dealing with." Prescott was sniveling like the coward he was.

Little Nicky came up from behind him and shoved him down into a chair by his shoulders. As soon as his ass hit the chair, he saturated his pants with urine. He knew what was in store for him. The longer he held out on the information the more he was going to suffer.

Little Nicky was waiting for my go ahead to begin his meticulous work to get the answers we so desperately needed. It was Little Nicky's personal best time at getting someone to talk.

Cameron, Little Nicky and I emerged from the speakeasy with the knowledge we needed to find Lottie. Louis stayed behind to clean up the mess Little Nicky left, which wasn't as bad as I had hoped it would be. Prescott spilled the beans almost immediately.

Lottie was being held in an old farmhouse about a half hour outside of the city. We all piled in the car as Little Nicky revved the engine, taking off like Lottie's life depended on it, because it did.

TABITHA KRUEGER

We made it to the farmhouse, right where Prescott had said it would be. The door was left wide open. With guns drawn we cautiously made entrance into the house. The open basement door across the room caught my attention, and I immediately made my way there. Descending the stairs as quickly and quietly as I could I was astonished by what I found.

My eyes drank in the large man on the floor covered in blood. A perfect puncture wound to the heart. I had no clue who he was, I had never seen this greasy man in my life. There were bloody footprints that went halfway up the stairs. The feet were small, wearing high heeled shoes. She made it out of this basement on her own accord.

I took the stairs two at a time converging at the basement door with Cameron and Nicky. "No one up here." Nicky confirmed.

"One dead guy down there." I thumbed back to the basement. "It looks like Lottie killed him and fled up the stairs. Her bloody footprints go about halfway up the stairs." The house engulfed us in its silence. The three of us trying to figure out what our next move was.

I felt like there was more that Prescott could have told us, but he died before he got the chance. It was Nicky's personal best time at a confession because he got so mad when Prescott told us they had sent a man, the dead man, downstairs to rape and then kill Lottie.

The snow had seemed like a hinderance, but it could work to our advantage. "We need to look for footprints in the snow. If she made it out of the house, she would have left a trail." We all realized that if she had left a trail, the third man in this kidnapping scheme would have been able to track her as well. All three of us went in separate directions. I went around to the left side of the house, Cameron to the right and Nicky went down the driveway.

172

SPEAK EASY TO ME

Shortly after going our separate ways Cameron's voice rang through the open air, "Over here!" Nicky and I both sprinted to where he was standing. "She climbed out the window." There was an open window with tracks underneath it leading to the woods. We started running along with the tracks. Once we got to the woods there was an odd finding. The one set of tracks we had been following turned into multiple, going every which way. Like we had done back at the house, we each followed a separate set of tracks.

I ran forward and came where the tracks kept going, all the other tracks went down to one set of footprints. "She went this way!" I did not wait for either of the other men to join me before I continued running in the direction Lottie had gone.

I saw a clearing coming up with a barn in the middle. That's when I heard a sound that made my heart stop. A scream so loud and painful, I knew I didn't have much time to make it to Lottie. My feet propelled me forward without thought.

I made it to what had been the barn door, now just a bunch of wood splinters hanging on by a few screws. I saw him towering over Lottie. She was on the ground and he had her pinned, his hands around her throat.

"Lottie!" I screamed in absolute panic. The disgusting man in front of me turned to me and gave the most chilling smile I had ever seen. He returned to his work killing Lottie. I heard the slicing sound of a knife, followed by blood spurting all over.

"Lottie!" I screamed again, this time, my heart completely shattered at the amount of blood loss pooling around Lottie.

CHAPTER 16

LOTTIE

My head was pounding. The top back of my head felt like I had been hit with a mallet. I went to raise my hand to my head but neither of my arms moved. I slowly started opening my eyes through the grogginess and was met with darkness. I tried again to raise my hand but was met with resistance. I knew the harsh stiffness and itchy material was rope. My hands were tied together behind my back.

I was searching for anything that would give me a clue as to where I was or how I got here. My eyes were still adjusting to the darkness. All I could make out was the outline of a door to my left. There was a mustiness in the air that suggested the room I was in was damp.

I moved my feet, but they were tied to the legs of my chair. I started breathing fast as the panic started to rise. My mind was racing, trying to recall what had transpired before I woke up in this damp, dark dungeon.

The memories started flooding in quicker than I wanted. The images of Cameron and Maggie on the desk in the study.

SPEAK EASY TO ME

Russel driving me to Le Mier. Then the memories I wished I could forget invaded my mind. My heart breaking all over again.

I walked into Le Mier immediately heading to the bar expecting to see Emmett there. Louis was behind the bar instead. Though I had never been formally introduced to him, I had seen him with his shirt off when I had inspected him for knife injuries. I felt like that was more than enough introduction to forgo formalities. "Where's Emmett?" I asked.

Louis didn't answer right away instead he looked at a spot behind me. "He's not here right now." He said sternly. Liar. I pushed away from the bar and went to where his eyes had been betraying his words. It was the hallway to Emmett's office.

I made my way down the short hallway until I was standing in front of Emmett's office door. I was going to knock, but then I heard a commotion in the room and flung the door open. There, to my absolute horror, was Emmett on top of Brooke on the floor. Her legs were wrapped around him. I felt like I was going to be sick. The bile in my throat threatened to erupt.

I was done. I was completely done. Everyone in this city was a vile person who didn't care about anyone, but themselves. I was through dealing with any of them. I would take the blame for any consequences that befell the farm. I would rather spend the rest of my life paying off an impossible debt to Uncle Lon than deal with any of these people ever again.

I threw out some words to Emmett, which I couldn't recall at the moment. Then I proceeded to run out of Le Mier before I could lose my lunch. I didn't care who I ran into as I plowed through the dance floor, stepping on more than one person's feet. I threw the door open and was met with snow hitting my face offering me instant relief.

I continued my hurried pace to an awaiting Russel who hadn't left the front seat of the car. I went around the back of the car to get

TABITHA KRUEGER

into the passenger seat. I was reaching for the door handle when a felt a hand go over my mouth and an arm wrap around both of my arms. I tried screaming, but the hand at my mouth muffled any noise that may have escaped.

I heard Russel's car door open with Russel saying, "What the hell?" before I heard a pop. That sound was so distinct, I knew it was a gunshot. An all-consuming fear I had never felt before overtook my body. I started struggling more. I had a flashback to when I was attacked in the barn when I was 19. I leaned my head as far forward as I could before rearing it as forcefully back as I could. My head hit its target. My captor's nose crunched under the velocity of my head. The spray of blood that accompanied his cries of pain were the last things I remembered before blacking out.

Now that I knew what happened to get me here, I was still unclear as to why. My thoughts then went to Russel. He was shot and I hadn't heard anything from him after that. But if these men wanted him dead, why not kill me too? Why take me? A hostage is harder to handle than a dead person.

I had nothing. I didn't have money for a ransom. I didn't have any connections to anyone except loosely to Morelli and even then, I wasn't part of his gang, I didn't have any information on him.

I was told Cameron had enemies, but that turned out to be Emmett. I didn't think Emmett had enough time to finish his business with Brooke and make it out to the alleyway to take me. Plus, there were at least two men, the one who accosted me and the trigger man who shot Russel.

I heard a door open beyond the door to the room I was in. There was a light turned on that now seeped through all the nooks and crannies in the door. Footsteps clunked down the stairs that must lay right outside the closed door, getting closer with each step.

I was in a basement. This really might be my dungeon.

SPEAK EASY TO ME

My panic was setting in again. I fought against my restraints hoping that by some miracle they would have magically loosened in the five minutes since I had last tested their strength.

The door creaked open revealing a silhouette in the doorway. He sauntered over to the light switch and the room was flooded with a dim light. I had to blink a few times to make sure what I was seeing was real and not from the hit to my head. There, standing on the other side of the room where I was tied to a chair, was Nathaniel.

"Hello, Lottie." He said just as normal as ever like I wasn't being held prisoner in a dank basement.

"Nathaniel?" Maybe I was reading this wrong. He had to be here to rescue me because nothing else made sense. "Untie me." I gestured to my hands and legs, pulling at the ropes.

"Why would I do that when I'm the one who tied you up?" The smile that crept across his face was frightening. He sauntered over to me, grabbed a chair that I was out of my view then sat in the chair facing me. "Lottie, Lottie, Lottie. What have you gotten yourself into?"

"Nothing. I haven't done anything. What the hell is going on, Nathaniel?" Nathaniel had been nothing but nice to me, despite the little hiccup with the whole Emmett/Holden situation. He had profusely apologized to me for that. He was the one person who had treated me halfway decently. This wasn't adding up.

"You really have no clue why you're here, do you?" I shook my head as even simple words escaped me at the moment. "My plan had been going so well until you had to screw it up." I don't know if he thought I would know what he was talking about from that little tidbit, but I was still clueless.

"You just had to play along a little while longer. Emmett was so close to ending Carmeron, he just needed a small

177

TABITHA KRUEGER

nudge and the job would have been done. Emmett would have killed Cameron, taking both Cameron and Emmett out of the equation." He kicked at my chair leg, making contact with my ankle and pushing my chair cockeyed. The squeak of the chair scraping the cement floor made my skin crawl. "But no! You had to go and cut Emmett completely off and for the first time in his miserable existence, he listened did what someone else told him."

Nathaniel leaned forward violently grabbing my chair and pulling me closer to him while straightening the chair. I flinched at his harsh movements making him laugh with evil satisfaction. "Aww. Are you scared of me Lottie?" He moved his face just inches from mine. Our noses were just a hair's breadth away from touching. "Good."

He leaned back further in his chair, crossing his legs in front of him and linking his hands behind his head in a relaxed pose. "The question is what do I do with you now that you're of no use to me?" Nathaniel was certifiably crazy. He kidnapped me because he thought I had sabotaged his cockamamie plan.

"You see, you had been crucial in getting rid of both of the pains in my ass in one fowl swoop. Now, I don't know what you'd be good for besides squeezing a little money out of both of them." This all had to be a joke. There was no way this man was this delusional.

I couldn't hold back my laugh. "Wait a minute. You want to try to extort money from two men who want me out of their lives?" I couldn't stop laughing now. Tears from the laugher, anger and sadness running down my face all at once. "You are an idiot." Nathaniel's face getting less amused the more I laughed which encouraged me to keep going. "I'm an idiot. We are all fucking idiots." My laughter was finally dying down. I let out a big sigh.

"Cameron wouldn't pay a cent to save my life. You're

SPEAK EASY TO ME

actually doing him a favor and removing me from his life. And Emmett? He was about to be balls deep in Brooke when I busted into his office, so I would say he's moved on." I tried wiggling in my chair to sit up better, straighter, as I faced him head on. I had nothing to lose at this point.

"Do you know why your father wanted me to marry Cameron? Why your estranged country bumpkin cousin was chosen to marry a very eligible bachelor that could have his choice of any woman in this city? Did that ever cross your pea-sized brain?" He was staring at me like I was speaking a foreign language.

"Your father figured out we had been working with a bootlegger running from Canada down to Chicago. His gang would stay at our house between runs. I would occasionally drive for them as well. It was very easy to avoid cops by being a dumb woman who could barely drive." I smiled as I thought about the time I almost hit a cop car to demonstrate how inept at driving I was.

I was making a run from Canada down to our farm, where Morelli's men would take over getting the delivery down to Chicago. There were cops two towns over that had started following me too closely for my liking. I sped up and got some good distance between us. I spotted a cop car parked in town. I set eyes on my target and stepped on the gas. I was hurdling forward, full barrels of whiskey covered in the back of the car. I slammed on the breaks at the last minute, narrowly avoiding a collision with the parked police car.

My plan was either going to be genius or the dumbest thing I had ever done. The cop came barreling towards me. His face was so red with anger I swear I saw steam coming out of his ears. "Are you crazy lady?" He barked at me through my window. I opened my door and jumped out.

"I am so sorry. I thought I was pressing the break, but it must

179

TABITHA KRUEGER

have been the gas." I couldn't think of another valid reason my car would be going that fast in town.

"Women do not belong behind the wheel of a car. It's dangerous, as evident with you." I just sheepishly nodded my agreement, head hanging down.

The two cop cars that had been chasing me were approaching. The set up to my plan had worked, now only if the execution followed as smoothly. I made sure my back was to the approaching officers praying they wouldn't recognize me. I could hear the tires slowing on the gravel road as they crept toward us.

Before they could say anything, the cop that was berating me chirped up, "Women drivers." He huffed out a huge breath. Thumbing my way he continued, "She doesn't know the difference between the gas and the break." The husky cop let out a bellow. "I swear, women should not be allowed to drive." The cops that had been in pursuit of me grunted their agreements before driving on without giving me a second glance.

The cop watched as I got back into my car, a gloating expression dressing his weathered face. I just politely smiled and nodded at him. As I drove away, I dramatically gave him a swerve or two just to drive home how bad of a driver I was. After that, I was never chased again on my runs.

"Your father wanted a piece of the action. He knew we were doing something illegal to keep the farm afloat, but he couldn't figure it out. He offered my father money, not only to rescue the farm, but to get me out of the bootlegging aspect of the business, in my father's eyes. What easier way for me to be out than if I was married to a man who was against bootlegging in the first place? Now the farm is used just as a resting point between Canada and Chicago during runs."

"You're Charlie?" Nathaniel came to the realization that Charlie wasn't a man like everyone had so naively assumed.

His eyes and smile were filled with amusement as he put it together.

"That's what I'm told." I said, slightly raising my shoulders as much as I could to shrug. "You see, I am no use to anyone anymore. I'm not running anything for the gang. I'm not engaged to Cameron, I made sure of that by throwing my ring into the roaring fireplace in your father's study. And I made it more than clear that I wanted nothing more to do with Emmett." I was trying to reason with a madman. I knew he had already made his mind up, but I had to try. "Just let me go and I will go back to the farm and not say a thing to anyone."

Nathaniel stood up, looked me up and down and gave me a small smile as he said, "I don't think so. Nice try though, Lottie." He moved his chair away from me by swinging it on its leg, facing it away from me.

He raised his hand to turn the light off. I did not want to be sitting in the cold room in the dark. I pleaded, "Could you leave the light on, please? I just want to be able to see." He contemplated my request.

"I guess I could grant you one last wish. I'll be back down later, Lottie. I have to go get some supplies." He said ominously before shutting the door and turning a lock I hadn't noticed he had turned to enter the room. Then he proceeded to whistle as he walked up the stairs.

I didn't know how much time I had before he would returned. I started frantically looking around the room to assess it. There was an old wooden work bench in the back of the room that I could barely make out since my head didn't turn far enough to get a good look.

I was able to glance down at my feet to inspect the rope. The rope was sturdy enough, but it looked old. There was fraying throughout the cords. I took my fingers and felt the rope around my wrists. It too seemed to be frayed. I worked

TABITHA KRUEGER

at trying to pick at the frayed pieces to no avail. I let out an exasperated sigh.

I heard a squeak coming from my right. I looked over and saw a huge rat sitting in the corner of the room. It spotted me at the same time and started making its way over to me. I closed my eyes and willed it to stop, to just stay over on its side of the room. Its beady little eyes were shining in the dim light of the bulb hanging from the ceiling as it made its way closer.

"Don't come any closer, please." It wasn't my first time trying to reason with a rat, at least this time it was of the animal variety. The relying squeaks its only answer. The rat continued its path to me. It was now at my right foot, sniffing at my dress. I tried kicking at it with my tied foot with no luck. I felt the tug on my dress as it started climbing.

"No! No! No!" I scream whispered as I started frantically moving all my limbs. With all the movement my stifled movements made, my chair tipped over. My whole body landed on my left arm. I let out a loud yelp as the pain started rippling down my arm from my shoulder.

The rat had jumped off my while I fell. It stared at me from a corner across the room. "This is all your fault," I said to the rat who just sat there. I rested my head on the cold concrete as tried to figure out what to do.

I pulled at my ropes on my legs again. Then an idea hit me. My ankles were tied to the legs of the chair. I couldn't pull them off, but maybe now I could slip them off. With a few wiggles I got my feet below the legs of the chair. I then used the heels of my fee to push my roped ankles down as I gripped the back of the chair as best as I could with my tied arms and pulled up. I could feel the rope leaving the chair and with one final push, my feet were free.

The chair had a bar that ran from left to right across the legs designed to make the chair sturdier. I placed my feet on

SPEAK EASY TO ME

it and pushed the chair down slowly, letting the back of the chair slide out from behind my back and tied hands. I placed my feet on the seat of the chair for the last few inches left behind my back.

Still on my side, I bent my knees as far as I could to my chest. I brought my arms down to my butt. I knew it was going to be a struggle so I took a deep breath and yanked my hands as hard as I could down and around my butt and legs. Once my hands passed my feet my whole body sprung out, uncoiling itself. I laid there with my back on the concrete for a moment trying to catch my breath.

I pushed myself up on my elbows as I fully took in my surroundings. Taking inventory of where things were placed, if there were any other viable exits beside the door I had been facing. It looked to be the door was the only way in or out of this space.

I carefully got up to a sitting position. I wasn't sure how long I had been down here, tied to that chair, so I wanted to take standing up slowly, to make sure I had my bearings. I rose to my feet to gauge how weak my legs were. As soon as I stood up, I had to pee. I hadn't seemed to soil myself while I was down here, so I couldn't have been down here too long.

I went to the corner and lifted my dress to relieve myself. Once I was done with my business, I moved to the work bench. There wasn't much there. A few nails laid loose on the table. Nothing that would be helpful.

I noticed a small shelf under the main work bench. I kneeled down to see, but the light didn't reach all the cervices. I closed my eyes and stuck my hand in the darkness of the space. I felt a blade of some sort. I carefully grabbed it and pulled it out. It was knife. It wasn't particularly big or sharp, but it would get the job done. I finished ransacking the room with no other finds.

I heard the upstairs door opening. I rushed to right the

chair. I tried to be careful not to make any noise. I placed the knife on the seat of the chair and sat down. The footsteps were getting closer, closing in. I looked down and noticed the rope I had left lying on the floor. I scooped it up and tucked it under the skirt of my dress. The door to my room was opening as I placed my hands behind my back as if they were still tied.

When the door opened it revealed a man I had never seen before. He was larger, wearing a suite he hadn't gotten tailored. There was a stench to him as he moved closer to me. "Nathaniel told me you weren't pretty. But you'll get the job done." The tone in his voice told me he came down here for only one thing. He started to undo his pants. He was larger than me, but I would use that to my advantage.

In one motion I got up from my chair, grabbing the knife I had concealed. The man was too stunned to do anything. With his hands still on his pants I ran full speed the short distance at him knocking him backward. He fell to the ground with his head making a cracking sound as it hit the concrete.

I leapt on top of him and plunged the knife at his chest. I had hit my mark with blood spurting out once I removed the knife. I jumped up from the bleeding man and ran to the door. He was trying to roll over, but all movement stopped right before I shut the door and locked it. I wasn't taking my chances of him coming after me even though, judging by the red pool of blood around him, he had just bled out.

My first instinct had been to rush up the stairs, but I didn't know who else was in the building with me. The man I left on the floor had not been the man who had grabbed me in the alleyway, so there was potentially one other man, besides Nathaniel, that could be in this place. I crept quietly up the stairs, trying to avoid giving myself away to anyone waiting at the top. I wiped the blood off the knife on my dress. I secured the knife to me by way of the belt on my dress.

I had made my way to the top of the landing of the stairs. I listened closely with my ear pressed to the wood of the door. I couldn't hear any noise on the other side of the door. I took a breath to steady myself as I turned the knob so slowly on the door you wouldn't be able to tell it was moving on the other side.

Through the small crack I created, I looked around. I didn't see any other men in my direct line of sight, so I pushed the door open a little more. I repeated this pattern until I had the door open enough, I could fit through the crack. I softly closed the door behind my back as I kept my body facing forward, watching for any signs of danger.

I took in the room I was standing in. I was in an old, abandoned farmhouse from the looks of it. The sun was brightly shining through the windows which revealed a thin layer of dust on the remaining furniture and cobwebs hanging everywhere. My eyes zeroed in on the door 30 feet in front of me. The key to my freedom was within my grasp.

I counted to 30 in my head, not moving a muscle until the silence continued. I lifted my foot ever so slightly before taking a step. The floorboards creaked under the weight of my foot. I cringed as the sound echoed off the barren walls. There were no other sounds I could hear. Complete silence once again filled the room. I took another hesitant step.

I was about to start taking normal steps when the front door burst open. I had just enough time to duck into the room I was standing next to. I partially shut the door, praying to God above that the hinges were oiled enough. I looked around the room I was now standing in. There was a window directly in front of me. I could make it in five steps. I stood behind the door listening to whoever just walked through the front door.

TABITHA KRUEGER

Nathaniel's voice carried through the house, "Edgar went down there 15 minutes ago. I would think he would be done by now." He laughed as if what he said was the funniest thing he'd ever heard.

"That bitch is getting what she deserves right now. I hope he takes longer. Really makes her suffer. My nose hurts worse now than it did when she smacked it." It was the other guy that had been in the alleyway.

"Stop being such a baby about it." Nathaniel chided him. Their muffled voices flittered away, moving to a different part of the house. I took this opportunity to move to the window. I flipped the lock on top of the bottom window-pane. With painstakingly slow movements, I pushed the window open.

I sat at the open window for a minute. I listened to make sure the two men's voices were still faint. I had slipped out my window at my family farm enough to make a clean escape. The nearly foot deep snow helped cushion my land-ing. I was now on the outside. The farmhouse was surrounded by cornfields on three sides, with a tree line to my left.

As I was contemplating my next move, I heard Nathaniel's voice float out of the open window. "Go check on Edgar down there, see if he needs a hand." Both men cruelly laughed. I knew I needed to decide quickly. I chose to start running to my left. The snow may have helped soften my landing from the window, but it was extremely difficult to run through.

I made it to the tree line when I heard the farmhouse door crash open. "There is nowhere for you to hide, Lottie!" I kept running through the endless bare trees. I dared to look back at the farmhouse curious if the men had followed me.

I could see the two men in the driveway aggressively pointing in different directions. After some yelling back and

SPEAK EASY TO ME

forth between the two, Nathaniel got into a car that was in the driveway. The other man followed slamming his door shut. The engine roared to life before they went down the driveway and out of view.

The men thought I went down the driveway. I noticed the trail of footprints that marked my traveled path. They hadn't taken the time to look around the house to find my tracks. I had some time.

There was no way I could cover the deep treads in the snow. I had to improvise. If I left tracks all over, they wouldn't know which ones to follow first. I began frantically running around the area making sure to make my tracks as chaotic as possible. I ran in circles and zig zags. Some of the footprints intersected.

When my I was satisfied with my work, I ran a further into the woods and repeated what I had done. There is an eerie way the winter carries sound through leafless trees. I couldn't see the farmhouse any longer, but I could hear the car tires as they crunched over the snow as it pulled back into the driveway. The two men opening and closing their doors was my signal to start running again.

"We are going to find you Lottie and we are going to enjoy killing you!" Nathaniel's hollow voice reverberated throughout the quiet forest. I started running faster.

My legs were getting tired. The air couldn't get in my lungs fast enough. I had to stop for a moment to catch my breath. I took the time to look around. The snap of a branch in the distance had my legs moving beneath me. I was running so fast I didn't notice the change of height in the snow. My feet caught on the mini mountain of fluffy white coldness. I fell forward, throwing my hands in front of me, just in time to catch myself.

The trees had given way to an opening. There was a dilapidated red barn sitting alone in the vastness of the open-

187

ing. I picked myself up with the last bit of strength I could muster. With my legs fighting against me, I ran to the sanctuary of the barn.

I hurled myself through the barn doors. The musty smell of moldy hay and rotting wood hit my nostrils with such verbosity I almost threw up. I shut the doors behind me once I stopped gagging. The flip lock on the door was barely hanging on by one lone nail. I locked the door anyway.

I moved deeper inside the barn, my steps muffled by the hay lined floor. I moved past two horse stalls in various states of repair. I spotted a ladder that lead up to a loft. Climbing the ladder seemed to be my best option.

Each rung I climbed seemed like an impossible task. My legs were wobbly beneath me, my feet frozen and sore from the cold snow that had made its way into my shoes. The old wood groaned beneath my feet as I climbed higher. I was two rungs from the top when I heard male voices bouncing off the silence of the clearing. That was the last bit of motivation I needed to reach the top.

I collapsed with an "oomph" as I threw myself on the floor of the loft. I was sprawled on the hay lined floor. My chest rose with every deep, shallow breath I took. As I was on the floor trying to catch my breath the whole barn seemed to reverberate. The sound of wood splintering as something made contact with it filled my ears. They were trying to kick the barn door in. It wouldn't be long before they would be granted entry by the flimsy lock.

I got to my knees, my body full of exhaustion. The ladder was the only way to get up to the loft, to me. I used my hands to feel around to figure out if the ladder was attached to the opening in any way. It appeared to be free standing. With what little strength I had left I began pulling the ladder through the small opening.

I had stood up while my legs threatened to give out from

under me. I bent down and grabbed the top rung of the ladder. The sound of bending and cracking wood sounded throughout the whole barn. Nathaniel and the other man were now in the barn with me. I began working as fast as my body could go could get the ladder up.

The men spotted me immediately. Both men charged in my direction, running to grab at the ladder I was desperately trying to drag up to me. I had the ladder about halfway up to the loft when the man with Nathaniel grabbed the bottom rung. The tug I felt almost ripped my shoulders out of their sockets. I stumbled forward on my wobbly legs, falling onto the ladder.

The pain that ripped through my body as my full weight fell onto the aging wood was excruciating. The momentum of my weight on the ladder jerked it up, causing the bottom rung to crumble in the man's hand. Nathaniel grabbed the next rung, using all his strength to tug at it. No matter how hard he pulled, the ladder did not budge from underneath me. He gave one last tug and the moldy, old wood gave out, breaking in half.

"You're trapped Lottie. No way down now." Nathaniel's cruel voice chilled me to the bone. I rolled off the ladder, pulling the half I had been laying on the rest of the way through the opening. I dropped it to my right with a clunk.

I heard the men's voices but couldn't make out what they were saying in their hushed tones. The muffled talking was accented by the man saying, "Got it!" Followed by one set of footsteps shuffling along the hay on the barn floor. There was no opening or closing of the barn door due to it laying in shambles, chunks of wood spewed about the floor, the remaining wood in the doorframe just tatters.

"I am not going anywhere Lottie." Nathaniel matter of factly stated. I risked taking a look at him. He was striding over to a wall piled high with hay. He grabbed a handful of the dark yellow hay, looking it over. He then proceeded to gather a bunch in his arms and brought it over to where the ladder had been, below the opening to the loft.

"I'm getting up to you one way or another dear cousin. Prescott went to town to get another ladder." That was going to take a long time. The roads might not even have had the snow removed yet. My feet were wet and cold from the melting snow on my shoes and dress. The barn was poorly constructed, the walls having gaps letting the winder wind seep through the cracks. I wasn't sure how long I'd last before getting frostbite or hypothermia or both. I chill sent a shiver through my whole body.

"While Prescott is gone, I wonder how long it would take me to move all the straw." I was now looking down at Nathaniel through the loft opening. He was taking another bunch of hay in his arms. "From here to over there." He was going to pile the hay up to the opening.

"Or you could stop being such a bitch and just make this easier on all of us." He was now going between the hay pile and the new pile he was constructing to reach me. Armful after armful, I watched him make the pile taller.

I had to weigh my options, but I didn't have many choices. My only way down was through that opening. I couldn't get down without Nathaniel seeing me. There were no windows or other means of escape from up here. I could have either sat there like a mouse waiting for the strike, or I could prepare to be ready to fight.

It would take Nathaniel hours to move enough hay to make it up to the opening by me. It would probably take even longer for Prescott to return. I started moving the hay around the loft. I was cold and tired; two things that would hinder any chance I had at fighting for my own survival. I stood up, my legs finally feeling stable enough to do so. I began to gather the hay in the loft to begin to make a nest. I

SPEAK EASY TO ME

would take advantage of the fact Nathaniel could not reach me for a while. My footfalls on the creaky, weathered wood drew Nathaniel's attention to me. I worked quickly, but cautiously taking care to mind where I was stepping knowing the floor could give way with any misstep.

"You sound busy up there Lottie. Care to share your plans with me?" His words were coming out breathlessly. Moving hay was not an easy task, especially for someone who wasn't used to manual labor. He was tiring himself out.

"Not particularly." I quipped back as I burrowed into my own pile of hay. I had made plenty of beds out of hay on the farm to know the perfect construction needed for my comfort. I could sleep for an hour or so and be refreshed when I had to fight for my life with Nathaniel and Prescott. I took the knife, still streaked with some blood, from my dress and placed it next to me on the hay bed I'd made.

I'm not sure how long I had been sleeping. I woke up with an eerie feeling. It took me a moment to recall what I was doing in this barn loft. There was no sound except for the blood rushing in my ears. It was too quiet. I didn't make a move for fear of causing unwanted attention. A rustling came from right below the opening, next to my head.

Everything happened quickly while at the same time registered in slow motion. A hand rose from the hole in the loft floor. My muscles froze up not allowing me to move. I watched as the hand grabbed a handful of my hair yanking it so violently my head jerked to the side. I cried out in pain. With arms flailing about, I started hitting at the gripped fist in my hair. He wasn't relenting as his grip increased, causing a few hairs to pull out from the root.

He pulled me far enough to the opening that I could see Nathaniel's face below with his arms outreached. He smiled once he saw my face peering through the opening. "Too bad

191

TABITHA KRUEGER

Prescott is going to miss this part." An evil smirk overtook his face.

While he gripped my hair with one hand his other one used to steady himself using the side of the opening. I balled my fists up, blindly swinging, smashing the hand he used to keep himself steady. Nathaniel lost his grip on the opening and fell, ripping the handful of hair he had a grip on, out of my head.

The pain was so immense I blacked out for a moment with starts dancing in front of my eyes once my vision returned. I cautiously approached the opening to take inventory of Nathaniel's location.

He was sprawled on his back on the floor, legs and arms laid out in various directions. There was no movement from his chest, no audible breaths. Just then Nathaniel took in a huge gasp of air as he came back to life. Coughing and choking as he tried to fill his lungs with the air that had been knocked out of him.

I didn't want him to see me looking at him, so I crawled slowly away from the hole. I wasn't paying attention of where I was going. Before I knew it, I was freefalling to the floor below me. I barely had enough time to register what was happening as the rotten floor boards squelched underneath me before cracking, sending me plummeting to the ground. I landed on my side on the barn floor.

Instantaneous pain rang out from my side before reverberating throughout the rest of my body. I turned to lay on my back as the unbearable pain continued to hit me in waves. My side was damp and warm. I moved my hand to my side feeling a thick, slick wetness. I raised my hand and to my horror, it was covered in my blood. I put my hand back down by my side and felt the knife handle sticking out. With the all the blood on my hand I couldn't get a grip on the knife, the handle slipping out of my grip each time I tried to

SPEAK EASY TO ME

pull it out. Rule number one when things are impaled into you're body, you don't remove them. In this case though, I needed the knife if I had any hope in fighting against Nathaniel.

I could still hear Nathaniel coughing on the floor adjacent to me. I had fallen into the horse stall, so I could only hear him, not see him. The unmistakable sound shoes scraping along the floor had me start to panic. He was getting up on his feet to head in by me and finish the job.

I didn't know what to do. I started crawling out of the horse stall in survival mode. More open space meant more options to escape even if that meant crawling right to Nathaniel. There was a trail of bright red blood as I moved across the floor. Nathaniel was now standing as his full height even if he was a little unsteady. He lumbered towards me on clumsy feet.

I grabbed the side of my dress, putting it over my hand like a makeshift glove. I gripped the handle of the knife and pulled as hard as I could, dislodging the knife from my side. Nathaniel hadn't notice as he straddled me, a look of killing in his eyes. He wrapped his hands around my throat and started squeezing. I dropped the knife as my hands flew up to my throat, clawing at Nathaniel's hands.

Nothing can prepare you for the panic that sets in when someone is slowly squeezing the life out of you. My lungs started burning as they were gasping for air that wouldn't come. I could feel my arms start to feel heavier, my movements less and less. I could feel my eyelids start to voluntarily close no matter how much I fought them.

The last person I was going to see in this lifetime was Nathaniel. The man I hadn't known a few months ago, who had befriended me only to kill me in the end, was a special kind of cruelty. I had accepted my fate. I would be left dead in this barn where no one would ever find me.

"Lottie!" I could barely make out the voice in the background. Whoever it was distracted Nathaniel. He released his grip on my throat enough so I could get a gasp of air in my lungs. That breath was my last chance to fight. I grabbed the knife I had let fall out of my hand, gripping the handle that was still slippery, coated with my blood.

In one motion Nathaniel turned back to look at me as plunged the knife into his throat. His eyes got big as he registered what I had done. His hands lingered on my throat as I pulled the knife out and drove it in again. Blood gushed all over me.

"Lottie!" The distant voice shouted again in panic. Rushed footsteps approached me and the bleeding man on top of me. Nathaniel reached up to the sanguinary wounds on his neck, his efforts futile to stop the blood.

Two arms threw Nathaniel to the side. It was Emmett. He was the voice I couldn't quite hear. "Shit. Lottie." Emmett gathered my blood-soaked body in his arms. Nathaniel had crushed my windpipe while he was strangling me, making my words hard to say.

"You came for me?" I rasped as I took in Emmett's beautiful face full of relief and worry. He brushed my now crimson hair out of my face.

"Of course. I'll always find you, Carrots." He finished his sentence as Cameron and Little Nicky came into the barn. "Shit!" and "Holy fuck!" was uttered, but I don't know who said what.

I was suddenly surrounded by all three men looking me over. With my adrenaline leaving my body the pain shot through me. I had a tiny bit of strength left in me, so I informed them, "My side. The knife." Every word was a struggle. Along with my windpipe being injured, I had at least one or two broken ribs from the fall. Every breath was excruciating.

SPEAK EASY TO ME

I could feel Emmett's large hands gently ripping my dress at the side. He took off his coat and held it to my gaping wound trying to stop the blood. "Can you stand up?" He asked.

I nodded my head yes, not knowing whether or not I could stand, but not knowing how else I would get out of here if I didn't walk. All three men helped me stand. As soon as I was on my feet the world went black.

CHAPTER 17

LOTTIE

The lights were so bright it made it difficult to open my eyes. As I squinted, allowing my eyes to get adjusted to the light, I saw a figure sitting to my left. My eyes finally focused enough to let me take in Emmett, sitting in chair, head tipped back as soft snoring matched his breathes. The sight made a smile instantly cross my face.

I took a minute to look around the stark white room. No decorations hung on any of the walls. The people milling about the hallway were all dressed in white coats and dresses, carrying around clipboards. I was in a hospital.

I took in a breath causing me to hiss in pain arousing Emmett from his peaceful sleep. My throat was on fire and my ribs were sore. I put my hands on the bed and tried to push myself up to a sitting position which in turn had my side feeling like I was getting stabbed again. Emmett joined me on the bed, perching himself on the side edge.

"Don't move, Lottie. You're safe." Without leaving my side he shouted, "Doctor! We need a doctor in here!" A woman in a white hate and white dress poked her head in. She gasped, saying "Right away!"

SPEAK EASY TO ME

Emmett's large, calloused hands were cupping my face. He was looking at me so intensely, it was as if he never thought he'd see me again. The look of relief on his face comforting.

"What? How'd I get here?" The last thing I remembered was standing up in the barn. Everything had gone black. I had no memory of anything from that point in time, to now.

"We carried you after you passed out. Oh God Lottie. I thought you died!" His rough thumb was stroking the side of my cheek as he recounted the saga of getting me to the hospital. "You lost so much blood."

A tear escaped his eye, running slowly down his cheek. He made no effort to stop its running. I lifted my hand to wipe it away the dampness on his cheek. He put his free hand over my hand, turning his head ever so slightly to place a gentle kiss on my palm. Emmett then placed my hand on his cheek holding it there with his hand.

He closed his eyes as he drank in our respective hands on each other's cheeks. "I never thought I'd feel you again. I still can't believe you're here." He took his hand off my cheek, taking both of my hands in his as he brought them up to his lips, gently placing kisses on my knuckles. He was kissing the hands of a killer.

I had killed two men in the span of a day. The elation of being alive was replaced by feelings of dread and sorrow. "I killed two men, Emmett." A hoarse whisper escaped my mouth. I felt my throat starting to close up a bit, causing it to burn like the tears in my eyes were doing.

"Don't you dare cry for those men Lottie." Emmett cupped my cheeks with his hands. The warmth of his touch made my tears flow more. It was as if the flood gates opened and every emotion I had felt was being released through the salty tears streaming down my face.

Emmett held my face so gently as he looked directly into

TABITHA KRUEGER

my eyes. He wanted to make sure I took in what he was saying. "They were both going to do atrocious, unimaginable things to you. They do not deserve one more ounce of your compassion. You did absolutely nothing wrong. Everything you did was right." He kissed my forehead. "I am so proud of you. I am amazed by everything that you are." Another forehead kiss. "You got out of a situation I do not think I would have been able to get out of. Those men all made their own decisions and had to deal with the harsh consequences."

There was a group of people who rushed into the room in a flurry at that moment. Emmett's hands left my face as he was pushed off the bed by the medical professionals now tending to me. He pushed a doctor back and the older man scolded him, "You stay out of our way, or you will be escorted out of this room." There was a stare down between the weathered doctor and the man who had been comforting me. "You were needed earlier, that is no longer the case." Emmett took heed and sat back down in the chair he had been sleeping in.

After a few minutes of poking and prodding most of the doctors and nurses left the room. Now it was just the older doctor, two nurses, Emmett, and myself in the room.

"You are one lucky young woman, Mrs. Emmett." I whipped my head to the doctor about to protest the use of the incorrect name. Seeing the confusion on my face, Emmett shook his head no, moving his arms in a way to indicate not to bring it up.

"If it wasn't for your husband rushing you here in time, you wouldn't be here with us right now. It truly is a miracle you survived at all." I had all my focus now on Emmett, who was sheepishly standing in the corner of the room, staring back at me. He told them he was my husband. I wondered how much of the story he had fabricated on how my injuries had come to be.

The doctor looked down at his clipboard as one of the nurses fussed about taking my blood pressure. The doctor commenced his findings. "The blood transfusion seems to be successful so far, but it can take months to be completely sure. We would like for you to stay two more days, just for observation."

He flipped a page on the clipboard before continuing, "You also have three broken ribs, a concussion, and a crushed windpipe." He took a beat before the final injury, "And a stab wound to your side. You need to take these next few days to rest." The doctor looked over to Emmett before he made his next statement. I didn't like the accusatory look thrown at Emmett. "Please be careful in the future Mrs. Emmett, next time you might not be so lucky." He made a quick exit from the room, followed by the nurses.

Emmett was back at my side holding my hands in his. "I needed a blood transfusion?" My voice still raspy. I had been so stunned I hadn't been able to ask the doctor any questions.

Emmett nodded, "As it turns out you and I are a perfect match in more than one way." A cocky smile engulfed his serious face.

"You?" His blood now ran through my veins. We were one in the most basic sense of being.

"I would have given my heart if it meant that you lived. Ripped my chest open myself if that's what it took." The sincereness of his declaration took me off guard. "Rest." He kissed the hair on the top of my head. "I'll be here when you wake up." Emmett took his seat in the chair again. Sleep sounded like the best idea. I was positively exhausted.

According to the clock on the wall it was 7 am when I woke back up. The sky was starting to come to life with the red and golden sunrise brimming up from the horizon. Emmett was still fast asleep in his chair, head bowed down, soft rumblings of snores intermittently coming from him.

TABITHA KRUEGER

I gingerly slid out of my hospital bed and padded into the bathroom. I relieved myself before washing my hands. I had just turned the water on in the sink when the bathroom door flew open. Emmett was staring at me with his dark eyes wild with worry.

"Lottie. You scared me. I woke up and you weren't in bed." I chuckled a little bit making me wince from the sharp pain the radiated from my ribs. This big, commanding man in front of me who looks like nothing in the world could scare him, was scared because I wasn't next to him.

"I had to pee." My voice seemed to be coming back a bit more, losing some of the raspyness. "I didn't know I needed to check in for that." I gave him a playful little smile as I passed him, making my way back to my bed.

"I just want to know you're alright. After everything that's happened, that you've been through, I want to make sure you're safe." The heat from his hands permeated my nightgown as he placed his hands on my shoulders.

"I am safe, because of you." I pulled my knight in shining armor into an embrace. I didn't know how else to thank him for saving my life. If he hadn't shown up when he did I would have died in that barn with Nathaniel.

Emmett's arms easily wrapped around my body. He took great care to not squeeze too hard. I took a deep breath, risking the pain, just to have his scent in my nose again. He smelled of laundry soap and cedar. We both reluctantly broke the embrace.

"You need to get back in bed." In one motion he folded my bedding down allowing me to climb in. He helped me arrange my pillows before pulling the blankets over me. "I am going to go get you food and something to drink. I'll be right back." He bent down and placed a chaste kiss on my lips.

As I watched him walk out the door a flood of memories

came back. I don't know if it was the blood loss, concussion, or both, but it seemed that my memories of certain events had been hidden away. Now those memories been unlocked with his kiss. Images of Emmett and Brooke tangled up together on the floor of his office made my stomach churn. The scene in Uncle Lon's office of Maggie laid out on the desk as Cameron thrust into her came into focus.

I jumped off the bed to run into the bathroom, my stomach releasing what little contents had been in there into the toilet. Emmett found me on my knees as I clutched the side of the cool porcelain.

"Lottie! Are you okay? Do I need to get the doctor back in here?" Concern laced his words and his face. I didn't even know if I could look at him so I kept looking into the bowl of the toilet.

"I need some time. Alone." The bile from my stomach had my throat in pain once again. "I need time to process everything." I didn't want to start an argument. I had a feeling that if I brought up the whole Brooke situation he would stubbornly refuse to leave until I forgave him. It would be easier if he was out of the hospital before I revealed my feelings.

I couldn't see him, but I could hear the hurt in his voice, "You can't do that with me here?" He placed a comforting hand on my back. The hand that had been on Brooke. I dry heaved again. There was nothing left in my stomach to expel.

I looked up at him. His eyes searching mine for an answer to my sudden change in mood and attitude. "Please, Emmett." When I looked at him I couldn't see anything but his unbuttoned pants as he stood up from between Brooke's legs.

His nod was so subtle I had almost missed it. "If that's what you need right now, that's what I'll give you." He stood up and reluctantly moved to the doorway of the bathroom, looking back at me one last time. I kept my head down so I wouldn't be tempted to relent and let him stay. I needed to decide on my own what I wanted and that would almost be impossible with him doting over me.

I crumpled to the floor as soon as I heard the click of the door closing. I wished I had hit my head harder to permanently block out the heart breaking images that danced through my head mockingly. The more I tried to think of other things the more the images became clearer. Dying wasn't the worst thing that could have happened to me. Being stuck in this endless purgatory in my mind was.

I had to force myself to eat and drink the next two days. The doctors wanted me to rest and to all their delight, that is exactly what I did. I slept for two days straight. I was awake long enough to eat, drink and use the restroom, otherwise I was sleeping. I don't know if the doctors would have been so happy had they known I was sleeping to escape my reality.

Emmett hadn't come back to my room for those two days. He respected my wishes, but he also refused to leave the hospital. The nurse informed me he had camped out in the lobby of the hospital threatening anyone who dared to try to make him leave.

"He is still down there Mrs. Emmett." The young blonde nurse, Joan, informed me. "He has new clothes on though. Not sure when he changed or who brought them to him." I politely smiled at her.

"Thank you, Joan." I wanted to lighten the mood. "You can tell him to stop sulking and let him come up." She returned my now impish smile. Seeing a man of Emmett's stature sulking around like a toddler had put everyone on edge. It did not matter that even though he had been virtually invisible, hardly moving from the chair and table he had claimed in the lobby, he still had a menacing presence about him.

The previous day I had sneaked out of my room to risk a glance at the magnificent mountain of a man occupying the

SPEAK EASY TO ME

lobby. Emmett had been sitting in a lone chair at a small table tucked away in a corner. There were no books or signs of food or drink in his vicinity. The look on his face was very serious. His eyes wandered in my direction causing me to duck behind the door I was peaking around.

I was as ready as I could be for him as he hesitantly entered my room. He lightly rapped on the door. "Hello, Carrots. May I enter?" I inclined my head in answer.

I was sitting up in bed with the blankets covering my legs. Emmett pulled the chair he had previously sat in as close to me as he could. "How are you feeling?" His eyes lingered on my throat, the once dark purple imprint of Nathaniel's hands had begun to fade into a yellow outline.

I put my hand under his chin to bring his gaze to mine. "I am feeling better. Just sore now." My physical injuries were on their way to mending, but the ones I held in my head were still very raw and festering. My eyes must have given me away.

"You're lying." Emmett could read me like a book. It was his job to know when someone was telling the truth.

"I cannot stop thinking about what I walked in to with you and Brooke in your office." He went to make an argument.

"I," he began. I threw my hand up to cut him off before he could continue.

"I can't handle this right now. All I have been picturing is you and her together and it is killing me inside. I cannot unsee her legs wrapped around you. And I really cannot hear your excuses right now. Nothing you say to me right now can take away these feelings."

Tears started rolling down my face. "I know you saved me. I owe my life to you, but I can't get past this. Every time I look at you, I am reminded of how you have made me feel."

Emmett grabbed my hands in his and started frantically

203

TABITHA KRUEGER

kissing the back of my hands. "Tell me what I have to do to fix this. I will do anything you ask of me." The quiet pleading in his eyes made my next words near impossible to say.

"This." I gestured between the two of us, "We can't be fixed. The damage is too far gone." Emmett's thumbs were wiping away my tears as his own were falling from his sorrowful eyes.

"I am so sorry for all of this Lottie." I nodded my head in understanding, not able to form any words. "Would it be alright if I drove you to your uncle's house?" There was desperation in his voice that I never wanted to hear again. "Please allow me that much."

"Okay." I said, much to Emmett's relief. I would let him win this last battle of the war he was losing.

The doctor came in shortly after with my discharge instructions. I still had no idea what the story was that Emmett had given the hospital staff when I arrived. I got the courage up to ask once we were in the car headed to Uncle Lon's house.

"I was wondering, what did you tell everyone about what happened to me?" He was somber as he kept his eyes straight ahead.

"I told them that you had been mugged. That you had left to run an errand and never returned home so I went looking for you. I found you like that in the alleyway downtown." The car was silent as I absorbed the information. "They wouldn't let anyone in the room that wasn't family. I lied and said we were married so I could be with you." His fingers tightened around the steering wheel with the last sentence.

"And my Uncle Lon?" I could only imagine what story they had told him. He never came to the hospital at all, not that I was surprised.

"Cameron took care of him. I am not sure what he told him, but he never once stopped by or called the hospital."

204

SPEAK EASY TO ME

The distain dripped from Emmett's words regarding my uncle. I doubted Uncle Lon had even informed my family of my being in the hospital.

"What about Nathaniel? Does Uncle Lon know about him?" I am not sure what set Emmett off, but my line of questioning had him yelling.

"I don't know Lottie. I have no clue what everyone else was doing or what they know. I have spent the last three days inside that fucking musty hospital, not leaving once. I just sat there, waiting for you." His face was getting red with anger. "You made it clear that you want nothing more to do with me. All I wanted was to spend my last few minutes with you, take you in as much as I can, and all you can talk about is subject matter that I don't want to hear."

I turned my face to the passenger side window so Emmett couldn't see the tears freely flowing down my face. The car came to a sudden halt, throwing me forward slightly. Emmett threw the car into park as he turned to me. I refused to look at him.

"Lottie I'm sorry. I am so frustrated with all that is going on and you are the last person I should be taking it out on. I have fucked up at every turn when it comes to you. That's my fault, that's on me. I wish I could blame you for not wanting to be around me, but honestly, I don't want to be around me either at the moment."

I turned to look at him. He was pouring his heart out to me, the least I could do was give him my attention. He did save my life after all. His face was also wet from tears. "You have made me a better person, Lottie. You have given me a new lease on life I had no clue existed before. All I want is for you to be happy, even if that happiness isn't with me." Emmett's hand softly caressed the back of my head, his thumb softly rubbing the space in front of my ear.

"I love you, Lottie. I have since the moment I met you. It

took me almost losing you to come to that realization." Emmett leaned in and gently placed a kiss on my lips. "I don't say anything." His words barely above a whisper. I took his hand and sat back in my seat. We continued the drive to my uncle's house holding hands in the silence.

Emmett drove the car up the driveway. "Thank you, for saving me." I said as I opened my door. Emmett kept his eyes fixed forward.

"You saved yourself, Carrots." His forward-facing gaze unwavering.

"I love you too, Emmett. I always will." My car door shutting was followed by the tires as they screeched out of the driveway.

The last week had drained every bit of energy I possessed out of me. I trudged into the house not knowing what to expect. Every inch of this house had soured in my mind. Every last inch covered in memories I wished to forget. I no sooner walked through the door before Uncle Lon was shouting my name from the study.

The last time I was in the study I had caught Cameron and Maggie on the desk and then threw my ring into the roaring fire of the fireplace. As I entered the room, I noticed Cameron was sitting in one of the green sitting chairs. Uncle Lon was sitting behind his desk. I wondered if he knew what activities had taken place there. It made me smile thinking he had no idea someone's bare ass had been all over his papers.

"Listen here," Uncle Lon started his long-winded speech. I was not in the mood to hear anything that was going to leave his big dumb mouth.

"No, you listen here" I pointed my finger at his as I continued. "I have been to hell and back and I refuse to take any more shit from you." Uncle Lon was up and out of his seat as my words kept spilling with venom from my tongue. "You think you own everyone and everything and you don't even know what's going on under your own roof, under your own nose."

I was now standing toe to toe with my red-faced uncle, his fists balled up at his side. "You will watch your tone with me, girl, or" All he had was empty threats. I had already been through the worst-case scenario.

"Or what? You'll kill me? Good. Go for it you pompous prick. See how well that works out for you. Ask Nathaniel how well that worked out for him." I could see Cameron's eyes get big as saucers as he leaped from his chair.

"If you know where Nathaniel is and you don't tell me," Uncle Lon was so close his spit was hitting my face as he bellowed.

"He's in hell, where he belongs." Uncle Lon took a swing at me. He was so large and cumbersome I was able to see it coming from a mile away. I ducked down causing his swing to propel himself forward, almost falling on his face. My quick movements may have saved me from his punch, but my sore body rang out in pain.

Cameron ran to my side reading the pain on my face. "Are you alright?" I just nodded as I took in a deep breath trying to let the pain pass. Cameron turned his attention to my uncle. "If you ever raise a hand to her again I will make sure your body is never found." I thought it was ironic that the man who had left bruises on me a month ago was now threatening to kill another man for potentially hitting me.

Uncle Lon was stumbling for words to hurl back at Cameron when I spoke again. "I am going back to my family's farm in Wisconsin in a car provided by you. Once I leave this house you will never contact me or my family ever again. If you attempt in any way to break the rules I have just set before you, I promise you, you will not like the results."

I highly doubt anyone had ever talked back to my Uncle Lon like Cameron and I had just done. We left him red faced

TABITHA KRUEGER

and still sputtering incomprehensible words. Cameron followed me out of the study and up the stairs to my bedroom.

I was going to pack enough to get me home. I started gathering my things as Cameron stood in the doorway watching. "You're really leaving?" He asked me as he leaned in the doorway.

"Absolutely. This town is toxic. I just want my old life back." I could tell he wanted to say something but didn't know how to say it. "Don't hold back now, say whatever it is that's on your mind."

He moved into the room and in three steps was sitting on my bed. "What about Holden?" He was quick to correct himself. "Er Emmett?"

I continued to gather my things as I replied, "What do you mean?" Trying to act as nonchalant about Emmett as I could while my heart was racing.

"I'm not stupid Charlotte. I know you have feelings for him." He waited a moment for me to answer and when I didn't, he continued, "And I know he loves you." His words had me stopped in my tracks. My hand on the hanger was unmoving. "That man doesn't care about anyone but himself and that is something my father had a hand in. That was, until you."

I took my hand off the hanger as I listened to Cameron go on. "He was ready to burn the city down to find you, Charlotte. For a man like Emmett, that doesn't happen. He never allows anyone close to him for *business* reasons." I knew what he meant when he emphasized 'business'. Emmett was an enforcer and didn't want anyone else tangled up in his lifestyle. Loving someone meant that they would be in danger.

"If you are leaving because you want to, fine. But don't run away from him Charlotte." Cameron had gotten up from the bed and was standing at my back. His warm breath was

SPEAK EASY TO ME

brushing the back of my neck. "I was a fool for ever treating you with anything other than the utmost respect. You deserve better than me and that's Emmett, as much as I never wanted to admit that, it's the truth."

"I can't." A sob escaped my throat. "I can't." The damn was broken once again and the tears flowed freely. Cameron gathered me in his arms as I cried.

"Shhh. It's okay, Charlotte." Cameron's soothing voice echoed in my ears. He kept me wrapped in his arms as he led me to my bed, moving all the clothes and toiletries I had placed on the bed, on the ground. He curled up behind me and just held me as I cried myself to sleep.

I woke up hours later feeling more rested than I had in a long time. The weight of Cameron's arms still wrapped around me. I snuggled deeper into his warmth. His snoring stopped for a moment as he pulled me in closer.

The smell of cedar flooded my nostrils. Cedar? My eyes shot open as I bolted upright. The twisting along with the pop-up sitting had my side aching. The man I was staring at wasn't Cameron. The warm comforting arms I had woke up in belonged to Emmett.

"Carrots!" His arms snaked around my waist as he sat up alongside me.

"What the fuck are you doing in my bed?" I demanded. I placed my hand on my side trying to mitigate the pain shooting through it. Emmett placed his hand gently over mine on my side.

"If you want me to leave, I will." The room was dark except for the light coming in from outside. I didn't want him to leave. I didn't want to say it out loud though. When I no longer protested his presence, his words came out soft and slow.

"I came back, after I dropped you off. I couldn't leave the way we parted be. If you love me and I love you, what's stop-

209

TABITHA KRUEGER

ping us from being together? Our wires have been crossed for so long, that now we are on the same page, why shouldn't we give us a chance? A real chance." The moonlight shone through my bedroom window illuminating Emmett's sharp features. Even in the shadows of the moonlight I could see how handsome he was.

The beam of moonlight danced in his eyes. "I marched in, ready to fight any argument you had. I saw Lon in the study and demanded to know where you were. He told me you went to your bedroom with Cameron and pointed at the stairs." He let out a soft laugh. "I came running up. Hoping to stop whatever *activities* were happening."

"It hurts to breathe let alone participate in any *activities*." He let out a belly laugh this time. Wrapping his arms around me again, he carefully pulled me down onto my side. We were laying face to face, just a few inches apart. This felt more intimate than when we had sex.

"I came charging in your room prepared to beat Cameron when I had seen you two laying in the bed." There was a quick flicker of jealousy in his eye that was gone just as quickly as it had appeared. "A floorboard squeaked when I took a step forward catching Cameron's attention. He motioned for me to be quiet as he pulled away from you." I felt Emmett's arms tighten around me in an unconscious possessive move.

"He motioned for me to follow him into the hall and told me what you said to your uncle. Just when I think you can't impress me or surprise me anymore Carrots, you do." I could see the pride beaming off his face, even in the dark. I never had anyone proud of me before. I knew my parents were, but they never told me as much.

"You should have seen his face. I thought he was going to keel over from a stroke." We both laughed. It felt good to laugh despite the aching it brought to my injuries.

SPEAK EASY TO ME

"That's my girl." The laughter fading from his voice as he stared into my eyes. There was shift in the air ramping up the heat between the two of us. Emmett intertwined his legs with mine. "Is this, okay?" I gave my head a slight nod in response. He used his legs to pull me even closer to him.

"I never got to properly thank you, earlier." Emmett pulled his head back slightly, our eyes met. "Thank you for saving my life. More than once." I could see the corners of his mouth turn up.

"I would do anything for you, Carrots." The truth in his words sent a shiver down my spine. He's proven he would do anything for me.

"I know you would. You already have." I leaned in slightly, fumbling around a little in the dark searching for his lips making Emmett chuckle. My mouth found his, quieting his laugh. Our tongues met in the middle. We had never kissed this slowly before. The other times we had kissed it had been frenzied and wanting. This time was slow and passionate.

Emmett pulled away leaving both of us breathless. He placed one final closed mouth kiss on my lips. "Let's get some sleep, Carrots. Tomorrow is going to be a long day." I snuggled in closer to Emmett as our breathing synched. I fell asleep to the sound of his breathing and the smell that was distinctly his.

CHAPTER 18

LOTTIE

The warmth of the sunlight penetrating the bedroom had me rousing out of my sleep. I rolled over, fully expecting to find Emmett laying next to me, but was met with an empty bed. The side of his sheets were cold to the touch.

Where he had been laying just a few hours ago laid an envelope with my name scrolled across the front. I sat up in the bed as I took the folded paper out of the envelope. It read;

DEAR CARROTS,

I do not know what I did in this life or previous to have had the pleasure of knowing you in this life. You have opened my eyes and heart to the possibilities that the world can hold. As much as this pains me, I have to let us go our separate ways. You may think me a coward for doing this through a letter. I cannot do this face to face for I fear I would not be able to keep my resolve. You have taught me how to be selfless in a world where selfishness is the only way to survive. It is because of this newfound selflessness that I have to let you go. I cannot risk your life for my own selfish wants and desires. You mean too much to me. I would never be able to forgive myself if there were repeat events of the ones that had just transpired. To see you in that state and have no control over what happened to you, I just cannot do that. I want you to go back to Wisconsin and settle down with someone who is worthy of having you. I want you to have lots of babies because this world needs more people with your fiery spirit and extraordinary mind. Don't take this letter as me not loving you; I love you beyond words. Take care of yourself Carrots.

Love forever and always,
   Emmett

THE TEARS WERE DROPPING onto the letter faster than I could wipe them away. Their wetness smudging the dark ink on the page. He was gone. I was truly never going to see him again. He knew last night that it was our last time together and all he wanted to do was cuddle in bed. I don't think I will be able to recover from this heartbreak.

I was all packed and on the road in less than an hour. I had not seen nor heard anything else from my uncle before I left. He did have a set of car keys sitting on the small wooden table by the front entry way.

I had made good time getting to the family farm in Wisconsin. To say my family was surprised to see me would be an understatement. My family had been about to sit down for dinner as my car pulled into the driveway. By the time I pulled up to the house everyone had filed outside to see who the mysterious car belonged to. I was rushed by a mob of family when my car door opened, and I emerged.

I warned my family as soon as I set foot out of the car that

I was injured and I would tell them all about it over dinner. I was helped inside the warm house. My sisters and parents were on pins and needles as I recounted my kidnapping and harrowing escape. I left out certain details that weren't pertinent to the story.

I had also explained that I was no longer engaged to Cameron as we had parted on good terms. I also reassured my parents that Uncle Lon would not be coming to collect the money he had already given us or contacting us ever again for that matter.

Falling back into farm life had been much easier than I had expected it to be. The only thing I missed from Uncle Lon's house was the claw footed bathtub. With four younger sisters the hot water in the house didn't last terribly long.

I had finally started reassembling the pieces of my heart slowly, but surely. Each day I awoke the pain was less and less. It had been two months since I had left Chicago, and everyone in it, behind me. The crisp May morning air was refreshing as it came through my bedroom window. I was ready to start my daily chores.

I was bounding down the front steps when I saw a car I didn't recognize driving up in the distance. The approaching car drew the attention of anyone who was awake on the farm. I was quickly joined outside by my parents.

The car stopped right in front of us as the engine was killed. The dapper man who stepped out from behind the wheel was donned head to toe in expensive looking clothing. He looked to be about the same age as my father. There was a brief case clutched in his left hand.

"Miss. Charlotte Bradley?" His voice was mature. I raised my hand and took a step forward.

"That's me." I said sheepishly. I could not image what this man wanted with me.

"Wonderful. I was afraid I had the wrong house." He

SPEAK EASY TO ME

closed his car door and started walking toward me. "Miss. Bradley. I am Shephard Samson attorney at law. Is it alright if we step inside?" He was no longer addressing me, but looking to my parents. My father stepped aside and gestured the man to enter the house. We all filed in behind him.

My father sat at the head of the kitchen table holding his hand out in invitation for the attorney to take the seat next to him on his right. Mama sat to my father's left. I pulled up the chair next to Mama.

"What is this all about?" My father demanded. Shephard opened his briefcase and shuffled through a small stack of papers before pulling out a one singular piece of paper.

"Well, Mr. Bradley, I am here on behalf of one of my clients. He passed away and left his entire estate to Miss. Charlotte Bradley." All eyes fell on me. I had no clue who would leave anything to me, let alone a whole estate.

My mother read my mind, "Who?" It was such a simple question with a devastating answer.

The attorney was referencing the piece of paper in his hand. "One Mr. Holden Carl Emmett." My whole world stopped. The guttural sob that left my body was something I had no control over. Emmett was dead. It was one thing to never see him again, but for him to be dead, was unimaginable. The room was spinning. My ears started to ring drowning out the words my parents were speaking. I pushed away from my chair and ran outside.

As soon as my feet left the last step of the porch stairs I fell to my knees. I couldn't breathe as I was desperately gasping for air. He couldn't be dead. I had it in the back of my mind that we would eventually be together again because we were meant to be.

The sobs racking my body made me shake so much I threw up. Mama was by my side in a matter of moments. She

215

was also on her knees as she engulfed me in an embrace, pulling me close to her.

My parents knew who Emmett was. I told Mama all that had transpired between the two of us. She knew every sorted detail from our first meeting to our last night together. My father didn't know about my relationship to the extent that Mama did, but I revealed enough to let him know how special Emmett had been to me. I told them as a way to be reminded Emmett was real and what we had together actually took place.

Once my body was void of all tears Mama helped to scoop me up from the ground and walked me back into the house. The two men still sat stoically at the table. Quiet sobs still left my body, but my senses had returned enough for Mr. Samson to continue the proceedings.

The man who had just told me my whole world was shattered wasn't done shocking me. "You are now the owner of Le Mier and his house on Monterey Street. They are yours to do with as you wish. I have a broker on standby if you wish to sell the properties. The choice is yours to make." I could not care less about the properties. They could rot as far as I was concerned.

"There is also the account at First National Bank in the amount of $105,142.53." My jaw was on the floor. My mouth went dry.

"What?" I never would have guessed that Emmett had that much money. His house was extremely moderate. There was nothing elaborate about how he dressed or the car he drove. His suits were tailored to perfection, but other than that there was no indication he had more money than most people of the time.

Mr. Samson opened his briefcase again. This time he had a check in his hand. "The money was already withdrawn saving you a trip and the paperwork to take it out." He slid the check across the table to me. I took the small rectangle of paper in my hands and examined it. I would destroy this check without hesitation if it meant I could have one more minute with Emmett.

"Your father can take you to any bank you like to open an account. The check is good anywhere." I passed the check to my father. He was in disbelief.

I still had so many questions. The most important one on my mind was his funeral. "What is being done about Emmett, I mean, Holden's funeral? He didn't have any family left." I mentally started taking inventory of what I would need to pack for his funeral. I had never been to a funeral before, so I wasn't quite sure what the protocol was.

"There won't be a funeral," was all the attorney said. He was closing up his briefcase to leave.

"No funeral? I'll plan it and pay for it with the money I just got." There was no reason he shouldn't have a proper burial.

"It's hard to have a funeral with no body." So many more questions were just opened with nothing really being answered. I hadn't even thought to ask about how he died.

"What? No body?" Nothing this man was saying made any sense. I was hoping I would wake up any moment from this nightmare.

My father took over the conversation. "How did the young man die?" My father's eyes were on me to gauge how his line of questioning affected me.

"He was on a boat with six other men. The boat was found capsized with no living survivors. Only one body has been recovered so far with no hopes of recovering more." The news was like getting gut punched all over again and this man was telling me like he was reading it from the printed pages of the newspaper.

I abruptly stood up. I didn't want to hear anything else

TABITHA KRUEGER

this man had to say. Every piece of information he revealed was worse than the last. Nothing he said would bring Emmett back. "That's enough! Please leave right now." I was standing up and walking to the door to open it. "You can find your way back to your car on your own." The three remaining people at the table were all standing up now as well.

"Miss. Bradley," the bearer of bad news pleaded.

"Charlotte!" My dad chastised me. I knew I was being rude, but it didn't matter to me.

"No. I can't hear anymore. I don't care what else you have to say Mr. Samson. You've said plenty already." He gave me a curt nod as he gathered his briefcase and left the house.

As soon as the click of the door indicated our uninvited guest left the house my father started in on me. "That is not how we treat guests in this house, Charlotte Elizabeth." My mother was standing by him with a look of sympathy on her face.

"A guest is wanted. That man will never be considered a guest in my book." I was storming away into my room. "And tear that check up. I don't want it." The minute I did anything with that check it was real. It would mean Emmett really was never coming back.

My heart couldn't handle the reality of the situation. If my heart had been hanging on by a thread when I left Chicago, this would break the thin tether holding it together. You can't live without a heart.

Breathing felt like I was betraying Emmett. Every breath I took without him was one too many. I laid in bed for days. I didn't eat. I barely slept. The only reason I drank anything was so I could replenish my tear reserves. When I thought, I was done crying my heart would break again causing the flood of tears to continue.

Estelle had to move out of our bedroom because she

218

couldn't take my sobs anymore. I didn't blame her. I was not pleasant to be around. I didn't even want to be around me.

I was finally sleeping soundly for the first time in a week when I was awaken in the middle of the night by a noise. *'Ping. Ping'* There was something hitting my window. *'Ping. Ping. Ping.'* Something was hitting my window. I threw my robe on and walked across the room to investigate.

There was a shadow below my window. I saw the arm of the shadow cock backwards before a pebble hit my window. *'Ping'* The first night I was able to sleep, and some idiot thought it would be a good idea to wake me up. I stepped into my house shoes before running down the upstairs steps, two by two. I threw the door opened so hard it banged against the side of the house as I was sure there would be chipped paint.

"What the hell do you think you're doing?" I assumed it was one of the new farmhands that were hired recently. They were in their early 20's and liked to play pranks.

"I'm glad to see you haven't lost your fire, Carrots." My legs locked up as the familiar voice stepped out of the shadows. I took a minute to look over the man now standing in front of me. I had finally lost it because I could swear that Emmett was standing in front of me. I took a small step forward so I could get a better look at this handsome man's face.

"Emmett?" My throat closed up as I said his name. He took a small step forward, matching mine.

"It's me, Carrots." He had now advanced into my personal bubble. He was so close I could reach out and touch him, which I did. I placed my hand on his face. He was real. Emmett was truly standing in front of me, in the flesh.

I swung my hand back and smacked him right across his left cheek. The loud slap rang throughout the darkness.

TABITHA KRUEGER

"What the fuck, Lottie?" Emmett's hand flew up to his slowly reddening cheek.

"You are supposed to be dead!" Every angry word was accentuated with a push into his chest. "You're supposed to be dead." Emmett wrapped his arms around mine so I couldn't hit him anymore. He brought me in close to his body as he was comforting me. He was really here with me.

He was supposed to be lost forever, but he wasn't. He was right here in front of me wrapping me in a tight embrace. Every single wish I had made the last week was to see him one last time and now I was. The anger and fury were overshadowed by the overwhelming feeling of relief.

The sobs of relief had now replaced the endless tears of sadness and loss. He was here in front of me breathing the same air I was, but not for long. I was going to kill him myself. I broke free of his encasing arms.

"No! You don't get to come here and comfort me. What the hell is going on Emmett?" I was screaming so loudly I was surprised it took this long for all the lights in the house to turn on.

"I know you're mad. I know that." He was trying to calm me down, but right now, nothing felt like it was going to work. "Let me explain myself and if you never want to see me again, I will understand. But I did this for you. For us." I wasn't in the right mind space to hear anything he was saying.

The screen door squeaked as it was opened behind me. I looked back to see my father and mother running down the porch stairs toward where the source of commotion was coming from, me. My father stepped in between the two of us in a protective mode.

"Who are you and what are you doing on my property, son?" I didn't want Emmett to say anything to my parents, so I answered for him.

"Apparently Emmett isn't as dead as we were led to believe." I crossed my arms as I stared daggers at the number one source of misery. My parents looked from me to Emmett and then back to me. "But he's about to be because I am going to bury him alive myself!"

"Emma, take Lottie inside. Now!" Mama put her caring arm around my shoulders and led me inside, leaving Papa and Emmett outside alone.

Mama sat me down at the table and put the kettle on. She knew there was no going back to sleep for any of us tonight. We had sat in silence as we sipped our tea. I was on my second cup when the front door opened as Papa and Emmett stepped through the threshold.

My cup clinked on the saucer as I placed it down. My chair scraped along the hardwood floor as it was thrown back when I abruptly stood up to protest Emmett's presence in the house.

"Lottie. Sit back down." Papa was not suggesting I do as he said. "Please let Emmett explain himself." I opened my mouth to protest, but he cut me off. "I think you really need to set your anger aside and just hear him out. If, after he tells you what he told me, you still want to kill him, I will help you dig his grave." If my father was on his side, maybe I should hear what he had to say. There had to be some logical explanation to this madness.

I looked between Papa and Emmett. "Fine," my anger seeping into my agreeance. Papa motioned for Mama to follow him out of the room to give Emmett and me privacy.

I crossed my arms in front of me and stared Emmett down. He stood by the door like a child about to get scolded for swearing in church. "Is it okay if I join you at the table?" I kept my gaze focused on my teacup and made no effort to hide my scowl. He took my non-answer as an invitation to sit down in the chair opposite me.

TABITHA KRUEGER

He cleared his throat before proceeding. "Lottie, I know I have caused you an immense amount of pain and I am truly sorry for that. Honestly, if this could have been done differently, I would have done it." He got my attention enough for me to glance up at him.

"After losing my family, I vowed to never let anyone get that close to me again. I never wanted to be put in that position of experiencing that kind of loss ever again." He shifted uncomfortably in his chair. "You have made me lose my goddamned mind, Carrots. Every rule I have set for myself you had me break. After finding you in the barn, thinking that the blood I saw running like a river was yours. Lottie, it broke me. It broke me in a way that was different from when I lost my parents or my brother because they were family." He reached across the table and placed his large, warm hand over mine. "Losing you meant that all my hopes and dreams of my future family were gone. The family we were supposed to build together." I looked into his red-rimmed eyes. "Do you know how much I wanted to stay curled up in that bed with you? But I realized in that moment that any amount of time you spent with me put you in danger. Fuck, Lottie. You weren't even safe from your own cousin because of me." The tears were welling up in his eyes. "Seeing you in pain is worse than any amount of torture I could and have, gone through."

My eyes were now welling with tears as well. "Emmett," I was trying to comfort him.

"Please, Lottie, let me finish before you say anything." I nodded my head for him to continue. "I knew the only way you would ever be safe was if I was dead. There was no one else on the boat with me except the captain, who had pissed off my boss. I took the opportunity to forge the passenger manifest to include people who never existed. I knew that if the authorities found an empty boat and me missing, it

222

SPEAK EASY TO ME

wouldn't have been enough to convince them I was dead. I killed the captain and then took the dingy to shore. The boat capsizing was just a lucky miracle that made it more believable." He had gotten his composure back. The tears that had been running down his face had dried up.

I took a moment to let what Emmett had just told me sink in. It was all a rouse. He planned this and knew what it would do to me. My voice caught in my throat as I asked, "How long had you been planning this?" I could see the look of shame written all over his face.

"I didn't know how I would do it, but I knew when I left your bed that morning. I went straight to my attorney's office and drafted up my will, which left everything to you." He moved his hands off mine and placed them under the table on his lap.

"And you didn't have the decency tell me?" The anger was slowly seeping back in.

"It had to look real, Lottie. I knew people would be sent to watch you. The feds have phones tapped now. The city is full of eyes and ears hiding in plain sight." Even if what he said was true, it didn't change my hurt feelings.

I slowly stood up from the table prompting Emmett to follow suit. "I hate you." I said with distain before I took the stairs up to my bedroom. I didn't hate him. I could never hate him. I was just so angry and hurt, I wanted him to experience even half the hurt feelings I had. I peaked out my window a few hours later and I found Emmett sleeping in his car. I couldn't blame him for not wanting to drive back to Chicago at his late hour.

I woke up to find Emmett's car still parked in front of the house the next morning. I got dressed and went outside to investigate. I looked through the car windows met with only empty seats. Emmett was nowhere in sight.

I made my way to the barn where I knew Papa would be.

223

TABITHA KRUEGER

Papa was in the barn like I had expected, but I did not expect to see Emmett standing next to him. He had traded his nicely tailored three-piece suit he normally wore for a pair of overalls and a dirty button up shirt. He was mucking the stalls. Good, I hoped he fell in shit.

I turned and immediately walked out. Emmett came running after me. "Carrots. Wait." He caught up to me rather quickly to my dismay.

"You can go ruin someone else's life, now." I kept my quick pace as I refused to look at him. He did make a pair of overalls sexy as hell though.

"I'm not going anywhere." He stopped walking. Yelling after me as I continued my path. "I work here now." I stopped walking so fast I almost stumbled forward.

I turned around and marched right up to the handsome bastard's face. "You what?" I demanded.

"You father needed another farmhand. Since my schedule is fairly open right now, I took the job." I let a condescending laugh leave my lips.

"You're going to farm? You won't last a month here." I chided him.

"You care to make a wager?" I stared at him as I crossed my arms. "If I make it a month, you have to give me another chance." Like hell that would be happening. If the work didn't drive him away, I'd find other ways to make his life miserable while he was here.

I smiled sweetly while all the thoughts running through my head were evil. "Fine." I turned on my heels as soon as I saw the triumphant smile starting to spread across his face.

To my surprise, Emmett was doing way better than I had thought he would. He was a fast learner when it came to farm work. He didn't blink an eye when I made sure all his meals were the absolute worst; I'd give him the crusted on crud at the bottom of the pans after cooking, I'd save all the

SPEAK EASY TO ME

burnt pieces of food for him, my personal favorite was purposely leaving his sandwich out causing the bread to get stale and hard. He ate every bite with a smile on his face. He was lucky I didn't poison him.

We were two days shy of the month deadline when I started to get desperate. I had one last ditch effort in my back pocket. I know it was a low blow, but I had run out of ideas. One of the newer farmhands, Milo, had asked me out on a date a few days prior. I had turned him down, but now I needed him for my plan. If Emmett saw me moving on maybe he'd finally get the message that things were truly over between us.

All the men had gone to the farmhand house across the property for the night. I made my way over to the house knowing I had to see this plan to the end. I knocked on the front door. I had made the mistake once of walking in without knocking. I had seen things that were burned into my cornea that could never be unseen.

The chatter inside the house stopped once the door was opened. Emmett standing on the other side of the door. He had a smile on his face that I was about to wipe away. "Carrots." He said hopefully.

"I'm looking for Milo." Milo was a good-looking guy. He wasn't as tall as Emmett or as handsome. He had a crooked smile and a mop of red hair. Milo must have heard me because he ducked in front of Emmett, whose hand was still on the door, to greet me.

"Lottie. What brings you here?" Milo had this puppy energy about him. He was always happy and I swear, if he had a tail it would always be wagging.

"I was hoping your offer still stands for dinner tomorrow night?" Emmett's knuckles turned white as he gripped the door harder.

Milo was oblivious to the giant of man standing behind

him. His smile grew bigger as he answered, "Of course. I'll pick you up at 6?"

I smiled back. "It's a date then?"

Milo inclined his head, "It's a date." I turned and started walking back to my house. The regret instantly setting in. There were heavy footfalls behind me that were quickly catching up to me.

"Lottie!" Emmett was pissed. He made no effort to hide his anger. He ran in front of me causing me to stop abruptly so I didn't run into him. "What are you doing?" I went to step around him but he matched my movements, blocking me from leaving.

"No. You don't get to run away form me this time." He crossed his arms as he stood his ground. I went to go around him again and he once again matched my movements.

"I am not going anywhere, Lottie. I don't want to be anywhere else except here. If you think you need to go out with Milo to get back at me or to prove a point, go for it. It won't change my feelings for you. You could sleep with every man in that house and I would still want you as much as I want you now. I would have to kill them all, but I would still love you just as much as I do now. As much as I always have." He went down on one knee.

"What are you doing, Emmett?" There was a panic in my voice once I realized what he was doing.

"I love you Carrots. You are it for me. I never wanted anyone as much as I want you and I never will. You can run away from me all you want, but I will be right behind you. We have had a rough start, but I want my ending to be with you. Please, marry me, Lottie." I was completely stunned. All thought left my mind. Emmett pulled a black velvet box out of his back pocket.

"I bought this the same day I bought the green dress for you. I knew any woman who would make me want to go through that much effort just for a dress was the woman for me. I knew you were mine right then and there. If you say no now, I will keep asking you every day of my life until my dying breath."

He opened the ring box to reveal the most stunning ring I had seen. Cameron's engagement ring was beautiful, but it was all for show. The ring in Emmett's hand was white gold with a simple emerald cut diamond in the middle. Classic and timeless. He was describing this ring to me at Le Mier when I had tended to the three men after the knife incident. He was telling me truth.

Sometimes you don't know the answer to a question until it's presented to you. My sisters and I would play a game where you were given two things to choose from at a rapid fire speed. No time to think, you just say the first thing that comes to mind between the two choices. This was one of those times that I didn't even think about the answer. "Yes." I said it so quietly as I started at the man kneeling before me.

Emmett's head shot up to look at me. "Yes?" He had to confirm he'd heard me correctly. "You said yes?" the joy beaming from his eyes made it clear I had made the right decision.

I nodded my head aggressively as my cheeks hurt from smiling so big, "Yes!" Emmett jumped up from the ground so quickly I wasn't prepared for him to scoop me up in his arms and spin me around.

He placed me back down on the ground. Emmett's hands engulfed my face as he cupped my cheeks and kissed me deeply and passionately. Our kiss was broken when there was a voice in the distance, "Does this mean our date is off, Lottie?" Milo teased from the front porch of the farmhand house.

I yelled back laughing, "No!" Which earned me a glare and a poke in the side from Emmett. He grabbed my waist

TABITHA KRUEGER

and pulled me in for another kiss. He pulled away and took my hand, placing my engagement ring on my left ring finger, sealing it there with a gentle kiss.

I was ready to start my life with the man that had turned my world upside down more than once. Who knew this was just the beginning of our crazy life, not the end? I didn't think life could get even crazier than it had been, but boy was I wrong. Being married to an ex-mafia enforcer had its own set of wild rides.

THE END

ACKNOWLEDGMENTS

I would like to start with thanking my amazing husband. You are my biggest supporter and motivator. You held down the fort while I was typing away, making my dream a reality. I am so proud to call you my husband and best friend.

To my daughter, Clara. You are the best part of me and I hope you know how much you have motivated me to finally pursue my dreams.

To my editor, Partners in Crime - you made such a stressful process for a new author so relaxing and non-intimidating. You answered every question I had and helped me along the way.

To Grace - Thank you for being my reading test audience. I you cheered me on the whole way and helped me bring this story to life. You gave me the confidence to keep telling Lottie and Emmett's story.

To my mom and mother in law - I would like to thank both of you for taking the time to read and help proofread and self edit. You are both amazing women and I am so blessed to have you both in my life.

To my dad and step-mom - You both have been such great supporters of me and I could not be more grateful for both of you.

To all my other friends and family - Don't think that all your support and hype goes unnoticed. You are all so wonderful and I am truly blessed to have such a great group of people in my life. I appreciate every encouraging word and gesture you have given me.

To all of my readers - Thank you so much for allowing me to share Lottie and Emmett with you. I hope you have enjoyed their journey as much as I enjoyed sharing it. I am looking forward to all the other stories and characters I get to share with you. Your support and continued reading mean the world to me! Thank you for allowing me to live out my dream.

ABOUT THE AUTHOR

Tabitha Krueger's debut book may be historical romance, but she enjoys writing many sub genres of romance. Her heroines are always plus size with a dash of sass accentuated with witty humor and her MMC love them even more for it.

Tabitha is just a Wisconsin girl at heart, born and raised, and currently resides in the cheese state. Enjoys spending time with her husband and daughter along with their dogs and turtle.